Praise for BOOK ONE of the *Mysterious Ways* Series

*The author has the capacity to lure the reader into the scene.
... I definitely recommend this book to anyone who needs a
spiritual pick-me-up or reassurance that they are not alone.*
~ MICHEALLE HOBLER, reader, Milliken, CO

*A novel for all ages about the power of miracles and the
bonds of trust ... transformational and heartwarming.*
~ *MIDWEST BOOK REVIEW*

An exciting adventure story carrying a message of value.
~ BOB SPEAR, *HEARTLAND REVIEWS*

*The writing flows gracefully. ... I highly recommend this
moving story.*
~ MANUELA POP for BookPleasure.com

*I could identify with Charlie's sense of loneliness and the
transformation that took place as he accepted faith into his
heart.*
~ MARC SHKOLNICK, alumni exec. dir, Colo. State Univ.

*Many times I pictured myself in the scene. I can still feel the
wounds on my leg from the bear attack.*
~ PAUL WORLEY, pastor

*The whole Mysterious Ways series looks really interesting. I
may have to add those to my wish list.*
~ HomesteadBlogger.com

ROCK OF REFUGE

❧ BOOK TWO ❧
MYSTERIOUS WAYS

A Frontier Novel by
Donna Westover Gallup

CLADACH
Publishing

Cover Art from the painting "Summer Reunion" by Dan Young
See more of Mr. Young's work at www.danyoungstudio.com.

This is a work of fiction. Names, characters, places, and incidents either are the product of the author's imagination or are used fictitiously, and any resemblance to actual persons, living or dead, business establishments, events, or locations is entirely coincidental.

Library of Congress Control Number: 2007940020
ISBN-10: 0975961977
ISBN-13: 9780975961971

To Blaine Austin and Brian Paul,
Nana's little cowboys.

"The Lord is my rock, my fortress and my deliverer;
my God is my rock, in whom I take refuge."

Psalm 18:2

1871
Colorado Territory

1

THE CLOCK ON THE FIREPLACE MANTLE
had lost its melodious charm for Charlie long ago and
was now droning out the morning hour in a monotonous
chime. A deafening silence would soon follow, broken only
by the annoying 'thunk' of the clock's large hand as it moved
across its aged face to announce another thick, tension-filled
minute. Charlie squirmed in his chair and fought the urge to
yell out loud; nothing in particular, just something to get his
grandfather's attention. Yet Grandpa didn't seem to notice a
thing. The old man just sat at their small table, nonchalantly
enjoying his breakfast and smiling mischievously. Tired of
waiting, Charlie pushed his chair back with a huff and began
to gather the dishes from the table.

Grandpa seemed to take even longer eating as Charlie
filled the basin with hot water to wash his breakfast dishes.
Occasionally, Charlie would throw a cold look in the direction of the table, trying to speed the old man along. Irritat-
ingly— Charlie thought purposefully— the old half-breed
would raise his fork ever so slowly and take another bite of
food or sip from his coffee cup, all the while remaining quiet,
and now and then smiling at Charlie. When he finished
eating, Grandpa laid his fork across his plate and grabbed his
coffee cup, finishing off the warm liquid in one gulp.

Charlie turned from the counter, expecting him to say something at last, but instead, Grandpa wiped his mouth with a napkin and carefully pushed his chair back, rising slowly while he stretched, his old knees popping loudly as he did so. Looking innocently at his grandson, he turned and shuffled into his bedroom. Charlie's eyes narrowed as they followed the old man's every step. Shaking his head, he reluctantly turned back to the dishes. He had to admit that there were times, more often than not, that the cabin wasn't big enough for the two of them anymore. Sometimes he felt closed in, even suffocated by the small rooms and the wooden walls.

He leaned over the basin. Through wisps of steam, he caught the glum reflection of his own face staring back at him. *Why am I feeling this way?* he sighed. *I love Grandpa. I love this cabin and the farm. It's been my home since I was three years old. So what is this apprehension I'm feeling? What's wrong with me?*

Questions pummeled his brain until Grandpa's voice bellowed from the back room and startled him from his thoughts.

"There's a heap of heavy sighin' comin' from in there," the old man called out. "Somethin' got yer goat, son?"

"Figures you'd hear that," Charlie muttered testily as he grabbed Grandpa's dishes from the table. "Been tryin' to get you to talk all mornin' and you act like you don't hear a word, but then you can hear a bee buzz a mile away."

"I heard that, too," the old man replied as he shuffled out of his bedroom and over to the fireplace to reach for the coffee pot. Taking a clean cup from the counter he poured himself another drink and said, "Ready to talk now if ya want to."

Charlie fumbled with a fork and watched Grandpa from the corner of his eye. "Don't know what good it would do."

Grandpa shrugged his shoulders. "Maybe none, but it won't hurt nonc either, so just spill it out."

Charlie didn't look up from the basin but absentmindedly wiped at the same fork. "Well, I don't know . . . ," he said with irritation. "You were actin' like you didn't care earlier, so maybe I should just forget it."

Grandpa raised his bushy silver eyebrows. "Forget what?"

Charlie glared at him, but Grandpa just sipped his coffee. "Go ahead; say it," he said.

Charlie dropped the fork. It plopped into the water and tiny bubbles scurried into the air. He blurted, "Well, first it was Wilbur, then Mary Lou, and now you."

"Whoa." Grandpa held up a hand. "That's a passel of folks. I thought it was just me that was frustratin' the daylights outta you, but since there's a list, let's go over them one at a time so I can keep track. What's goin' on with Wilbur?"

Charlie shifted his weight from one foot to the other, ignoring Grandpa's sarcasm. "You know. He's done moved into town to take that job at the post office."

"Yeah, and that has you all miffed?"

"No," Charlie answered coldly. He fished the fork from the basin and laid it on the counter, "it's just that . . . that . . . well, yeah, I guess it has. I mean, he didn't even talk to me about it. Just up and moved. I didn't even know he was lookin' to leave the farm. Wilbur's been my best friend since we were young'ns. Why didn't he let me know he was leavin'?"

Grandpa looked over the rim of his cup and answered evenly. "Maybe he doesn't consider movin' to Pueblo such a big deal."

Charlie swished the rag inside a bowl. "That's not it," he muttered. "The point is, he didn't talk to me about it."

Grandpa leaned against the counter, his gnarled fingers woven around the warm cup of coffee. "Sounds like what most people do when they make up their minds about somethin'. He mighta been afraid you'd try to talk him out of it."

Charlie stopped swishing the rag across the dish he was holding. *Would I have done that?* he wondered.

"What are you really upset about, Charlie? That Wilbur didn't let you know, or that he decided it was time to leave the farm for an adventure, and didn't ask you to go with him?"

The question agitated the boy. He wasn't sure why, but it did. Setting down the plate, he grabbed an iron skillet and picked at the burnt egg remnants that were stuck on it.

"Ponder that question," said Grandpa, "and let's move on to the next person in line. What's goin' on with Mary Lou?"

Charlie threw a glance at the old man and sighed as images of Mary Lou bounced in his head. She was the youngest of the Tuttle family and Wilbur's only sister. She had finished the last of her lessons at the schoolhouse and was talking about going east in the fall to attend finishing school. Still cross, he grabbed the wash rag and vigorously scrubbed the skillet, but to no avail. The egg wasn't budging. "Dumb ol' finishin' school!" he mumbled under his breath. *What in the world is a finishing school anyway?* he thought. *Finish what?*

Grandpa leaned against the counter patiently until Charlie stopped messing with the skillet and, in defeat, stared blindly at the cabinets in front of him. "She's leavin' too," he snapped.

"Ahh, another one gone on an adventure without you."

He pulled out a chair and made himself comfortable at the table. This part of the conversation involved a girl and he was definitely interested in hearing what his grandson had to say about her, considering Charlie rarely mentioned girls.

"You and Mary Lou weren't really that close, were you?"

"Not really." Charlie scrubbed the skillet. "She was always there, tagging behind Wilbur and me."

"You fancy her?"

Charlie turned and looked at the old man like he was crazy. "I just said she irritates me. She's a pest and not exactly what I'd call pretty, though she does have nice blue eyes."

Grandpa took a swallow from his cup. "Uh huh. That's how it starts. The little pest soon becomes a bug, a love bug that bites when you least expect it. Guess you got bit bad."

"No, sir," disagreed the boy firmly. "It isn't like that. Me and Mary Lou have always just been friends." He set the wet skillet on the counter with a thump, squeezed the water out of the rag, and hung it from a nail to dry. Pulling the other chair out from the table, he sat across from his grandfather. "I mean, she's cute, but we hardly ever talk. Most of the time

I make her mad by sayin' the wrong things, especially when I make fun of her front teeth."

Grandpa looked at the distraught boy and hid the smile that tried to curl at the corners of his mouth.

"You tease her about her front teeth?" he asked in mock surprise. "Didn't I teach you to treat a girl better'n that?"

Charlie's chin hit his chest. "Yes, sir," he mumbled. "But she isn't a regular girl. I can get on her nerves faster than anythin', and she always knows how to get on mine."

Grandpa rubbed his chin. "Her leavin' upsets you?"

Charlie grabbed Grandpa's empty cup and stomped to the basin. The heels of his heavy boots raked the floor boards.

"When she leaves, there won't be no one left," he said.

Grandpa's eyes grew wide with surprise. "There's me."

"Yes, Grandpa, but even *you* are changin'."

Grandpa rose from his chair and leaned against the counter again, folding his arms across his chest. "And that brings us to person number three on your list of most aggravatin' folks. So, how am I changin'?"

"'Cause you know when things are botherin' me and you always sit and talk to me, but not this mornin'. This mornin' you didn't say nothin'. No words of wisdom, no direction, just a silly smile. I figure you're just gettin' too old or I'm gettin' to be too much of a bother."

"Well," said Grandpa with a sigh. "I am gettin' older, no denyin' that. And you're like a son to me and could never be a bother, so I don't think either one has anything to do with what's ailin' you. Maybe you're just feelin' sorry for yourself."

Charlie spun on his heels and faced his grandfather. Crimson color snaked over his cheeks and neck. "I . . . I am not feelin' sorry for myself," he stammered. "Why should I?"

"Your friends are growin' up and movin' on with their lives. And you feel like you're stuck here with an old man and a farm, the same ol' life. That's what's eatin' at you, isn't it?"

The boy's jaw muscles flinched as he turned sharply away. Without answering, Charlie grabbed the basin and pushed the back door open with his shoulder. The dirty dishwater hit the ground with a *whump!* and splashed out in all directions. The earth ferociously drank up the liquid.

Inside, Grandpa picked up a towel with one hand and grabbed the wet skillet with the other. Rubbing briskly, he looked towards the open door. "Here's some advice for you. I took both Bessie and Nellie out to the pasture this mornin', so now'd be a good time to go clean out their stalls."

Charlie leaned in and plunked the empty basin on the counter then stepped off the stoop. Watching Grandpa's face, he pushed the door closed with the tip of his boot. Grandpa threw Charlie a wide grin as the door shut between them. Charlie, scowling, strode away from the cabin and his grandfather.

Grandpa hung the skillet from a nail on the mantle and shuffled back into his bedroom where he pulled the ledger from the dresser drawer. Sitting on the end of his bed, he stared at the book. There was nothing he could do. The numbers were what they were and he had to make do. Finally, he squeezed his eyes and pushed the worry from his face. "Charlie must never know," he mumbled as he laid the book back in the drawer. "He's got his whole life ahead of him, Lord, so there's no need to worry him about mine." Slowly he slid the drawer closed. "No need to worry," he whispered.

2

THE ANCIENT SHED STOOD ON A RISE THAT overlooked the cabin and outbuildings of the Smith farm. Its dark red paint no longer shone brightly in the summer sun, but displayed the weather-worn boards beneath its chipped and peeling face. The windows, dark with the dirt left by many a storm, reflected nothing but the tops of tall prairie grasses that were growing up along the walls, with remnants of tumbleweeds clinging to them as if they were a haven on a rough sea.

The doors, leaning slightly off kilter, groaned in protest as Charlie pulled them open, then finally gave way as the rusty hinges released their grip. Sunlight flooded the darkened barn, casting the young man's long, thin shadow across the wooden floor planks. He stepped across the threshold toward the tool bin, the floorboards creaking beneath his feet. Above him, sleepy birds fluttered in the rafters and a handsome brown barn owl turned his disc-shaped face toward the intruder.

The summer had started out unusually hot and dry, enhancing the odors of the old barn. The scent of sweet hay and musky manure mingled with leather, dirt, and old wood. These were smells Charlie had come to love. Inhaling deeply, he felt the edge of aggravation slide away.

Pushing aside hand tools of all sorts as he hummed softly, Charlie rummaged mindlessly through the cluttered tool bin until he saw the handle of the old ax. Pulling it from the bin, he held it in his hands, rubbing his thumb across the dull, chipped blade. His memory raced back seven years, back to the winter when he was a ten year old boy, scared and alone. Grandpa had fallen ill, leaving Charlie to take care of the farm. He could hunt, fish, mend the corral, milk the cow, till the earth, and do a whole passel of other things back then, but there was one thing he didn't know how to do, and that was to swing an ax.

Instinctively, Charlie gripped the splintered handle and rested the iron head on the floor. In one fluid motion he pulled the ax over his head then swung it down, stopping it just before the blade crashed into the boards at his feet. A wave of energy surged through his body. He smiled.

No need to be afraid any longer.

Years of working the farm had made him strong, and although he was only seventeen, he was tall, muscular, and could swing an ax as easily as the next man. In fact, the wood pile was now his chore because it was Grandpa who couldn't lift an ax anymore.

Funny how quickly things change.

Cradling the old ax head in the palm of his hand, he looked up at the new ax that was hanging on the wall, its smooth head glistening in the morning light. Something new usually replaced something old; eventually, something had to give up its place in line, or move on to make way for the new.

"Grandpa was right," he whispered. "I *am* feelin' sorry

for myself. It's time for Wilbur and Mary Lou to move on and experience something new, that's all. I'm ready for a change too, but it's not my turn yet. I've got Grandpa to take care of and he comes first." In his heart he meant every word. The desire to go out and seek new adventures would have to wait for the time being. Grandpa came first.

The thought brought no comfort to him, though, as he gently placed the old ax back in the bin where he'd found it and grabbed the pitchfork.

"This is your adventure for now, Charlie, so you'd better get to work," he mumbled. He laid the pitchfork in the wheelbarrow then pulled on a pair of work gloves. Frowning, he pushed the wheelbarrow to Bessie's stall.

The stall gate was already open, pulled back and tethered to a nail. He poked his head in and looked around. A pile of clean straw had been pushed into a corner and served as Bessie's bed. She never moved it once she had it the way she wanted it, and she never messed in it. But the rest of the stall was a different story. Horses weren't proud when it came to the call of nature. Her water trough was nearly empty and the tiny window, as proven from its outward appearance, was black with dirt.

Charlie pushed the pitchfork's three prongs deep into the hay and loaded the wooden tines until they bent from the weight. Despite the occasional sneeze, it felt good to be out there working his muscles and letting go of what troubled him. Beads of sweat rolled down his face and dripped from his nose with each thrust of the pitchfork. But Charlie didn't mind.

Time passed steadily and soon the wheelbarrow was

almost full with the last load. He stood up, mopped his face with the back of his glove and looked around, listening closely to the silence. Had he heard something?

Charlie always enjoyed his space, his time alone, and he needed it; but now for some reason, he had an odd feeling that he was being watched and, for a moment, felt a bit uncomfortable. He shrugged and whispered, "You're being silly, Smith," then swept at the last strands of hay with the fork. But the feeling nagged him, like the fly that kept zipping around his ear. Every so often, he'd spin on his heels, hoping to catch Grandpa peeping over the rails, but his attempts to catch any perpetrator were futile. Grandpa was in the cabin and he was alone in the barn.

Throwing the last of the straw into the wheelbarrow, he leaned on the handle of the pitchfork again and peered around. The fly landed on his cheek and he flicked it off with his fingers just as another one buzzed his ear.

"So, what do you prefer, Charlie?" he asked out loud. "To be in the house with the walls closin' in on you, or out here where spooks stare at you from the shadows?" Shaking his head, he laughed nervously. But the laugh stuck in his throat when, from the corner of his eye, he caught a slight movement in the next stall. Slowly, he turned his head.

Disturbing emotions stirred within him. The last time he had been caught off guard, he'd almost been killed by a mama grizzly. He was only ten years old at the time, and right now, he felt like he was ten again. The memory of the bear attack still haunted him. It was because of her, because of the she bear, that he hated unexpected surprises. Now, his natural defenses pricked his nerves and he struggled to remain calm. Sweat dripped from his hair to the floor like sprinkles of rain.

He stared back into the dark eyes that glared at him from between the slats. His heart pounded in his chest. The longer he looked, the harder it was to breathe. Instinctively his fingers twitched. Slowly he moved his right hand to his hip, but—to his dismay—it came up empty. Grandpa's pistol was in the cabin. He didn't carry it all the time, but he wished he had it now.

3

THE ANIMAL SNORTED. CHARLIE JUMPED.
But a pang of relief shot through the pit of his stomach.
His arms sank to his side and his shoulders sagged as the
pitchfork slid from his fingers and hit the floor with a bang.

"Bessie, what are you doin' in here? 'Bout scared me half
to death. I thought you were outside with Nellie."

He could feel the frustration from earlier that morning
start to creep back to the surface as he marched out of one
stall towards the next. "What's the use," he muttered. "I'm
not gonna get this barn cleaned out if I have to keep stoppin'
for this and fussin' over that. I thought Grandpa said he put
you out with the cows."

Charlie gave the gate a yank and let it swing free to
bounce off the wall behind him as he stepped into the stall.
He was annoyed and he didn't care who knew it, but the
horse didn't excuse his rude entrance. Throwing his large
head up and down, the animal whinnied loudly and pawed
the floor with his front hoof. Charlie froze. Expecting to see
Grandpa's old mare, instead he'd come face to face with a
large gelding the likes of which he'd never seen.

With a quick glance, Charlie figured the big fellow to
measure about sixteen hands high. Even in the dimly lit stall,
his black coat glistened, blending hues of green and blue

into the inky black mix. In contrast, his mane and tail were flaxen gold. "You're the most beautiful thing I've ever seen," whispered the boy.

The horse didn't take to the compliment immediately, but grazed the boy with its large roaming eyes while its broad sides heaved in aggravation. His ears, pinned back against his head, warned Charlie to be careful. His long, golden tail twitched with short, deliberate strokes and his dark eyes darted nervously from the boy, to the bouncing gate, and back to the boy.

Without taking his eyes off the animal, Charlie reached carefully for the gate and stopped its unnerving racket. A hush fell over the room as the two sized up each other. Each waited for the other to move. Charlie slowly removed a glove. With palm flat, he held out his hand and offered his scent as an introduction.

Still unsure, the horse tossed his head with vigor; his long mane a whirl of gold. "It's okay, boy," Charlie said softly. "Nobody here's gonna hurt you. You just surprised me, that's all. I didn't mean to surprise you back." He kept his hand out and whispered, "My name's Charlie. It's okay, boy."

The horse's nostrils flared. Guardedly he stretched his neck toward Charlie's hand. He rooted the open palm with his wet nose and twitched his lips across the boy's fingers, looking for a treat. The big animal threw his head up again and stepped back, snorting loudly in disappointment.

Charlie stepped back too. "Wow," he said breathlessly. "Where'd you come from, boy?"

"I bought 'im for you awhile back," answered Grandpa. Startled, Charlie spun round and found the old man leaning on the stall rails, a toothpick hanging from the corner of his broad smile.

"What?" cried Charlie.

"Yep. I've had my eye on 'im for quite some time and was finally able to buy 'im a few weeks ago from Ben Jacobs down the way. He couldn't deliver 'im till yesterday, though, and since you were late gettin' home from the Tuttle's, I decided to keep 'im a surprise till now."

"But, but Grandpa," stuttered the boy. "Why? I mean he's beautiful and all, but we can't afford to go and buy another horse just for me."

"Never you mind what we can and can't afford, son. I bought 'im 'cause you're gonna need 'im. Can't go on no cattle drive without a horse now, can you?"

Charlie's eyes widened. "Cattle drive? You mean I get to help drive the cattle up to Fort Collins this year?"

"Yep, I reckon you can now. Only got a couple of months to work with this fella, though. The two of you'll need to be ready to go by September."

"September? But the soldiers usually come late fall."

"They're comin' early this year. The government's slowly dissolvin' the fort. Seems it isn't needed anymore since the Indians settled down. But some of the soldiers've decided to stick around and settle those parts. Why, I even heard they're gonna start a college up there to teach young'ns about farmin' and such. Named somethin' like Colorado Agriculture College." Grandpa twisted the toothpick and shook his head. "How 'bout that?" he mumbled, "gotta go to college to learn about farmin' these days."

He looked at the boy and chuckled. "Just think, I taught

you all I know about it for free." He looked at the floor and chuckled again. Turning the toothpick with his tongue, his gaze drifted beyond the walls of the barn and out into the meadows where the cows were moaning as they made their way to the lower pasture to feed. Uncertainty clouded his eyes for just a moment.

He turned back to Charlie and smiled. "Anyway, this last batch of cows to go up will be the beginnin' of a couple a' herds for some of the folks that'll be homesteadin' up there. I figure this'll be your only chance to go."

Turning back to the horse, Charlie slowly held his hand out again. The wary gelding stepped toward him. "Been wantin' to go on a cattle drive a long time, Grandpa. Can't hardly believe it."

"Well son, you're almost eighteen. You finished your schoolin' over a year ago, so I figure it's time you had a chance to see somethin' besides the likes of Pueblo and this little farm. Time for you to venture out a bit, see some of this territory before it gets all built up and closed in. Cattle drive'll do you good."

"Do they know I'll be joinin' 'em this year?"

Grandpa nodded. "Yep, they do. When Sergeant Barlow let me know he was leavin' and business would be conducted by Sergeant Wilkins, I started correspondin' with him."

Charlie pushed the hair out of the horse's eyes and stroked the long dark nose.

"Grandpa, I'm sorry—"

Grandpa held up a hand. "No need, son." His voice dipped almost to a whisper. "You know, I was seventeen once myself, and it really isn't all that different now than it was back then. In fact, if I 'member right, I ran off to Alabama to fight some Indians just to spark some excitement in my life when I was your age." Grandpa chuckled again. "I don't want you goin' and doin' nothin' foolish like that."

"I won't," mumbled the boy; remembering the old ax and the commitment he made that morning. *I ain't doin' nothin' without you, Grandpa.*

Grandpa rested a foot on the bottom rail and leaned his elbows on the gate. "What I'm tryin' to say is, I know there're lots of changes takin' place for you right now, inside and out. A body hardly knows what to do with hisself. Itchin' for your own space, but not wantin' to leave where you are. I understand your confusion, your irritations, Charlie."

Charlie nodded and slowly stroked the horse's mane. "Thanks, Grandpa," he whispered. "I know that doesn't sound like much, but I do mean it."

"That's good enough for me," said the old man. "Just work hard and be ready when the soldiers come. They'll be expectin' you to pull your weight. As for my expectations, I just want you to meet folks along the way and learn a thing or two. But mind you make me proud, boy. Make me and Jess proud."

Charlie met his grandfather's eyes. "I'll do my best, Grandpa." His mind wandered to their friend Jess. He'd met him for the first time the winter Grandpa fell ill and Charlie had faced the most desperate time in his life. He and Grandpa needed help something awful when the big mountain man seemed to come out of nowhere, just in time to save them both. Not only did Jess touch his life, he touched Charlie's heart, and changed him forever. Grandpa was Charlie's hero, but Jess… well, Jess was something else.

"Good," continued Grandpa. "Now that's settled, you can finish your chores in here and then go ridin' for awhile. See how he sits." He pulled the toothpick from his lips and threw a teasing glance over at the boy. "Might wanna take 'im over to the Tuttle's and show 'im to Mary Lou."

Charlie furrowed his brow and shook his head. "Mary Lou'll like him, but she won't ride 'im," he said impatiently. "She's been listenin' to the schoolteacher talk about how things are done out east. Says ridin' western style is for boys and she won't mess with a horse until she's in finishin' school where she'll learn to ride side saddle, all prim and proper."

Grandpa snorted. "Well, sounds like she's got a bunch of silly notions in her head about how things are out east." He grunted as he turned to leave. "I been there and it isn't all it's cracked up to be. Silly girl." He waved a hand. "Well, take 'im out anyway and give 'im a good start."

"Wait a minute, Grandpa," said Charlie. "What kind of horse is this? I've never seen a quarter horse like him."

Grandpa turned back and shook his head. Pulling on the toothpick, he said with an air of authority, "He isn't a quarter horse. He's what they call a Rocky Mountain horse. He's just as hardy as a quarter though. Can cut cattle, pull a wagon, and does a hard day's work like the best of 'em, but he rides a bit smoother than a quarter horse. And I thought that might come in handy, with as much ridin' as you're gonna be doin'."

Charlie laughed softly. Grandpa was right, there was a lot of riding to do between the farm and Fort Collins.

"Best of all," Grandpa continued, "they're bred right here

in the territory, so they're used to mountain ridin'."

The old man gently stroked the horse's long neck. "Jacobs said the breed comes in lots of colors and oftentimes the tail and mane can be totally different from the coat, which is what I found most intriguin' about this here boy. You'll be able to pick 'im out in a crowd."

Charlie patted the muscular neck. "He's really some-thin'."

"Yep, he is," nodded Grandpa in agreement. "Just remember, though, when you're ridin'—he isn't Bessie. This here young'n is high spirited and ready to get goin' in the blink of an eye. Jacobs said he can run like the wind."

"I bet he can. I can't wait to find out."

The two stroked the golden mane in silence for a few moments, then Grandpa took a step backwards. "Well, I'll leave you to your chores and then to—"

"Grandpa?" Charlie cleared his throat, then added quietly, "Would you mind if I borrowed your saddle?"

Grandpa smiled broadly, his high cheekbones sharp and defined. His eyes twinkled merrily.

"Naw, I don't mind."

Charlie gave a short nod in appreciation, but Grandpa continued to talk like he didn't notice. "But you don't need to be usin' that wornout piece a' leather. Why, it's so old, it's barely a saddle anymore. Just a patch a' hide with danglin' stirrups. Not worth nothin' to no one but me."

The old man chuckled and pulled on the toothpick again, lost in another memory. Charlie stood and stared at him, a bit confused and hoping for a little clarification.

No more games, Grandpa. Is it 'No,' you don't mind or 'No,' I can't use it? What's it gonna be?

Grandpa just stared at the floor.

It was breakfast time all over again. Charlie inhaled deeply, trying to let the irritation go, then calmly said, "Well, okay then. I guess I can handle him bareback for a while."

The old man threw his head back and laughed loudly enough to startle the owl that was roosting above his head.

"Now, as much as I'd enjoy watchin' you ride this horse bareback and cattle train him all at once, I don't think that'd be too wise. We might be part Indian, but we aren't that big a part—so why don't you use the saddle down there?"

Charlie closed his eyes. It was getting harder to stay calm. He turned from the horse and faced the old man.

"What saddle?" he asked briskly.

Grandpa raised his arm and with a thin, boney finger, pointed towards the back of the barn.

What now? Charlie walked to the gate and glanced down the length of the barn. "Where?" he muttered.

"Back there," said Grandpa.

Charlie looked at the old man and frowned. "You mean in that musty ol' room? I hate goin' back there."

"It's just a room, boy. Gotta get over bein' afraid of your own shadow if you're gonna go out into the big world."

"I'm not afraid. Just cautious. I don't go where I don't have any business goin', that's all."

Looking determined, Grandpa nodded toward the back of the barn. "Well, you've got business back there."

4

CHARLIE LOOKED INTO THE DARKNESS. RAYS of sunlight were finding their way through varied knot holes or cracks in the walls; puddles of light flowed across the darkened floorboards. Yet these barely affected the dim, hazy recesses of the barn. Somewhere back there was a small, dank room that Charlie had always tried to avoid.

He knew Grandpa used it to store things like Great-Grandma's spinning wheel and worn out trunks full of old stuff; but he'd had no idea there was extra tack back there. Even if there were, as far as he was concerned it would be pretty much used up and on its last leg; nothing he'd want. But the suspense got the better of him. He had to go see.

He stepped gingerly out of the stall and around Grandpa, who still hadn't moved, just pointing with his gnarled finger, as if in a trance. Charlie smirked, then went down the corridor uneasily, as if expecting something to jump out at him.

Grandpa sniggered, but Charlie didn't care. Keeping his hands waist level as a precaution, Charlie crept along the wall, turning once slightly to glance back at Grandpa.

A few wisps of sunlight slid into the dim room between streaks of dirt on the window pane. With little light to guide him, how would he find anything of interest in there?

He squeezed his eyes shut and pinched the bridge of his nose to help his eyes adjust to the darkness. The room had that musty smell he remembered.

Several boxes were piled against the walls; an old trunk rested in a corner; broken farm tools dotted the floor. The spinning wheel sat in a far corner covered with dust, its large wheel supporting a mass of spider webs that stretched from the top of the arc to the floor. Indian blankets from eras past, their bright colors muted by age, hung from rusty nails randomly pounded into the walls. A couple of old buffalo hides, their brown fur dotted with lint and coated with a fine powder lay folded neatly on top of a box. A large, cracked mirror leaned lazily in a corner, the broken glass tilted just enough to reflect the feather-like cobwebs that draped across the ancient beams overhead. Loose silken strands floated eerily towards the floor. Charlie shuddered.

His eyes searched nervously for something familiar—a stirrup, a bridle, anything.

"Calm down, Charlie," he whispered. "Grandpa taught you better. Pay attention, look around. See what the shadows reveal to you." He took a deep breath, slowly let it out, then methodically scanned the room again, this time paying attention to what the contents told him.

Up against the back wall, next to the old spinning wheel, a bundle looked out of place. While everything else in the room had accumulated years of dust and cobwebs, this quilt didn't look so old. He studied it for a minute and then recognized it as the cover from Grandpa's bed, and from beneath it protruded the familiar shape of a saddle horn.

With a goal in sight, Charlie grabbed the old doorframe

by the tips of his fingers and forced himself over the threshold. Wiping spider silk out of his face and gently pushing remnants of the past aside with the tip of his boots, he made his way across the room. He didn't know why he was bothering with this. After all, it was just another piece of old, dilapidated leather, its usefulness long gone. Squatting in front of the bundle, he pulled back the corner of the quilt.

The black leather had been oiled to such a high gloss it shimmered in the dimly-lit room. Fancy, hand-tooled designs fanned across the skirt and down the fenders to the oak stirrups. Positioned just right, golden rays of sunlight danced across the silver conchos, making them twinkle like stars against a blackened sky. A new saddle! Nicer than Charlie had ever imagined possible. Wide-eyed he stared, hardly breathing.

"Well, do you like it?"

Charlie snapped around. He'd forgotten Grandpa, but the old man had quietly followed him. The boy nodded, unable to speak. Turning back to the saddle, he slid his hand across the smooth surface of the seat. He never dreamed he'd own such a fine piece. "It's beautiful, Grandpa," he murmured. "But—"

"None of your business how I paid for it," scolded the old man. "But it *is* paid for, every stitch of it."

Charlie closed his eyes and took another deep breath, again swallowing the mingled scents of the barn. "Lord," he prayed as the smells engulfed him, "thank you."

"Sometimes," Grandpa whispered, "you find good things in unusual places. You just have to believe."

Charlie nodded in agreement and stood to his feet, the

beautiful saddle still holding his gaze.

The horse nickered, reminding Charlie there was work to be done. A childish grin spread across his bronzed face as he turned to his grandfather, but the old man had slipped back to the cabin.

Alone, he stood in the haze of the barn and gazed out the open door to the hills beyond. He thought about his home and of the man who meant the world to him. This man who raised him since he was three years old and had taught him all he knew about life: how to live with honor, integrity, and dignity; how to peacefully stand for what he believed was right and decent; how to defend himself should the situation prove necessary; and now, how to sacrifice for someone he loved.

He didn't know what Grandpa had given up so he could have these things, but he knew this was Grandpa's way of acknowledging the fact that he *was* growing up. Whatever the sacrifice, the old man must have considered it worthwhile.

In the haze, Charlie smiled, feeling like a man, and feeling proud of his grandfather and of the example he had lived in front of Charlie everyday.

As he watched, a soft breeze played with the grass just outside the barn doors. He closed his eyes again and waited. Soon, the familiar sound of rustling leaves flowed down the hillside and into the yard. It was a sound that once haunted him, but now brought him peace.

"Thank you, Grandpa," he whispered as he gathered the saddle and tack in his arms. "And you too, Jess. I can't think of a better name for him than Star. His full name will

be North Star, Jess, but we'll just call him Star for short."
Charlie chuckled at the memory of their introduction so
long ago. "The two of us will always make the two of you
proud, I promise."

In the cabin, Grandpa pulled a chair up to the little kitchen
table and sat down, filled with mixed emotions. He was
thrilled that Charlie loved and appreciated his gifts, and he
knew the boy would always take care of what he possessed,
but settling his spectacles on his nose, concern filled his
thoughts as he pulled a folded, dirty piece of yellow paper
from his shirt pocket. Opening the frayed letter, he sat
back in his seat and readjusted his glasses. He'd already
memorized the message, but he read it again, slow and sure.
When he finished, he folded the paper along the worn
creases and tucked it back into its hiding place, patting the
shirt pocket hidden under his vest. "Well," he chuckled, "I
just told my grandson that good things can be found in
unusual places. I wonder what good will come of all this?"

Looking into the fire, he grew solemn. He felt a hundred years older and bone tired, but he had no choice.
Patting his chest pocket again, he sighed heavily. "Better
get ready for my own adventure. Been puttin' it off long
enough."

≫ **5** ≪

EVENING SHADOWS SLID ACROSS THE FACE of the mantle clock. The hands were pointing to the seventh hour and the clock was chiming when Grandpa heard the outhouse door slap shut. Charlie hobbled into the cabin, from his hat to his boots covered with dust that flew off in puffs as he moved. He went straight to the wash basin, hung his hat on a peg, and sloshed water on his face and hands, cleaning them just enough to be acceptable for supper.

Charlie threw a wide 'Smith grin' at his grandfather, who fought with all he had to keep from laughing. He couldn't help but notice how the once-confident, long-legged strides of a farm boy had been reduced to the short, child-like shuffle of a new cowboy. He knew by the way Charlie's legs were bowed, that his bottom half was aching something fierce. But, from the smile the boy was sporting, he was obviously happy with what he and his horse had accomplished their first time out. When Charlie moaned, Grandpa bit his lip.

Grandpa grabbed a pan of cornbread from off the fireplace rack. From the corner of his eye he watched Charlie wobble over to the Dutch oven hanging in the fire. "Been ridin' much?" he asked matter-of-factly.

"It was a day," Charlie said with a smile, though his

eyes winced in pain. "Jacobs was right. He does run like the wind. But what Jacobs forgot to mention is he can stop on a dime. Sometimes he stops so fast, it's hard for me to stop with 'im."

The old man laughed and wiped his hands on the towel, his old gray eyes sparkling with delight. "Did he throw ya?"

Charlie pulled the Dutch oven out of the heat, and lifted the lid. The sweet aroma of beans and ham hocks hit him square in the face and his mouth watered so fast he almost drooled.

"No sir," he replied as he turned and took a spoon from the table. "He tried a couple of times, but before I put 'im up for the night, we came to terms on who was boss." He scooped a spoonful of the thick juice and blew on the rising steam. "He's a fine horse." He sipped the steaming broth. "And he'll be a good friend to me, just like Bessie is to you."

"Good, I'm glad," said Grandpa, as he slid a bowl of butter across the table. "I hope you have 'im just as long, too. Now, how 'bout some supper? Looks like you're hungry."

"Starvin'," answered the boy, a bead of bean broth sliding down his chin.

Grandpa motioned to the table. "Then sit down, and I'll ladle up some grub."

The old man grabbed a couple of bowls while Charlie made sure everything else they needed was on the table.

"He gave you a good workout, huh?" asked Grandpa.

Exhausted, Charlie fell into his chair and began tugging on a boot. "You betcha he did, but he was pretty lathered up by the time we called it a day. I'd say we're about even."

Grandpa sat the bowls down. "Keep them boots on till

after supper. I don't want piles of dirt around the table while we're eatin'."

Embarrassed, Charlie slid his foot back into the boot. "Sorry," he mumbled.

"Coulda left some dirt outside for other critters, ya know." Grandpa chuckled. "Didn't hafta bring it all in the house."

Laughing, the two sat down to their supper of beans and cornbread and thanked the Lord for His bounty. Charlie silently acknowledged that the bounty consisted of not just the food that was before him, but of all that he'd been given, from the first day of his life until this moment. He'd lost both parents at an early age; but he was raised by loving grandparents. Indeed, he was a very rich young man.

Famished, Charlie finished off a bowl of beans and two pieces of cornbread before speaking a word. Finally, he came up for air and sat back in his chair. He buttered another piece of cornbread.

"About this morning, Grandpa—"

"No need, son." The old man waved off an apology. "Everythin's fine. Just tell me about you and your horse."

"Well, sir," started Charlie again. "Before I do that, I have to let you know that I asked the Lord to forgive me for my attitude this morning and I need to ask you to do the same. I'm not right sure what got into me, but I hope it's gone."

Grandpa looked over at Charlie and his watery eyes smiled before he broke out into a soft laugh. "This is just the beginnin', son. You wait till girls come into the picture."

Charlie didn't respond to that comment. Between bites

he talked on about how he and his horse had galloped and how he took to cow cutting maneuvers real fast. It was obvious Jacobs had trained the horse well, but after working together that afternoon, it seemed like he and Star had been made for each other.

"By the way," Charlie added, "his name is Star, and I'm teachin' 'im all kinds of things."

"Star," repeated Grandpa. "I like that name."

Charlie cast a look at Grandpa and smiled awkwardly. "Sorry, don't mean to talk with my mouth full."

"It's alright tonight," smiled the old man. "So, what kinds of things are you teachin' him?"

"How to come to me when he hears a certain whistle and how to let me stand on him, or crawl around his legs without him movin'. You know, stuff like that."

"That takes a lot of trust between horse and rider, son. I don't know if you should be workin' on things like that the first day out."

"I'll be fine," said Charlie between bites. "And besides, we'll have to start trustin' each other sometime, won't we?"

Grandpa blew at his broth. "Mary Lou like 'im?"

Charlie dug around in his soup before answering. "Yeah, she did, but she wouldn't ride 'im. Said he was too big. I tried to tell 'er that he was as meek as a church mouse and wouldn't hurt 'er, but she wouldn't believe me."

"Well, her loss," mumbled Grandpa.

"She's leavin' sooner than I thought." Charlie frowned. "Her folks'll be takin' her out east in a few weeks. Mrs. Tuttle got all teary-eyed when I told her about the cattle drive. Said she'll be all alone now until one of her children gives her grandbabies and Heaven only knows when that will be."

Grandpa grumbled something, but his thoughts turned to other matters.

Charlie, soon lost in his own thoughts, chewed quietly for a moment, then turned his attention to the last piece of cornbread. He drenched it with butter, then finished it off in three bites.

Grandpa laid his spoon aside and rested his arms on the table. He cleared his throat and looked at Charlie. "Mind if I ask you somethin'?"

"No, sir. What is it?"

"Remember the last time we were in Pueblo, gettin' seeds and starters for the spring plantin'?"

Charlie bent over his bowl again. "Yeah, I do."

"Well, remember when you were loadin' the wagon and I walked over to the post office?"

Now it was Charlie's turn to lay his spoon aside. Swallowing the last bite, he sat back in his chair again. "Yes, sir, I remember."

Grandpa rubbed his whiskered chin. "Well, I got a letter that day, and it seems I've been summoned to the city."

Charlie's eyes grew wide. "Denver? You hafta go to Denver?"

Grandpa cleared his throat again. "Seems I gotta go see a judge."

"How come?"

Grandpa shifted in his seat. "Well, a cousin of mine, Ralph Smith, up and died awhile back, and although I haven't seen him in over fifty years, the letter said he left me some real estate somewhere near Saint Louie. It also said he had a passel of debt, so I'm thinkin' they're callin' on me to allow them to sell the real estate so they can settle the debt."

"So, why can't you go see Judge Carlyle in Pueblo and settle it there?"

"'Cause this particular judge in Denver specializes in these matters. Judge Carlyle doesn't reside over probate cases. They're more complicated than what folks around here are used to dealin' with." Grandpa sighed wearily. "More trouble than I need right now. But Ralph is dead and I'm alive, so I'll be the one to settle the matters."

"If you gotta go, couldn't I go with you?" Charlie asked as he swiped at a blot of dirt on his pants.

"Nope," stated Grandpa matter-of-factly. "You gotta get ready to go on that cattle drive. Besides, I can take care of my business in Denver and be back here before you leave, so I can tend to the farm while you're gone. If both of us were gone, things would go to pot. The place needs upkeepin' and there's lots to do before the weather changes."

"The weather changes? It's only July, Grandpa. Even if I leave in the middle of September, neither one of us would be gone that long. This isn't like one of those Texas drives where a poke can be on the trail for months. I'll only be gone a few weeks." Charlie thought for a moment and then continued. "In fact, why don't you wait and travel as far as Denver with us? That way you and I can experience a part of the drive together."

Grandpa pushed himself away from the table and started gathering up the bowls. "I like that idea, son, but I'm thinkin' I shoulda gone to Denver long before now."

Charlie shook his head. "I don't see where waitin' a few more weeks is gonna make that much difference, Grandpa. That judge hasn't been beatin' down the door tryin' to get you to Denver. You only got one letter and that was months ago, so I think he can wait a few weeks longer."

Grandpa set the dirty dishes by the basin and scratched his chin as he so often did when he was in deep thought. "But who'll tend the farm if we're both gone? It takes at least a week to ride to Denver and a week back, not to mention how long I might be holed up there tryin' to settle all this."

Charlie stood to his feet, his voice rising with him. "Ask Mr. Tuttle." He stopped and scratched his head. "No wait, they'll be takin' Mary Lou back east right about then." Turning to Grandpa, his face brightened. "Okay, then ask Mr. Jacobs if he'll keep Nellie for awhile and stop in a few times to check on things here. He can use or sell whatever milk she gives, the cattle that are left here after the sale can graze in the south pasture, and the chickens won't be layin' as much by then. And he can have the eggs. That'll be all that needs to be done till we get back."

Grandpa reached for the butter dish, but stopped. Slowly he nodded his head. He rubbed his chin again. "Well, I reckon you're right, son. I like the idea of not havin' to go it alone. This way, I'll be in good company at least part ways."

The familiar sparkle returned to Grandpa's eyes and he started to make plans as he finished clearing the table. "We'll take a ride over to Jacobs' ranch first thing in the mornin'. If he can help, then we'll head over to Pueblo so I can send the judge a telegram and let him know it'll be a little longer before I get there; 'cause I hafta agree with you, I don't think time could matter that much."

"Good. It's a deal then," said Charlie. "Tomorrow we're off to Jacobs' place and then to Pueblo." Grandpa picked up the last of the supper dishes and headed to the basin.

As he was speaking, Charlie looked at him. Not just at him, but at his features. The idea about traveling with Charlie and the soldiers had put a flicker of light back in the old man's eyes, but that excitement couldn't hide the changes that had occurred slowly over time.

Dark circles had crept in and settled under Grandpa's eyes. And the sparkle that once reflected the amber brown was filmed by milky gray, making them faded and dim, like a candle slowly fading for lack of oxygen. His brow was always furrowed, as if in deep thought or great pain. Charlie wasn't sure which, but he was sure his grandfather looked old and tired. Charlie wondered whether Grandpa could make a trip to Denver, some hundred miles away.

He got up quietly and pushed the chairs under the table. "I'm glad we'll be travelin' some together, Grandpa," he said. "Maybe you should stay in Denver and wait till I come back through, so we can travel home—"

"Nope. I'll head back here when I'm done. I might be old, but I can still ride a horse and make a fire."

There was no point in arguing, so Charlie headed out to the well for a bucket of water. Over his shoulder he said, "Okay, Grandpa. We'll both do what we set out to do and meet back here in no time at all."

6

BEN JACOBS SHIELDED HIS EYES FROM THE morning sun with one hand and looked up to where Grandpa was sitting in the buckboard. Ben's face was as tanned as cowhide, hard lines running from the corner of his mouth to his chin, but his eyes were soft and merry, reflecting the heart of the man.

"Be glad to, Stuart," he said. "Nellie won't be no trouble and I'll ride over once or twice a week just to have a gander at the place. How's that sound?"

Grandpa looked down from the wagon seat, holding Bessie's reins in his fingers. "Much obliged for the help, Ben. I don't think we'll be gone long, but I'll feel better knowin' things are taken care of at the farm."

"It's a deal, then," said Mr. Jacobs, slapping the wagon wheel and extending his hand.

Grandpa leaned down and shook it. "Done deal," he said with a grin.

Ben Jacobs tipped his hat a little to wipe the sweat off his bald head, and looked over at Charlie. "So, whatcha think of that horse?" he asked smiling.

"He's the best!" replied Charlie. "We had a pretty good workout yesterday and I plan on givin' 'im more of the same when we get home."

Jacobs nodded. "He's a good hoss. Won't never disappoint ya."

Charlie agreed heartily, "Nor me him."

"That's good to hear, Charlie. I'm glad he's got such a fine home."

Grandpa tipped his hat. "Thanks again, Ben."

Stepping away from the buckboard, Jacobs returned the gesture. "That's what neighbors are for, Stuart. Don't worry 'bout nothin' here. Just travel safe and God be with you both."

Grandpa clicked his tongue and Bessie turned them slowly toward Pueblo. When the way was clear, she broke into a trot. Charlie turned in his seat and waved his hand to their old friend just before he disappeared from sight beyond the hills.

Grandpa and Charlie got a room at the small boardinghouse in Pueblo and then headed to the post office. It didn't take long for Grandpa to write his message to the judge in Denver, nor for Wilbur to send it. Not wanting to disturb Wilbur at work, they agreed to meet him for a quick dinner at the boarding house later that evening and then went to the general store to place their order.

Grandpa handed the list to the mercantile clerk: twenty pounds of coffee beans, ten pounds of sugar, and a few spices he thought they'd need on the drive. Despite Charlie's protests, he bought the boy a new slicker and hat. He did let himself be talked out of buying spurs. Charlie insisted Star wouldn't need them.

Each picked out a couple of wild rags; a saddle blanket; a canteen; two sets of long johns; two pairs of jeans; three long-sleeved shirts; a few extra pairs of socks; and a couple of tin plates and cups. They'd need those. The storekeeper fitted Charlie with a pair of chaps, the kind with rawhide fringe hanging down the legs, a leather belt with a large silver buckle, and a leather vest that fit tight around the chest. Ammunition and rope were added to the mix and before they finished, the clerk had persuaded Grandpa to buy a box of waterproof matches. They were just little slivers of wood with white phosphorus on the tips, but Grandpa figured they were worth a try if the gunpowder got wet and they needed an emergency backup. They were sold in airtight boxes, so they'd be safe in the saddlebags when it came time to cross rivers or a sudden rain storm hit. When they finished shopping, Grandpa made arrangements to have the order filled by morning when they'd pick it up before heading home.

Sleeping until sunup was a luxury that wasn't afforded them very often so they took advantage of it whenever they went to Pueblo. They lay in their beds, comfortably tucked under their sheets and blankets until bright golden hues split the thin, dark horizon in the east.

At a little table in the parlor they ate breakfast and watched the sun inch upward into the eastern sky, little by little chasing away the shadows.

Wilbur was already gone, which disappointed Charlie. They were all too tired to do much talking the night before, and Charlie was hoping they'd be able to do some catching up before he and Grandpa went home. But Wilbur had a job to do, and Charlie admired his work ethic.

By 7 o'clock, the small town was buzzing. Grandpa and Charlie met the store clerk outside the mercantile on the boardwalk where he was sweeping dust off the steps. Their order was stacked neatly on a bench. Grandpa followed the storekeeper inside to pay for their merchandise while Charlie loaded it on the wagon. Teams of mules pulled loaded wagons up and down the street, their harness chains jingling with every step. Children scurried to the corner schoolhouse, hoping to beat the morning bell. Business doors were unlocked, and signs in the windows were turned from "CLOSED" to "OPEN."

It was always nice to come to town.

Grandpa bade good-bye to the clerk and walked out on the boardwalk. Filling his lungs with fresh air, he stepped carefully down the steps and made his way around the buckboard and placed his boot on the running board of the wagon, ready to heave himself up to the seat, when he heard someone running behind him.

It was Wilbur, wide-eyed and breathless. "Glad I caught you before you pulled out, Mr. Smith," he huffed. "Seems Judge Walker was eager to hear from you." He pulled a yellow slip of paper from his vest pocket and held it out.

Surprised, Grandpa pulled his foot down and turned round to meet the young man. "Why, thank you, Wilbur. I didn't think I'd get a response at all, let alone so soon after sendin' my message. Wonder what's the deal?"

Wilbur adjusted his visor. "Don't know, sir. But like I said, the judge musta been eager to hear from you. We usually don't get messages this early unless they're urgent."

Grandpa grunted and pulled his reading glasses from his shirt pocket and settled them on his nose. His crooked fingers shook slightly as he unfolded the yellow slip of paper. He was instantly lost in the message. He grunted now and then as he read, the furrow over his brow deepening and his face turning a light shade of red. Overcome with a mixture of curiosity and concern, Charlie stopped loading the wagon and joined Wilbur. They both watched the old man read the telegram. After a couple of minutes, Grandpa slid the glasses, along with the paper, into his shirt pocket and gave them a pat. Then he looked surprised to see Wilbur still standing there waiting for a response.

"Oh, sorry son." He smiled stiffly. "Haven't got a reply for the judge. Thanks again."

"You're welcome, Mr. Smith," answered Wilbur. "It was good to see you again." He punched Charlie in the arm. "And you too, Charlie."

"You too, Wilbur." Charlie punched him back. "Sorry we didn't feel much like visitin' last night."

"Oh, that's alright," his friend replied. "It's a long, tiresome drive."

"How's the job?" asked Charlie.

"It's a job." Wilbur chuckled. "If you've seen one dirty envelope, you've seen 'em all."

Charlie tipped his hat back a bit and nodded. "Yeah, I bet," he said, sliding his fingertips into his pants pockets.

"But sendin' and receivin' telegrams is pretty interesting," added Wilbur. "See those wires over yonder?" He pointed to the edge of town where a long row of wooden crosses with wires strewn from one to the other marched across the landscape. Charlie had seen them in the past, but never paid them any attention. "Those are telegraph wires," continued Wilbur. "The government has hung them pretty near all across the country, so messages can be sent from here to Timbuktu in just a few minutes. From what I hear, they even have big ol' cables under the ocean that run from the US of A to Europe!"

Grandpa had already climbed into the wagon. "You don't say," he muttered. "What'll they think of next?"

Wilbur didn't hear him. "Morse Code is fascinatin' stuff," he babbled on. "Just a bunch of dots and dashes, but it actually makes sense once you learn it. I'll have to teach you sometime."

"Okay. When you gonna be home next?" asked Charlie.

"Probably in a couple of weeks. I think I'll get to go home on a few weekends, but we'll have to see how the mail runs."

Charlie rested an elbow on the wagon wheel. "Well, I guess I'll see ya when I can. I'm headin' out on a cattle drive in a few weeks."

Wilbur whistled. "You don't say. Finally get to chase cows all the way up the territory, huh? Well, that sounds mighty sportin'."

Charlie punched him in the arm again. "Better sport than readin' a bunch of dots and dashes." He laughed.

"Yeah, you remember that, when you're ridin' through wind, rain, rivers, and cow patties and I'm sittin' in a nice, dry office readin' dots and dashes," teased his friend.

Grandpa picked up Bessie's reins. "Charlie, better finish loadin' up the wagon. We got a ways to go."

"Yes, sir." Charlie looked at his friend, a hint of sadness in his eyes. It might be a long time before they saw each other again. Charlie held out his hand, but Wilbur didn't take it. Instead, he threw his arms around his friend and locked him in a bear hug. "You be safe, Charlie."

Charlie hugged him back. Wilbur was as close to Charlie as a brother and he loved him as much. "I will, Wilbur. You take care too."

Wilbur stepped back and tipped his visor to Grandpa. "Good day, Mr. Smith." Before Grandpa could reply, the clerk turned and jogged back towards the tiny post office.

Charlie watched his friend run down the street then disappear into a doorway. "Take care of him, Lord," he whispered. Then eager to know what the telegram said, he turned to his grandfather.

Grandpa could feel the boy's curious stare burning a hole in his back, but he didn't turn. Holding the reins, he glared at the road ahead.

"Don't keep me waitin', Grandpa," fussed Charlie as he walked up to the front of the wagon. "What did it say?"

Grandpa didn't look down at Charlie, but stared straight ahead, his jaw muscles flexing as he fidgeted with the leather reins. "Nothin' important. Judge Walker wants me in Denver as soon as possible, and on my calendar, soon as possible is sometime in September."

Since the message had obviously irritated Grandpa, Charlie didn't want to push the issue, but neither did he want any surprises. With a hand over his brow, he squinted up at the old man. "You won't get into some kind of trouble with the law if you don't show up right away?"

Grandpa shifted in his seat. "For what?" he snapped. "For takin' care of my own business before I run off and take care of my dead cousin's passel of troubles? I don't think so."

Charlie quietly finished loading the wagon then climbed up beside his grandfather. Neither one spoke until they were out of town and on their way home.

The wagon bumped lazily on the dirt road, creaking as the wheels dipped low into the deep furrows. Grandpa leaned forward in the seat and rested his elbows on his knees, the reins drooping idly from his fingers as he surveyed the road ahead. "Bet she's some gray-haired, lonely old spinster who ain't got nothin' better to do than try to get people all riled up," he muttered under his breath.

The sudden remark surprised Charlie. "Who?" he asked.

"Miss Amelia Taylor, that's who."

"Who's that?"

"She's the one who actually sent that telegram," Grandpa grumbled. "She's the judge's secretary and the one who 'insists that I get to Denver as soon as possible.' Well, she can insist all she wants, but she's still gonna hafta wait. I'll get to Denver when I'm good and ready."

"Grandpa, you're gettin' yourself all worked up 'bout nothin'. I'm sure she didn't mean to sound bossy. Just encouragin' you to find the time to come up, that's all."

"And I told 'em yesterday when I'll be comin' up. She just needs to tend to her own business and let me tend to mine."

"She'll learn *that* when she meets you, Grandpa."

"Dern tootin' she will. I bet she's one of them old bitties

that wears her hair in too tight a bun, pullin' her eyes back and makin' her head hurt. And the only thing that makes her feel better is makin' everyone else's head hurt."

Charlie laughed and shook his head. "Let me drive, Grandpa. You climb in the back and rest awhile."

To the boy's surprise, the old man didn't argue, but handed the reins over and stepped across the seat into the buckboard. Charlie kept things steady until he thought Grandpa was comfortable, then he clicked his tongue and prompted Bessie into a faster trot.

Grandpa laid himself down among the supplies. He rested his head on a bag of coffee beans and pulled his hat down to shade his eyes. *I shoulda gone sooner,* he thought. *But I ain't gonna disappoint the boy now. He's countin' on me goin' part ways on that drive with 'im, and that's what I'm gonna do, dagnabit!* The wagon bounced along. *What did she mean this situation could affect my family, anyway? How could Ralph's death affect Charlie?*

He hadn't had an attack in a while and this one caught him off guard. He'd gotten himself all worked up and frustrated, too occupied by the telegram to recognize the pressure that had been subtly building inside his chest. Now desperate for relief, he fumbled through his pocket, hoping he'd remembered to bring his medicine.

"Let's see," he mumbled, "a small comb, a couple of pennies, my pocket knife . . ." Sweat rolled down the side of his head as the pressure intensified.

He threw his hand into his other pocket and felt around:

a roll of money, a kerchief, and to his relief, a little glass bottle. He pulled it out and tried to steady his shaking hands as he struggled to unscrew the cap, but they wouldn't cooperate. The small amount of liquid inside the bottle sloshed against the brown glass as the wagon rocked to and fro. Unable to open it in time, he slid the bottle into his vest pocket and pulled his hat down over his face. Gritting his teeth, he braced himself for the wave of paralyzing pain. His hands dropped to his side and his fingers dug into whatever bag lay nearby. Pain like dull arrows hit hard, shooting down his left arm and up through his jaw. He battled for breath beneath the crushing weight on his chest.

"Lord," he whispered. "They're gettin' worse each time, but I got important business to take care of in Denver, and from what she said in this last telegram, the outcome will impact my family. So if I can make a deal with you, if you can wait till I've settled these matters, make sure my boy's future isn't marked in some way, I'll gladly surrender to you then."

The wagon creaked as Bessie pulled it towards home. Charlie relaxed the reins and whistled softly as the morning sun warmed his face and warded off the crisp remains of the previous evening. In the buckboard, sweat poured down the old man's face and stung his eyes as he scuffled again with the small bottle of medicine.

The doctor had said the liquid would relieve the pain and even help him sleep, but warned that it could be addictive if he wasn't careful. Normally, Grandpa wouldn't have anything to do with something addictive. He refused to drink alcohol for that very reason. Said he'd seen what it could do to a man. And since the attacks usually didn't amount to more than a feeling of severe indigestion, he figured he could just walk them off and save the money, instead, to get Charlie outfitted for the cattle drive.

But the doctor had insisted, so he had bought just a couple of tablespoons of the serum to keep in his pocket in case of an emergency. That was a few months ago. Now he was glad he had. This one felt worse than indigestion.

He rolled onto his left side and with the back of his right hand wiped sweat from his eyes. He moved slowly, due partly to the pain, but mostly because he didn't want to attract Charlie's attention. The boy didn't need to see him this way. He rested his head on a bag for just a second.

His breath was quick and shallow. He felt he was going to suffocate, but he couldn't move to alleviate the pressure. His left arm throbbed in agony. With clenched teeth he stifled the urge to moan. He knew opening the bottle was going to take all he could muster, so he closed his eyes and wrapped his gnarled fingers around the glass container and, ignoring the wrenching ache in his jaw, forced the lid into his mouth and held it tightly between his teeth. Concentrating, he twisted until the metal cap gradually gave way and began to turn.

His sweaty hand shook as he tipped the bottle to his lips, spilling a few drops on his chin as the wagon wheels vaulted down the heavily rutted road. The mixture felt thick and cloying in his mouth. He fought the urge to gag and spit it out, swallowing hard instead. Finally, with the medicine down, he tackled the painstaking task of securing the lid back onto the bottle and sliding it into his vest pocket.

Exhausted, he rolled onto his back and waited for the agony to pass. Several tumultuous seconds ticked by before the laudanum took hold and the attack subsided. In its place a wave of peace rolled over him, leaving him feeling at ease and comforted. He closed his eyes and pulled his hat over his face. "Thank you, Lord," he mumbled.

His skin was damp and pale. Sweat plastered his hair to his head and soaked his shirt and vest. But inwardly, though his heart had been seriously damaged, he was at perfect peace, happy with the deal he had just made with the Lord.

Charlie threw a glance over his shoulder to check on Grandpa and was pleasantly surprised to find him asleep. Turning back to the road, he smiled.

7

MRS. TUTTLE, JOLLY SOUL, OFTEN HOSTED
events at the Tuttle cabin. This time it was a farewell luncheon for Wilbur, Mary Lou, Grandpa, Charlie, and anyone
else who was going out on business or adventure. She was
a gracious hostess who greeted each guest with warmth and
charm, often bringing a bit of laughter to the conversations
as she made her rounds. It was only on occasion that she
would be seen dabbing her eyes with her lace handkerchief,
in the event that someone would mention how different
things will be without Mary Lou. Charlie didn't care for all
the hoopla. He would rather have left on the cattle drive
without much ado, but he went to the luncheon for Mrs.
Tuttle's sake.

The circuit preacher stopped by early afternoon to say a
few encouraging words about life's journeys and to offer up a
prayer for guidance and protection for all who were about to
embark on the unknown.

Neighbors came from miles around, their wagons loaded
with food and children, and as usual, the day was spent
eating, scolding, talking, playing games, and laughing. Now,
as the sun was sinking in the west, folks were loading up
and going home.

Grandpa, complaining of indigestion, had left an hour

ago. Charlie had stayed to hear some of the old timers tell their stories. When the last man emptied his pipe and thanked Mr. and Mrs. Tuttle, Charlie was still there, hoping that he and Mary Lou would have the chance to talk; but it didn't look promising. Mary Lou hadn't seemed to be as set on their meeting as he had, so he figured it was time to call it quits.

Then as he led Star out of the corral, he saw Mary Lou sitting on the creekside alone, staring into the trickling water and he knew it was now or never, so he led his horse to the water and let go of the reins.

"Mind if I sit a spell?" he asked.

Mary Lou didn't look up. She just shook her head.

Charlie sat beside her. Nervously he pulled on a long blade of grass until it popped out of the ground, then began twisting it around his finger. The sun was already setting below the treetops, its late rays glistening through the branches. Time passed; the two still hadn't said much and he was getting uncomfortable.

"When do you think you'll be home next?" he asked.

Mary Lou shrugged her shoulders. "It depends."

"Depends on what?"

Making sure her skirt covered her legs, she pulled her knees up and hugged them to her chest. "Well, it depends on the weather, if I'm working or not, my friends . . . you know, things like that."

Charlie looked at her sideways. "May I write you?"

Mary Lou giggled. "Do you know how to write, Charlie Smith? I didn't think you paid that much attention in school."

Charlie grinned and threw the broken blade of grass into the water. "Well, I did pay attention some. Not as much as you, but some."

A cool breeze stirred in the branches above them, cuing the katydids to begin their evening song. A strand of blonde hair gently brushed across Mary Lou's cheek. She glanced over at the boy. "Of course you can write to me, Charlie," she said quietly. "We'll still be friends. Just 'cause I'm going away doesn't mean we have to act like complete strangers."

Charlie smiled. "Well, I'll see if I can't throw a few words together once in awhile and send them to you."

"I'd like that," she said smiling. Looking over her shoulder at the cabin, she nodded. "We've got to get up early to meet the stage in Pueblo tomorrow afternoon, so I should be heading in now."

Charlie got to his feet and helped her up. She nervously brushed at her skirt. In all the years they had known each other, they had never stood this close. Mary Lou tilted her face toward his and smiled. At first, he only noticed her slightly crooked teeth, as he usually did, but then he looked into her face. For the first time, he realized that the childhood freckles had melted into a soft pink complexion. Holding her gaze, he looked into her dancing blue eyes. He could feel heat rising from his neck and his tongue swell in his throat, and despite the miserable first attempt (his tongue stuck to the back of his teeth and he couldn't pronounce a word), he finally managed to ask the question. "C . . . Can . . . I mean, may I kiss you good-bye?"

Her pink cheeks reddened, but she didn't lower her eyes. "We're just friends, Charlie," she whispered up to him.

Charlie could feel color fill his face. Embarrassed, he stepped back. "I'm sorry," he mumbled.

She touched his arm and searched his eyes. "It's not you, Charlie," she said pleadingly. "Please believe me. It's all this ambition that I have locked up inside of me. Ma was perfectly content marrying a farmer and raising a pack of children, and she's hoping we'll all have at least forty babies of our own. But I'm not like my ma. I want something different, something more than just a one-room cabin, a passel of kids, and a worn-out hoe. There's too much I want to do, too much I want to see right now, without worrying about a lovesick boy back home—a home that I have no intention of ever returning too."

Shoving his hands deep into his pockets, Charlie looked around for a hole into which he could crawl. He felt like a fool. He was a fool for even thinking about a kiss, let alone asking for one.

"What do you want, Charlie?" Mary Lou asked quietly.

Surprised, he peeled his gaze from the ground and threw an awkward glance at her. "I don't know." He shrugged. "I haven't given it much thought—"

"'Cause it's always been just you and your grandpa," she finished, a sarcastic edge to her tone. "And where will you be when your grandpa goes to Heaven?"

Charlie shifted his feet. "Look, Mary Lou, I don't want—"

"Well, you'd better start," she interrupted as lightning flashed in her eyes. "You'd better start wanting. Wanting a life other than what you have here; wanting a woman with grace and style; just wanting to live. You'd better start,

Charlie, or you'll be living the same old life fifty years from now."

He wasn't sure what to say. "I . . . well . . . I don't really see anything wrong with my life right now," he stammered.

"Yes you do," she scolded. "You're just as ambitious as I, or Wilbur, or even as much as your grandpa was when he was your age; but you're afraid to do anything about it; you're afraid to leave and live life. But your grandpa will leave *you* one day, Charlie, and you'll find yourself alone."

Charlie folded his arms across his chest, not sure what had started this conversation and uncertain where it was heading. His eyes avoided hers; he gazed across the yard. Mary Lou stared hard into his face.

"I waited for awhile, Charlie," she finally said softly. "I waited for you to ask me to the parties and dances, but you never did. You and I were never close, and I used to hope. But it was always you and Wilbur. I was just a tag-along. Someday you'll meet a girl and fall in love with her, but if you hesitate too long, you'll find her in the arms of another."

Charlie flushed with surprise. "I never knew you were—"

Without warning, Mary Lou stepped closer and kissed him on the cheek. "Live, Charlie," she whispered.

Then just as quickly, she gathered her skirt and ran to the cabin. Speechless, he touched his cheek with his fingertips, gently caressing the warm spot left by the brush of her lips. As he watched her close the door, he felt a sudden sense of sadness. He knew it wasn't because he had lost her—she was never his to lose—but because he had never bothered.

He turned back and looked at the babbling creek. Was life passing him by like the water that flowed at his feet? She talked like she could see right through him, like she could see the restlessness that had been tormenting him lately. But what he found most frustrating was the fact that she was right. He wouldn't leave Grandpa. Not right now.

Star came up from behind and nuzzled Charlie's shoulder with his wet nose until he was rewarded with a gentle rub. "Thanks, buddy," whispered Charlie. "I needed that." He pulled an apple, that he had taken from one of the food baskets, out of his pocket and held it out for Star. The horse sniffed and his great nostrils flared, then he eagerly gobbled it down and licked Charlie's palm to make sure he'd gotten the last bite. Charlie scratched behind one of Star's ears. It was getting dark. It was time to go.

He pulled himself up into the saddle and looked back at the cabin. "Good-bye Mary Lou," he whispered. "I hope you find what you're lookin' for. Don't worry 'bout me. If I end up livin' the same old life, that would suit me just fine." But in his heart he knew that wasn't true. He knew he wanted more.

 **8**

SEPTEMBER ARRIVED IN AN ARRAY OF COLOR
and a sense of anticipation. The evergreen slopes of the
majestic Rocky Mountains sported groves of golden aspen;
Charlie watched their leaves quiver in the light breeze from
the back door of the cabin. Out the front, the prairie
was adorned with soft hues of lavender, white, greens, and
browns. Not only did nature's royal colors signal a change
of seasons, but they meant the end of Charlie's waiting and
the beginning of his adventure. He had longed for this day,
and here it was.

The soldiers were busy rounding up the herd from the
top pasture and bringing them out onto the dirt trail north
of the cabin. Charlie gathered and packed Bessie and Star.
Checking their gear several times, he knew he hadn't forgotten anything, so he led the two horses to the shade of a large,
blazing red maple. Sergeant Wilkins came and stood with
them. This was his first cattle drive too, having only been in
Colorado for a couple of years.

He didn't resemble Sergeant Barlow at all. Instead of
being tall and thin, Sergeant Wilkins was short and round.
Charlie thought he had a friendly face. His clear blue eyes
and easy smile made the boy feel somewhat better, since he'd
be traveling with this stranger.

The sergeant patted Star's neck. "He's a mighty fine horse, Charlie," he said. "He should serve you well on this trip."

"He will, Sarge," replied the boy. "We've worked awfully hard these last couple of months and he can cut with the best of 'em."

"Good. We won't have time for training once we hit the trail."

"Don't worry 'bout me and Star. We'll do our part."

The sergeant smiled and nodded. "I know you will, boy. Before Sergeant Barlow retired and moved back to Kansas City to be with his family, he filled me in on how you'd been hankerin' to go on this drive since you were about ten years old. I've no doubt you're ready to be a good cowhand."

"We won't let you down, Sergeant."

The big man patted the horse one more time, then turned on his heels and headed for his own mount. Cutting the cool morning air with a shrill whistle, he held up a plump forefinger, swirled it in a circular motion, and then whistled again. "Head 'em up," he hollered, his round face reddening.

It was time to go. Charlie's heart raced as he grabbed the reins and led the horses towards the cabin. He saw Grandpa step out onto the stoop and close the door behind him. "It's time to mount up, Grandpa," Charlie called.

Grandpa smiled and reached for Bessie's reins. "And so it is," he said happily. He quickly slipped a package into his saddlebag and buckled it closed then grabbed the saddle horn and gave a good pull, checking the tautness of the cinch strap. Satisfied that the saddle was secure, he slid a foot into the stirrup, grabbed the pommel, pulled himself up with a slight grunt, and swung his leg over, slowly easing himself into the worn saddle. He was old, but Charlie loved to watch his grandpa in motion; he was still quite the horseman.

"We got all we need for this here adventure?" Grandpa asked as Charlie mounted Star.

Charlie settled into his saddle. "Yessir. Everything's in our saddle bags and what didn't fit inside is tied on."

"Good," said Grandpa. He scanned the prairie and then looked back at the cabin. "I hope—"

"Everything will be fine, Grandpa. God has everything under control."

The old man smiled at his grandson. "Yes, He does. He's got it all under control."

The soldiers had rounded up the hundred and fifty head of Hereford cattle that they'd purchased from Grandpa and started pushing them out onto the prairie. Charlie watched their white heads bob in the sea of dust. Swirling upward, the dust cloud stood on the breeze for a brief moment and then disappeared, making way for another wave. Excitement coursed through Charlie's veins. He'd watched this so many times before from the top rail of the corral, but this time he was watching it from his own horse. This time he was part of it and would live it.

Grandpa watched his grandson. Charlie definitely looked the part of a cowboy, sitting in his new saddle, riding a new horse, and wearing the new clothes and chaps. *He's a handsome one*, thought Grandpa. *Gonna hafta keep my eye on him, that's for sure.*

Star pranced back and forth impatiently; displaying the same eagerness as his rider.

"I hope ya like dust, son," Grandpa said.

Charlie kept his eyes on the cattle. "Why?" he asked.

"'Cause it looks like you're gonna be eatin' a lot of it over the next few weeks."

Charlie grinned. "That's okay by me."

"Then you better get on up there and start eatin' your fill. Me and Bessie will just swagger a bit to the west and try to stay out of it."

Charlie turned Star and trotted towards the herd. Over his shoulder he hollered, "Stay where I can see you."

"We'll be in plain sight," yelled Grandpa. Chuckling, he thought, *I don't know if you'll actually be able to see anything once you're in with the herd, but me and Bessie will be able to see you, or at least the big ball of dust that contains you.*

Star broke into a gallop. Grandpa paced Bessie and watched the boy fade among the cattle and soldiers. *He'll be grown up and gone just as quick as that*, he thought to himself.

A familiar, calming voice spoke. "I'll take care of him, Stuart."

"Please do, Lord," whispered Grandpa. "He's a good boy, but this land is bigger than he can imagine, full of bad folks and the like. I want him to grow up and become a strong Christian man; so don't let no harm come to him when I ain't around to take care of things."

"I'll never leave him, Stuart. And I can protect him like no one else can, even you. And while I'm taking care of him, I'll take care of you too; so go in peace, my friend."

Grandpa couldn't argue with that. Content, he gently tapped his boot heel to Bessie's side and led her into a fast trot, following the cloud of dust that was rising to the north.

 **9**

DESPITE BEING RAISED ON A FARM, WHEN IT came to driving cattle, Charlie was a greenhorn. There was no doubt about that, but he learned fast and that proved to be a valuable asset in the first few days of the drive.

Each day every man held a post and it was imperative that each maintain his post in order to keep the cattle moving, and moving in the right direction. The trail boss, whom Charlie hadn't yet met, constantly scouted ahead of the outfit searching for water and a safe place to camp for the night.

Because it was a small herd, only one man rode point—in front of the cattle—to lead them wherever the scout directed. Flank riders kept the cattle in line by riding alongside the herd and the drag riders kept stragglers from straying in the rear. With the exception of the scout, post assignments changed daily to relieve the men from breathing the thick dust stirred up by the herd. Charlie learned the responsibilities of each post as he pulled his weight with the chores.

For days the cattle plodded along under the warm, fall sun, across the rolling grassland. Not in a particular hurry, the men and their horses followed suit and didn't push the herd any faster than necessary. Except for the occasional cow that decided to wander off toward some imaginary sanctuary, Star hadn't had many opportunities to stretch his legs. He was anxious to run, but he obediently walked with the rest.

It was the walking that taught Charlie about saddle soreness. After ten or twelve hours a day in the saddle, he could barely swing his leg over the saddle horn to slide off Star when they finally made camp in the evenings. And when his feet hit the ground, it took sheer willpower to move anything from his waist down. He had never been so stiff and sore. But as the days passed, his muscles grew stronger and he became accustomed to the constant rocking motion of the horse beneath him.

Each day was much like the day that preceded it, but occasionally something new or unusual would be seen or heard. One such time happened on a late afternoon when Charlie saw a dark speck off in the distance on the prairie. For a long time it just remained a small dot, never moving or wavering and as the group got closer, Charlie understood why. The speck was actually a cabin. Getting closer, he saw a sign above the door which read, 'Log Cabin.'

No kiddin', he thought with a chuckle.

Then the sergeant's barking voice rose above the moans of the cattle. "We'll camp here."

With whistles and shouts the men led the cattle into a small meadow beside a stream. After Charlie had helped secure the animals for the night and had pinned Star to the ground where he could graze and drink from the stream, he headed towards the cabin. He was too curious to keep from asking why a cabin was way out here.

Just before reaching the door, Charlie tripped over something hidden in the tall grass, and when he righted himself, he was looking down the long line of a railroad track. Northward it went as far as the eye could see until it rounded a bend and disappeared. To the south, it stopped just a few yards away from where he stood. This scenario puzzled Charlie and he turned around several times, looking at the cabin and what lay around it. Both the track and the cabin were in the middle of nowhere. Mountains rose to the west; grasslands flowed to the east, where a few rocky outcroppings jutted up towards the sky. But there was nothing compelling that Charlie could see; nothing except cottonwoods and a small creek split the prairie.

Grandpa rode in and picketed Bessie. He stripped his gear from her back and laid it under a tree. He walked over to Charlie who had just introduced himself to a man standing in the doorframe of the cabin.

Charlie was saying, "Glad to meet you, Mr. Dooley." Then the boy turned and pointed to Grandpa. "And this is my grandfather, Stuart Smith. Grandpa, this is Mr. Dooley. He lives and works in this log cabin. Guards the track for the Denver & Rio Grande Railroad."

Grandpa grimaced under the pressure of the big man's handshake. Mr. Dooley was not only tall, he was thick: thick in the arms, legs, fingers, and neck. He was the biggest man Grandpa had ever seen, next to Jess.

The smell of sweet bacon floated from the cabin. A quick glimpse revealed a couple of tables and a few chairs scattered across the room. Charlie figured by the smell and by the apron Mr. Dooley was wearing, it was some sort of eating establishment. Probably for the railroad workers. He also noticed that the apron the big man wore was soiled with dirt and smeared with blood. He figured it wasn't any of his business, but it did look like the man had hunted and wrestled down whatever critter was on the menu. The picture of this large man wrestling a little varmint made Charlie smile.

Grandpa took his hat off and pushed his hair back with his hand. Scanning the mysterious railway, he said, "Where's this track headin', Mr. Dooley?"

The large man turned his grey eyes to the north. "It rides from here to Denver and back, for now. General Palmer plans to take it all the way to Pueblo."

Grandpa's eyes grew round. "Pueblo? Pueblo down the way?" he asked as he pointed south.

Mr. Dooley nodded. "Yep, tha'd be the one."

"When's it suppose to land in Pueblo?"

"Sometime next year, I was told."

Grandpa shook his head. "Well, I'll be. Pueblo's gettin' a railroad."

"Yep," said Mr. Dooley. "The railroad will join Denver to this here new town, and then go right on down to Pueblo."

Charlie looked around. "This is a new *town*?"

Mr. Dooley chuckled. "Well, it don't look like much now, but it's just startin'. It's gonna be called *Colorado Springs*, a place for rich folk to live, or just to come visit for vacations and such. General Palmer likes the lay of the land with the Indian's sacred stone gardens over yonder and Pike's Peak up there. They already got schools and libraries, parks and churches, and even a college all planned out."

"Is this the place where that Colorado Agriculture College is gonna be built?" asked Charlie.

"No," replied the man. "That's way up north, around Fort Collins. I don't know what this one'll be named, or what they'll teach, but they're makin' plans."

"Can't they put all that in Colorado City, just west of here?" asked Grandpa.

Mr. Dooley shook his head. "Won't do. Not for rich folk. Colorado City's a miner's town. Too rowdy for the folks Palmer wants to bring out here."

Grandpa snickered and rubbed his chin. "How ya gonna keep the two separate?"

Mr. Dooley stepped out of the cabin doorway and walked to the middle of the railroad track. He turned and smiled. Pointing down at the track, he said, "You're lookin' at the separator. Only citizens of good moral character will be settlin' in Colorado Springs. Any riff raff that comes floatin' in will be directed to Colorado City, on the other side of the tracks."

Grandpa shook his head again. "Ya don't say," he whispered. "Well, tryin' to convince folks who see themselves one way, but the railroad sees another way, ought to keep the railroad folks busy for awhile."

Dooley looked down at his bloody apron and then back at the two men. "It already has," he said with a gleam in his eye. "I convinced him to stay in Colorado City."

Charlie and Grandpa just stared and couldn't think of much more to say, so they took their leave and walked the horses to where the soldiers were setting up camp in the shade of a cottonwood.

"What do you think the railroad will do to Pueblo?" asked Charlie as he tied Star to the line.

Grandpa stared at the ground. "Well, it depends," he said thoughtfully. "It depends on what type of cargo the train will bring back and forth and how the town takes to it. We'll see."

"And what about *this* new town?" asked Charlie. He looked around at the emptiness, letting his eyes scan prairie and mountains. "*I* don't think it'll amount to much," he mumbled. "Probably won't get as big as Pueblo, anyway."

Grandpa looked at the boy. "Only time will tell, son. Only time will tell."

As the two entered camp, they heard one of the soldiers talking. It was McQueen, a robust Irishman. He was telling the tale of Robert Emmet, apparently one of McQueen's heroes from his homeland.

With rolling eyes and flailing arms, the soldier played out how Emmet had risen up and taken Dublin Castle, killing the lord chief justice in a bloody battle. McQueen explained how words to several Irish ballads were believed to be secret codes that had helped Emmet in his quests. Then the burly man broke into song.

> Oh my name it is Nell, and the truth for to tell,
> I come from Cootehill which I'll never deny;

Charlie sat down and leaned against his saddle. Without taking his eyes off the bellowing Irishman, he leaned towards the sergeant. "Has he been drinkin'?" he whispered. The sergeant shook his head.

71

I had a fine drake, and I'd die for his sake,
That my grandmother left me, and she going to die.
The dear little fellow his legs they were yellow;
He could fly like a swallow or swim like a hake;
'Til some dirty savage, to grease his white cabbage,
Most wantonly murdered my beautiful drake.

The Irish ballad went on for a while, but still no one moved. Charlie wasn't sure why, but McQueen seemed to be in a good mood, and he hoped he'd remain so by the end of the song, though the words weren't too promising; but at least for now he was singing. For that Charlie was actually grateful. He'd heard worse come from that soldier.

10

CHARLIE SAT DEEP IN THE SADDLE, TAKING note of the land around him. He was riding point and, since he was in front of the cattle, he could see clearly from beneath the wide brim of his hat, free from the dust and grass kicked up by the cattle's hooves.

He constantly scanned the prairie for a sign—from anything, man or beast—but he was mainly looking for man, or a man. The scout, that is. Today, his job was to lead the herd to wherever the scout stopped for the day. And he wouldn't see him, only his sign.

Occasionally, Charlie would relax and let his feet hang lazily in the stirrups. A gentle breeze swept across the prairie, swirling the tall grasses in unison like ripples on a large pond. Charlie's gaze followed the swells toward the eastern horizon.

A large flock of geese lifted from their hidden nests and soared into the clear sky, honking noisily overhead.

On the distant prairie a large herd of antelope grazed. Their beige coats almost made them invisible against the muted colors of the plains until they stirred and their white rumps revealed their position. There looked to be hundreds of them.

He watched as some of the young ones suckled their

mothers and then disappeared among the wildflowers to play or sleep. His gaze slid beyond them and searched the horizon for something more, but as far as the eye could see, there was only a vast openness, a beautiful display of nature, untouched by the boundaries enforced by man.

They drove the herd down the soft slopes of the rolling hills and into a small valley. Magpies scattered from a cluster of scrub oak and flew over the cattle, looking for something to steal and take back to their hideaways. "Camp robbers," mumbled Charlie. The birds squawked when they realized the stinginess of the cowboys; their saddlebags were strapped shut and their hands were empty.

Again a cool breeze stirred the grasses, this time bringing up the sweet smell of honeysuckle. Charlie inhaled deeply, trying to hold on to the scent as long as possible. Soon, it would all be lost to the approaching season.

Charlie wished the land would stay just as it was, changing with the seasons but forever a place of peace, solitude, and beauty. Deep down he knew it wouldn't, though, not with the railroad coming.

He turned his attention to the west where Pikes Peak loomed above them, dark and massive. Back home he could barely see its summit from the hills behind the cabin, but here the whole mountain was visible, rising in its full magnificence. Charlie studied the cold, forbidding peak. A translucent stream of white blew from the summit, like a white ribbon unfurled and thrown into the sky. But instead of flowing majestically over the prairie, it looked motionless, frozen in time. He knew the ribbon wasn't a cloud. It was snow—snow whipped by a raging wind on high. The stony cathedral was already feeling winter's fury.

He studied the mountain a second longer and tried to imagine what is was like for Zebulon Pike to climb the wild, harsh face of the mountain, some 14,000 feet up, just to finally reach the barren tundra; a place where the air is so thin even the trees refuse to grow. *Even so*, he thought, *the view from up there must be incredible. Maybe that's why Jess likes being a mountain man.*

Riding herd gave a man time to think. Even though there were hundreds of animals, several men, and a beautiful vastness of territory stretched out before them for miles just waiting to be explored, it was a lonely business. There wasn't time for socializing with the other men while the cattle were moving, so for at least ten hours a day it was each man to himself. Even he and Grandpa didn't see each other until they tethered their horses at camp in the evenings.

After supper, the crew's custom was to walk away from the chuck wagon and spread their gear on the prairie for the night. One might separate from the crew just to be alone, usually because he was sick, but most wanted the company of other humans at the end of the day. It was easier to socialize with people than with cows.

The dark prairie wasn't what most would consider a luxury accommodation, but Charlie found it comfortable and exciting. For the cowboys, the hard ground was their bed at night, the saddle their pillow, and a thin blanket and small fire the only warmth to cut the cold nights; but the beauty of the black canopy of sparkling lights above them, the songs of the meadowlark and coyote, and the smell of the rain on the breeze made up for the discomfort.

Once they were settled around their small campfire, the men talked, laughed, argued, or played cards, the latter usually producing the rest, but Charlie chose to lie back and look at the stars with Grandpa. One night, however, a thunderstorm gave them no choice but to huddle close with the cowboy soldiers.

It was late September and, for the most part, the weather had been typical for the high plains: warm during the day with an occasional quick scattering of rain in the afternoon; followed by a crisp, cold night. That was the usual, until the night rain poured down around them and six men huddled under a cramped canvas canopy. A seventh was out in the rain somewhere, standing watch. Cook, as the men called him, lay underneath the chuck wagon wrapped in his blanket. A tin cracker box pillowed his head and a worn, dusty hat hid his face.

Peterson, a tall and lanky southerner who had recently been transferred to the Fort, yelled, "Ain't seen a gully washer like this in quite some time."

Charlie nodded in reply, knowing his voice wouldn't be heard over the thunder.

"Blasted, God-forsaken country," grumbled McQueen, the words rolling off of his tongue in a thick Irish brogue. "One hundred-ten degrees durin' the day, thirty degrees at night, and when it rains, it floods the whole plain. Cain't make up its mind what it be want'n to do, 'cept make sure any human in the vicinity is as miserable as can be."

"Relax, McQueen," mumbled Sarge. "Griping about the rain isn't going to make it go away, so how about applying your red head to a game of cards?"

The Irishman must have known better than to spar with the sergeant, because he slipped the leather suspenders off his broad shoulders and sat down beside his boss. Charlie was amazed by the size of his arms.

"Sure," the Irishman responded gruffly. "Ain't got nuttin' better to do."

The two settled against their saddles and stretched their legs towards the fire. Sarge rummaged through his saddle-bags and found a deck of cards. As he shuffled them, McQueen pulled a twist of tobacco from his pant pocket and bit off a piece. He packed the wad into his jaw with his thumb, then rolled his tongue over it a couple of times. Looking satisfied, he hunkered back down against his saddle.

Chewing the tough tobacco, he picked up his cards and fanned them across his large, calloused palm. Occasionally he would lean back and spit the black residue out onto the rain-soaked prairie. Peterson pulled his gear in closer and joined the two but declined McQueen's offer to chew.

Grandpa leaned against his saddle and pulled his glasses out of his vest pocket. Then he rummaged through one of his saddlebags until he found his Bible. Charlie pulled closer to hear him read.

"What's that?" asked LeFaye, a young Frenchman about Charlie's age who had joined the ranks a couple years earlier.

"It's a Bible," said Charlie. "We read it every night. Slide on over if you'd like to hear."

LeFaye shrugged his shoulders and wormed his way in closer. No one else showed interest.

Grandpa opened the worn leather cover and flipped

through the pages. When he found the book of Philippians, he began to read aloud.

Charlie, straining to hear the words over the pouring rain, thought it ironic that the lesson was on contentment. No matter the situation, Paul encouraged the believers to be content. Charlie thought it was an appropriate lesson. The darkening sky was lit only by the frequent bolts of lightening. Then deafening thunder pounded the sky and shook the earth, as it rolled between the mountains. Rain soaked everything.

The sky grew blacker with every rumble of thunder, until Grandpa couldn't read anymore. Tucking his glasses back into his vest pocket, he bowed his head.

"What's he doing?" asked LeFaye.

Charlie lifted his head and opened one eye. "Same thing I am," he answered. "We're prayin'."

"Oh," replied the young soldier. "My apologies." Charlie opened both eyes and smiled. "It's okay. Lean in a bit and we'll pray together. Me out loud and you to yourself if you want."

The young soldier bowed his head. At first he seemed unsure what to do or say, but must have realized he had no reason to worry.

Charlie began to pray aloud. "Lord, at first I thought it was gettin' mighty miserable out here with the heat, the dust, and now the rain, but according to your Word, I should be content no matter what the situation. Help me to take your Word and hide it in my heart so it will guide me through the day. Help me make the right decisions and convict my heart when I don't. And help me to believe that

I can do all things through you. And Lord, I can even see that some good has come from this rainy night, since you've given me the chance to meet LeFaye here. Bless him, and show him what you want him to see, Lord. Thanks for the rain, and thanks for LeFaye. Amen."

The soldier lifted his surprised face.

"I've never heard my name in prayer before," he mumbled, "not out loud anyway. I know my mother prayed for me all the time, but only in whispers. It sounds kind of strange, but thank you for your kindness."

Charlie clapped LeFaye on the shoulder. "You're welcome. Thanks for joining us."

The young man smiled. "I'd like to sit with you and your grandfather again, if I may."

Charlie chuckled. "You may. We don't mind at all, LeFaye. If we can, we'll read from the Good Book every night."

With the Bible tucked safely back into the protection of the saddlebag, the men stretched out as best they could, resting their heads on their saddles and pulling their blankets tightly around them. It was only September, but the storm was blowing in a cold that could chill a man to the core.

Lightning struck the prairie close by and thunder rolled through the mountains again, but despite the raging storm outside their small tent, Charlie soon heard the sound of soft breathing coming from beneath Grandpa's blanket. "The man can sleep anywhere." He chuckled to himself. He slid his hands behind his head and gazed up at the tarp roof, finding a rhythm to the pattering of the rain on the tent above them. His eyes grew heavy and he felt his body sink into his blanket and begin to drift into sleep. But every so often he'd be drawn back to consciousness as the peace was broken by McQueen's cursing. Either discontented by the weather or the outcome of a hand of cards, McQueen was swearing and cursing the rain, the cows, the army, and whatever else came to his mind.

Charlie looked over at LeFaye. He didn't seem to be paying attention to the Irishman, but was staring at the top of the tent as if lost in thought.

"LeFaye," Charlie said, trying to speak softly but still be heard above the tapping of the rain on canvas. "You okay?"

LeFaye shifted in his blankets, but kept his eyes locked on the tarp above.

"On me mum's grave and beyond to—" ranted McQueen. "Argh, what'd ye do that fer?"

Charlie and LeFaye both turned in time to see Sarge withdraw his elbow from McQueen's ribs. Charlie and LeFaye exchanged glances and were glad their chuckles were muffled by the sound of the rain.

"What had you so deep in thought?" asked Charlie, now that he had LeFaye's attention.

"Oh, that." LeFaye glanced upward. "I was just thinking about your prayer and about God. That's all."

"What about 'im?"

LeFaye settled back into his blankets and threw his hands behind his head. "Well, I was just wondering if God knew who you were talking about when you mentioned my name in prayer, but then I had to admit that of course he did, even if by deductive reasoning alone, since I am the only Phillip LeFaye in the area."

Charlie laughed. "Want to know somethin' else, LeFaye? Not only did He know I was talkin' about *you*, but He knew before I asked. He knows your name, He knows the color of your eyes, He knows your laughter."

LeFaye turned toward Charlie, the glow of the campfire revealing his wide, eager eyes.

"He just wants you to get to know *Him*," Charlie added.

Outside, a jingle of spurs sounded above the slapping rain. A dark form of a large man came through the camp towards the chuck wagon. Rain muted the man's features; but when the lightning flashed, Charlie saw he was tall and walking like he meant business. He threw the carcass of a dead antelope over the tailgate of the wagon, and muttered something to the cook, before turning towards the tent. Then Miller, the trail boss, tucked his head and came in out of the rain. All eyes turned upward and followed him as he stepped across the mess of tack and tired men lying across the sheltered ground. Water dripped from his hat and slicker. He tapped McQueen's foot with the tip of his boot.

"Your watch now," Miller yelled above the downpour.

"Already?" complained the Irishman.

"The storm has them spooked, so keep a close eye."

McQueen struggled to pull himself to his feet. Miller grabbed his arm and yanked him up. "Have you been hittin' the bottle, soldier?" Miller asked tersely.

McQueen scowled and straightened to his full six feet, staring into Miller's eyes. Beads of sweat dripped down his round, fuming face.

"I don't drink when on the job, Miller. And I suggest ye mind yer own business."

Miller was slightly taller than McQueen, but not as square; yet Charlie could tell by the way his buckskin jacket fit his broad shoulders that Miller would be a fair match in a fight. Miller held the Irishman's gaze.

"So it must be your shaving soap that smells like whiskey."

McQueen's black eyes hardened, but Miller didn't flinch. After what seemed like hours to Charlie, McQueen relaxed his shoulders and turned his face from Miller's, but at the same time he pulled his Colt revolver from its holster and with a casual air, pointed the barrel at Miller.

A wicked smile slid across the Irishman's lips as he opened the cylinder and counted the cartridges inside. He slapped it shut and shoved the gun back down into his holster. He threw a warning glare at the scout, then grabbed his slicker and hat and headed outside.

He hadn't bothered to put on his shirt or reposition the suspenders that dangled at his waist before going out into the storm. As his silhouette disappeared into the glistening raindrops, Irish curses sliced the cold night air.

Miller pushed McQueen's saddle aside with his foot then threw his gear down beside the sergeant.

Isaac Miller wasn't a regular in the army but had signed on as trail boss days before the small detail left Fort Collins for the Smith farm. Although the Fort had been relieved of most of its military responsibilities, it was still protocol that those remaining never leave the area without a scout. The soldiers had been on alert since the major engagement between the army and the Indians at Summit Springs a couple of years earlier. Although a good scout, he appeared to be a loner. Peterson once said the man would rather sleep out on the prairie with one eye open and one ear to the ground during a buffalo stampede than to be with the rest of the men. But here he was in the tent.

Before sitting down, he turned to Charlie and tipped his hat. Charlie responded with a nod and watched closely while the cowboy soldier settled into the warm spot left by McQueen.

This one's different, thought Charlie. *Better keep a closer eye on 'im.*

Charlie let his head fall back onto his saddle and closed his eyes. Lulled into a trance by the rhythm of the rain once more, he yawned deeply. *But it'll have to wait till mornin'.*

The fire burned lower as the small detail shifted restlessly beneath their blankets. All of the men eventually slept. They had to. Tomorrow would be another ten hours in the saddle.

❦ 11 ❧

AT DAYLIGHT, THEY MOVED THE CATTLE northward and the crew joked that at least the trail wasn't dusty anymore. It was muddy, though, and each step made a sucking noise just before the black muck flipped up from the cattle's hooves and splattered against whatever was closest to them. Sometimes it was each other, sometimes a passing horse, but nothing escaped the dark coating. Then, as the noon sun burned overhead, the wet mud baked into a hard gray shell, eventually crumbling into a fine dust that once again found its way into every crevice and fold.

Charlie pulled a biscuit and bacon from his saddlebag. He was hungry and relished the small meal except for the annoying grit, which even got into his canteen.

That evening, after securing the cattle, he and Star headed for the nearby creek. It was a dark, chilly evening, but it was also time for a bath. Sitting on a rock, Charlie yanked off boots and socks, then stood and stripped off shirt, pants, and long johns. Amazing how much dust fell from his underclothes as he pulled them off and dropped them into the water.

Star stood on the bank and watched Charlie hop on

one foot, then hug himself tightly while his knees knocked against each other, then sit down, only to bolt straight back up, just to sit down again, and then jump back up. Star tipped his head and watched as Charlie repeated the same movement several more times.

Finally, shivering uncontrollably, Charlie forced himself to ease into the water. His teeth chattered violently and his skin covered with chill bumps, like the skin of a freshly plucked chicken. But he sat. And the flowing current washed away the sweat, grime, and dust.

Star must have figured it was safe to get a drink; but suddenly he raised his head. With his ears forward, he listened. His large eyes wandered from tree to tree as if he heard someone out there. He nickered, but Charlie didn't pay any attention.

Charlie buried his head under the water for a second, then when he came up, he didn't look at Star, but rubbed soap across his arms, down his legs, and under his arms, then splashed handfuls of water onto his face and over his head. Taking the soap again, he rubbed it into his hair, feeling little pebbles of sand come loose from his crusted scalp.

His hands and feet were turning blue from the cold. He dunked his head into the water a couple of times to rinse out the soap, coming up sputtering and shaking his head like a wild man. Then he rubbed the soap across his long johns and scrubbed them against a stone till bubbles saturated the cloth. He rinsed them as fast as he could then sprinted to the creek bank.

Climbing out of the stream, he grabbed his small towel and recklessly dried himself. He was soaked to the bone and shaking like an autumn leaf, but oh! it felt good to be clean.

He dressed and gathered his belongings. It was time for supper.

Cook filled Sergeant's plate with stewed rabbit and beans, and Grandpa motioned for him to sit next to him on a big piece of deadwood.

"We're not too far from Denver, Mr. Smith," the sergeant said between bites. "We'll hold the cattle outside town when we get there and I'll let the men ride in with you, if that's alright. They could use the break."

"I'd be obliged," said Grandpa. "It'll give me a few extra hours with my boy."

"He's done a fine job out here these last couple of weeks," said the sergeant. "It didn't take him long to figure things out on the trail. I see why you're so proud of him."

"There's more to that boy than meets the eye, Sarge. He's going to make a fine man some day, for sure."

Sarge raked a forkful of beans into his mouth. "Don't look now, Mr. Smith, but I think he's already become a fine man."

That surprised Grandpa. He still saw Charlie as a boy. Scanning the group for his grandson, he watched Charlie talk and laugh with his new friend, LeFaye. Sure enough, Grandpa saw a young man standing in the same boots a boy had been wearing just a few weeks earlier.

Charlie stood a little over six feet tall. Working the farm had firmed up his arms and broadened his shoulders, but the cattle drive had done something else. It had given him self-confidence. Charlie wasn't just stronger physically, but mentally too. He was no longer the little fellow that followed his gramps around the farm.

The boy's mousy brown hair, swept back behind his ears, stopped at the nape of his neck. His brown eyes danced as he laughed, and the high cheek bones that Grandpa had attributed to the family lineage were no longer dotted with freckles, but were bronzed by hours of working in the sun.

But what really amazed the old man most was recognizing for the first time how closely Charlie resembled his father. He was the spitting image of Teddy.

"Well, I'll be," whispered Grandpa.

"You've done a fine job, Stuart."

"I tried." When he turned back toward Sarge, the soldier was gone. In his place, a large mountain man shared the deadwood bench.

Grandpa wasn't surprised. He had become accustomed to thinking of his friend Jess being there all the time, whether he could see him or not.

"I don't know how it happened, Jess," he whispered. "He grew up right in front of me without me seeing it."

"That's okay, my friend. I watched him."

"But if I didn't even realize he was growin' so fast, how can I be sure I taught him everythin' he needs to know?"

"There's no way you could, Stuart. You're up in years and you're still learning new things, aren't you?"

"Well, yeah, I am, but—"

"He'll learn every day too," interrupted Jess. "Some things will be easy enough, others not so, but either way I'll be there to guide him and he'll be wiser and stronger for it. Keep your trust in the Lord, Stuart."

"Yes, I will." He watched the clouds glide across the darkening sky. "I know I don't have much time."

Jess shook his head. "Stuart, my friend, your life is in God's hands. Didn't I teach you that a few years ago?"

"Yep, you did." Grandpa chuckled. "I guess I'm just one of them mule-headed folks who hasta learn things over and over again."

Jess nodded.

"I should stop worryin' about every little thing and enjoy whatever time I have left, shouldn't I?" said Grandpa.

Jess slapped his knees. "After all these years, you've finally learned that! So you see, you *can* learn something new at your age."

12

NEXT MORNING, THE CREW'S GREENHORNS
saw firsthand what a storm can do to a little stream. On
a normal day, it was only a creek, passable with just a few
leaps and bounds by a good horse, but after the storm, the
water was running high and fast. As the herd approached
the churning water, the cattle hesitated to cross, pacing the
bank and moaning with disapproval. But once the first few
jumped in, and several white heads were bobbing across, the
rest followed, splashing into the rapids.

Grandpa tied Bessie to the chuck wagon and climbed
up beside Cook. The heavy wagon would cross with little
difficulty. Charlie and Peterson, who were working flank,
waded into the shallows and waited for LeFaye to bring up
the rear. Pacing through the surging water, Star made sure
no cattle ventured past his post. Peterson made sure none
floated downriver. It was up to LeFaye to make sure none
turned tail and ran back in the opposite direction.

The last cow jumped into the water. Charlie walked Star
back to the south bank where LeFaye and his mount stared
at the rapids. Peterson waited in the shallows. Noiselessly the
three measured the task at hand. Speaking low, Charlie tried
to calm his friend's nerves.

"Have you ever crossed a river before?" he asked.

"Of course I have," LeFaye said, but he swallowed hard. "One doesn't come all the way from the east coast clear out here without crossing a river or two, but I just never got used to it." He lowered his voice to a hoarse whisper. "This one just seems a bit more intense than any I've crossed before."

"Well, this really isn't much a river," said Peterson. "Shouldn't be too deep in the middle."

LeFaye looked at him. "It's water, and it's moving fast. Call it what you will; I don't like it."

Charlie nodded, resting his hands on the pommel of his saddle. He chose a direct tack and asked, "You trust your horse?"

"Yes," replied the Frenchman. "He's a good steed."

"Then give him the lead and take it slow."

LeFaye drew a deep breath and studied the flow in silence. After a long pause, he said, "Okay, Charlie. I'll follow you."

Charlie gathered Star's reins in his fingers. "Let's go, then." Gently, he squeezed Star's ribs with his knees and whispered, "Take it slow and easy, boy."

Star threw his head back and pranced to the water. Peterson took the lead while LeFaye followed close behind Charlie.

The water came up to Star's chest in mid-stream, a little deeper than Charlie had anticipated and the strong current forced the horses downstream. Charlie grasped the reins. Horse and man inched towards the opposite bank.

"Just a few feet to go, boy," Charlie said, trying to reassure Star.

Peterson's horse was nearing the north bank as well.

Charlie turned in his saddle to check on LeFaye. The soldier was steadily proceeding behind him. With his back against the flow, Charlie saw a sudden look of horror on LeFaye's face.

Charlie spun round in time to see the branch, with its long, jutting arms run into Peterson's roan. The animal panicked, jumping and bucking, running into the branch again until it finally floated on downriver.

Peterson overcompensated for his horse's reaction. Apparently fearing a fall, he yanked back hard on the reins. In response, the roan reared on his hind legs and dumped Peterson into the cold water. The soldier disappeared under the tumbling swells and the frightened horse bucked, splashed and kicked as it scrambled to the shore.

Charlie and LeFaye watched in horror. Peterson's arms thrashed above the water as the swift current carried him downstream. His head would bob above the surface for a few seconds and then disappear again beneath the white foam. He would reappear and gulp another breath of air before being pulled under again. He seemed to be trying to yell for help, but the water lapping into his face choked back the sounds.

If the current weren't so strong, he could just stand up, thought Charlie, *but if he keeps this up, he'll drown for sure.*

Charlie turned Star back to the water's edge and raced down the shoreline till he was ahead of the soldier. He pulled the lariat off of his saddle horn and threw it out into the raging water. Charlie could see Peterson's panick-stricken face. The man didn't know how to swim.

"Please, Lord, give him the presence of mind to grab

the rope," Charlie pleaded. Then he yelled, "Grab the rope, Peterson! Grab the rope!"

The young man turned his face toward Charlie's voice. Charlie didn't know if Peterson could see him, but he yelled again. In a split second, Peterson began to kick his feet and flail his arms.

"That's right, Peterson," yelled Charlie. "Grab the rope. It's right there."

Peterson groped for the lifeline. In the darkness, his fingers—which must have been stiff with cold—finally grasped the rough lifeline.

Step by step, Charlie backed Star up the embankment pulling Peterson until he finally lay face down on the thick grass, barely breathing.

Charlie jumped from Star and untied the blanket behind his saddle. Kneeling in the grass, he rubbed Peterson down from head to toe. At first, Peterson's blue fingers refused to let go of the rope. Finally, the young soldier started coughing up water, he caught his breath and relaxed enough to release the rope.

"Th . . . thanks," he said through chattering teeth.

"No need." Charlie wrapped the blanket tightly around his friend's shaking body.

Peterson lifted his head and glared upstream. "I swear I'll beat him for throwin' me."

"We'll talk about that when you're dry and not so angry," Charlie said sternly. He stood and pulled Peterson to his feet, holding his arm for a minute until Peterson's legs stopped wobbling. "A hot cup of coffee'll help you regain perspective."

Peterson responded with a raspy cough as Charlie gave him a boost onto Star. Taking the reins, Charlie led Star and Peterson back to the chuck wagon.

The men were huddled by the chuck wagon, waiting for Charlie's return. When the two came round the bend, the sergeant stepped out to meet them.

"Why didn't someone help me?" asked Charlie.

Sarge's face reddened. "We were told not to," he answered, impatiently.

"Not to? Who said not to?" coughed Peterson.

The sergeant nervously wiped his forehead with his hanky. "Can't say. But we were told to stand our ground and let Charlie handle things."

Charlie grew angry. "Well, I'm glad I was able to oblige. Next time it'd be nice to know someone was backing me up."

"I was."

Charlie whipped round to see Miller.

"I was right there," Miller said calmly.

"I didn't see you," snapped Charlie.

"That's not unusual, but I was there."

The sergeant cleared his throat. "The two of you can discuss this all the way to Fort Collins if you like. We've got to take these cows to Denver, though, so mount up." He turned towards his own horse.

"But, I'm soaked," said Peterson.

The sergeant didn't bother to turn around. "That you are," he yelled over his shoulder, "but that won't stop you from riding a horse, will it? We're too close to Denver to stop this early in the day. Mount up!"

Before Peterson could protest again, the big man mounted his horse and waved his white kerchief in the air.

Charlie watched Sarge start the herd as Peterson wrang water out of his shirt tail. "I ought to be feelin' just dandy by the time we camp tonight," the young man grumbled.

"You'll be fine," Charlie said.

Peterson snorted as he slid off Star and pulled himself up onto his roan. "I'm gonna be sore all over," he grumbled.

Charlie swung his leg over Star and settled into the wet saddle left by Peterson. "Yep, that you will be," he agreed, "but you'll be alive to feel it."

13

PETERSON'S UNIFORM HUNG ON A COTTON-
wood branch while he sat by the campfire in his long johns
with his saddle blanket draped over his shoulders.

Charlie and LeFaye sat with him. They relaxed against
their saddles. Miller brought three cups of coffee.

"Mind if I sit with you?" Miller asked.

"Not at all," Charlie mumbled.

The scout handed a cup to each of them then sat on the
ground. He leaned against a tree and looked over at the blue
uniform as it waved in the breeze. "Good thing Charlie was
paying attention this afternoon."

Peterson ripped a handful of grass out of the ground. "I
ought to whip that horse for throwin' me in the water."

Charlie blew on his coffee. "Actually, if we get right
down to the bottom of things, you shouldn't a' been riding
him in the first place. You don't know how to handle him."

Peterson glared at the young cowboy. "I'm as experienced
as any man here," he protested in his southern drawl. "I may
not know how to swim, but I do know how to ride, and that
there horse threw me for no good reason."

Charlie shook his head. "He threw you because you were
pulling back on the reins too hard. His mouth hurt, so he
relieved the pain the only way he knew how."

"I was trying to hold on," argued Peterson.

"Wrong move. He reared up to relieve the pressure. You just happened to be on his back at the time, so you were dumped into the creek. But the minute you let go of the reins, he stopped rearin' up, didn't he?"

Peterson took a gulp of the hot coffee. "It wasn't that simple. The log popped up and he bolted, and I—"

"Got scared and pulled back too hard," finished Miller.

Peterson seemed ready to protest again but stopped. He lowered his head and confessed. "I did do that, didn't I?"

"Yes, you did," said Charlie, grinning at Miller. Then to Peterson he said, "He got spooked and you made it worse."

"Guess he taught me a lesson, didn't he?"

Miller chuckled. "He doesn't know you don't know how to swim and could've drowned, or I'm sure he would've tried to be more understanding."

Charlie asked Miller, "Who told the troops not to help me with Peterson?"

"I did."

"Why?"

"'Cause they'd have only gotten in the way. You were doin' a good job."

"You said you were right there with me, but why didn't I see you?"

"You were too busy to notice. But I was there just in case."

Charlie sighed. "Well, I guess it could've ended a lot worse than it did."

"And I agree with Miller," said Peterson. "I'm very grateful you were paying attention."

Charlie sat his coffee cup down on the grass and cleared

his throat. He glanced at Peterson and then LeFaye. Would you two mind if I asked you each a personal question?"

"I don't mind," said the Frenchman. "I doubt there's anything about me you don't know. Not many secrets on a cattle drive."

"Well, there is one thing I don't know," said Charlie.

LeFaye laughed nervously and shifted his weight. "Then go ahead and ask."

Charlie searched his friend's face. Their eyes locked. "Phillip, if you would've been knocked into the river today and the worst happened, where would you have gone?"

LeFaye looked confused. "Down river, I suppose, unless you pulled me out and buried me."

Charlie laughed. "No, that's not what I meant."

"Well, what do you mean?"

"Where would your soul have gone?"

LeFaye set his cup on the ground. His brow furrowed. Finally he looked back at Charlie. "I don't rightly know, Charlie. I really don't know."

"Would you mind if I introduced you to a friend of mine?" asked the young cowboy.

Right then, Grandpa walked into the circle and almost interrupted, but Miller held his hand up, signaling for Grandpa to be still. The old man stopped in his tracks and looked over at his grandson. He glanced at the book in Charlie's hand, then quietly lowered himself to the ground.

"You mean God, don't you Charlie?" LeFaye's attention had not been diverted.

"I mean Jesus," answered the boy. "I met Him almost eight years ago when a friend introduced me to Him and

He saved my life, as well as my soul, and He's been my best friend ever since, next to Grandpa."

LeFaye hesitated for a minute, then said, "Ever since you prayed for me that night awhile ago, I've wondered about God, who He is, what He is like; so go ahead. I'll listen, but I've got some questions for you."

"I'll answer what I can; what I can't, we'll find out."

LeFaye laid his book beside his bedroll. Peterson pulled the blanket tighter around his shoulders.

Charlie opened the small, worn Bible to the book of Romans. He read and the two soldiers listened quietly.

"See here, this is how our sinful nature came about," said Charlie. "Man was made perfect, made in the image of God, but when Adam sinned, every man, including himself became a sinner and was doomed to die both physically and spiritually."

LeFaye looked stunned. "Well, that doesn't leave much hope, now does it?"

"Ah, but there is hope," said Charlie. "Listen to this." Charlie flipped the page. "Here it talks about the wages of sin. Being working men, we all know a wage is something a person earns, or deserves, for something he did. We, us humans, deserve to die because of our sinful nature, but God didn't end it there. He isn't willing to give us the wages we deserve, but wants to give us a gift instead."

LeFaye's watery eyes filled with doubt. "And that gift is eternal life?" he said with a hint of apprehension in his voice.

Charlie nodded. "Yes, it is."

"And folks just have to believe in Jesus to receive this gift of eternal life?" asked Peterson.

Charlie nodded again. "That's right. All anyone has to do is ask for forgiveness and believe in Him."

Now a dark cloud shadowed LeFaye's eyes. Sadly he shook his head. "I don't know," he whispered. "I don't understand how God could be so loving, so giving, and yet there be so much pain on this earth. I mean, my mother had done this very thing you speak of—believing, praying earnestly for a better life. In her faith, we left France and came to America where she believed we would find peace and happiness; yet she and my sister never had a chance to live. And even now we have war, killing, stealing . . . If God is so good, if He cares for us so much, why does He allow this? I don't understand."

Charlie closed the Bible and tucked it back into his saddlebag. Turning to his friend, he started to give an answer.

But McQueen yelled, "Because there ain't no God!" He pushed past Miller into the circle. "I've been listenin' to what this preacher boy has been sayin', and he's a liar. There ain't no God, there ain't no Heaven; and as for Hell, yer livin' in it right now."

Charlie started to jump to his feet, but a firm hand gripped his shoulder and pulled him back down. "Sit down," whispered Jess. "He'll learn, but not from you and not now."

Charlie spun round and stared with amazement at the big mountain man. Jess was sitting on the ground beside Charlie's saddle, smiling at him.

"Jess?" whispered Charlie.

"It's okay, son," Jess said. "I appreciate the loyalty, but fightin' him isn't in the plan right now, so keep talkin' to these two here, and I'll handle that one later. Just sit tight for now."

Just as Charlie leaned back against his saddle, Miller stood up from his resting spot against the tree. "Mind if I answer this one, Charlie?" he asked politely.

The question surprised Charlie. Miller had never said one way or the other if he believed in God. *But then again, I never asked*, he thought. Then to Miller he said, "No, go ahead."

Miller threw a warning glance at McQueen and then turned his attention to LeFaye. "When Charlie first started talking to you this evening, he read a verse from the Good Book that referred to Adam. It is true that because of him all men are sinners, but did you get the part before that, about when they were first created—about how Adam and Eve were made perfect?"

"Yes," said LeFaye. "I'm familiar with the story, how they ate of the forbidden fruit."

Miller nodded. "That's a good start." Shoving his hands deep into his pockets, he began to pace back and forth, pausing as if examining each word before he spoke.

"The reason why Adam and Eve ate the forbidden fruit is because, although they were perfect, they were made with the ability to choose. Then, they were free to act on that choice, foolishly or not. See, God created man with a free will, with the ability to make choices. Just as Adam could choose to walk with God, he could choose to walk away from Him too. But let's say God didn't make man that way. Let's imagine everyone was made without the ability to choose."

Miller stopped pacing and looked directly at McQueen. "What would things have been like then?" he asked.

McQueen glared back at the scout. "Ye don't know what yer talkin' about, fillin' this boy's head with lies."

"You're welcome to sit and listen," said Miller calmly. "We'll answer your questions too."

McQueen started to say something, but stopped himself. His hard eyes darted from Miller to Charlie then back to Miller. "I've had enough of this. Just keep yer God to yerself. I've no need for 'im." Turning sharply, he stomped back toward the chuck wagon. Peterson followed him with his eyes.

Taking advantage of the short distraction, Grandpa moved closer to Charlie.

Miller turned back to the Frenchman. "Where were we?"

LeFaye plucked a piece of prairie grass. "You were asking what it would be like if we were all born without the ability to make choices. I guess it would be like a marionette show." He chuckled. "We'd all be puppets on a string."

"Exactly!" Miller said. He picked up his pacing again and continued. "If we lived in a world where we didn't have the ability to make choices, there might not be any suffering, but there wouldn't be any life either. God was aware of that when He made Adam. If He didn't make man a living soul, man could not have a soul at all."

"But God has a will too, and it's supposed to be so good. If He is the Almighty, can He not stop pain and suffering? Can He not will it away?" asked LeFaye.

"Yes, He could," answered Miller. "But He won't for a couple of reasons." Using his fingers, Miller explained, "One, bad things happen in this world because man makes bad choices. There are wars, famine, sickness, greed—right down the list, all because of bad choices.

"And two, it is often through pain and suffering that folks turn to Him. Instead of nothing bad ever happening, He can take a bad situation and make it good, if we allow Him to. He can use any circumstance to help each one of us become the person He wants us to be. He didn't bring pain to mankind; man did, by choosing to sin. But when we turn to Him, God can take the pain in our lives, in the world, and make it good."

"Turning to Him is easier said than done," snorted Peterson. "Take McQueen for instance."

"That's because of pride," said Miller. "It would seem like a natural thing for the creature to willingly turn to the creator when it's hurtin', like a crying child to its mother, but often, we don't. Through stubbornness, pride, and arrogance, we figure we can handle things on our own, blame God when things go wrong, and keep going; but that becomes a vicious circle, with no end, no peace, and no redemption. Pain will always be a constant in our lives, and it refuses to be ignored; so how can we deal with it?—We turn it over to God."

"We can't do it by ourselves, though," said Grandpa to no one in particular as he fingered a saddle strap. "Only God can give real peace when the heart is broken. We surely do need Him."

Miller nodded. "And that's the other side of how God created us. God made us with a free will, but He made us to need Him, too. So when we don't listen to what He tells us, and we make stupid choices, really messing things up, we have a longing deep inside to make things right. Or if we're carrying scars from something that hurt us, pain too heavy for the human heart to handle, He takes it from us and carries it for us. He is what we need."

LeFaye closed his eyes and lowered his head. Tears dripped off his chin onto the dry ground beneath him.

Charlie scooted over to him and put an arm around his shoulders. "Let the Lord change things for you, Phillip," he whispered. "He can take the sin, the pain, the whole kit 'n caboodle, and give you eternity to get to know Him."

LeFaye sat in silence. Finally, he looked over at Charlie, and tears filled the corners of his eyes. "I can't, Charlie," he muttered. "I've too many questions about God that haven't been answered. I understand what you and Miller are saying, but I still don't know . . ."

"Can we answer anything else for you?" asked Charlie.

"No, not now. Maybe later."

Charlie looked over at Peterson, who lowered his eyes to the ground and shook his head.

"Okay," whispered Charlie. "Maybe later."

Charlie looked over at the spot where Miller had been pacing. Instead of a tall man standing by the tree, there was nothing except Peterson's uniform, flapping in the cool evening breeze.

14

OFF TO THE WEST, THE SUN WAS BEGINNING to set behind the Rockies, exhibiting a spectacular show of color in the sky. Shades of red blended with the blues of the evening sky and mingled with the remnants of thin, white clouds. One could almost imagine a giant union flag waving over the snow-capped mountain peaks.

Charlie and Grandpa watched sun's golden fingers slide away from around a small, jagged mountain range. "That mountain over yonder looks like an Indian layin' on his back, don't it?" said Grandpa.

"Yeah," Charlie said. "It does." Pointing, he added, "There, you can see the long feather lyin' to the south, and then there's his forehead, his nose, his chin, his belly, his legs, right on down to his feet." Charlie smiled. "That's amazin'."

"You should see it from the west side," said Grandpa. "It really looks like a Ute Indian from thata way."

Charlie stared at his grandfather. "You been on the other side of those mountains?"

"Yep," he said with a nod. "It was a long, long, time ago. Even before I met your grandma. I was just a young'n and lookin' for adventure after the war in Alabama."

"You never told me, Grandpa." Charlie was taken aback.

Grandpa shook his head. "No, I haven't told you a lot

about me, son. Guess I been too busy tryin' to teach you things that would count in your life, like huntin', trackin', usin' your senses, and things like that instead of borin' you about my past."

"But your past is a part of my life too," said the boy. "And it does count. It all counts."

"Then I'll have to make it a point to tell you some things once we get home," said the old man. "In the meantime, let's finish the business that brought us north."

Charlie had a million questions but didn't press the issue. They turned their horses toward the lights of the city as the first stars of the night twinkled above them in the dusky heavens. The day had begun its surrender and from somewhere below, the music of a tin-pan piano welcomed the darkness. The saloons and brothels came alive with each gaslit lamp. Laughter and loud, rowdy talk echoed through the streets, beckoning the gold panners in from the rivers and the cowhands from nearby ranches.

Charlie had heard about Denver. It was a young city, only thirteen years old, but because of the gold rush and the recent union of the Denver and Rio Grande railroads, it was a bustling city. Folks were still pouring in from the east by train, wagon, horse, and stage, hoping to find their fortune along the banks of the Platte River or Cherry Creek.

Makeshift tents, cabins, lean-tos, and Conestoga wagons lined the two rivers for miles, providing the only shelter for many families as they panned through the muddy waters of the rivers day after day. It wasn't unusual to hear a gun shot echo across the valley at any time, as killing became the accepted manner used to resolve claim disputes.

All this was on Charlie's mind as they rode into the
city. He was amazed at the crowded streets and boardwalks.
As the small band of soldiers and the two civilians slowly
picked their way through the crowded streets, he became
more aware of the sights and smells around him, the likes
of which he had never known in Pueblo. Large signs hung
above every building, announcing the type of business and
its wares, which included everything from land and mine
claims to prostitutes.

Men stood on the boardwalks conducting business,
chatting about politics, scrapping over gold nuggets or the
goings-on at a ranch. There were men in all styles of clothing: boots and chaps, pin-striped suits, string ties, or tattered
rags. A group of Indians, all wearing various types of animal
skins, rode past them, their eyes cast downward to avoid the
questioning expressions of the white men. Grandpa turned
in his saddle to take a second look at one in particular.

"Whoa, Bessie," he said. A light of recognition flooded
his eyes. Above the noise of the crowd he shouted, "Nakima,
is that you?"

An old Indian riding a black and white paint similar to
Bessie, turned in his saddle to see who had called his name.
Grandpa raised a hand. The Indian squinted and stared as
if letting his old eyes open up the memories in his head. It
didn't take long before his face showed recognition of the
old white. He turned his horse slowly and walked him up
beside Bessie. Neither spoke a word. Grandpa held out his
right arm, and the old Indian grabbed it, embracing it solidly
with his left.

"How are you my old friend?" asked Grandpa, his smile

stretching wide between his cheekbones.

"I am well for now, Eagle Eye," answered the old Indian, eyes glowing. "But the white man's government is making things difficult for me to remain well."

Grandpa nodded his head toward a building down the street. "Is that why you're here? Takin' care of business?"

The old Indian nodded. "There is a new council here, Government Agency for Indian Affairs. But the council is blind, deaf, and mute. They do not see our way, nor hear us when we speak, and to us, their words make no sense. I do not see a bright future for the Ute people if it is left in the hands of the white man."

"I'm sorry to hear that," said Grandpa. "I wish—"

"I do too," the old Indian cut in, "but it will never be." With that, he held out his left arm. "Take care, Eagle Eye."

Grandpa grabbed and embraced the leather clad arm. "Good to see you again, old friend," he said warmly. "I can only pray."

The old man and Grandpa held each other's gaze for a long minute. No more words passed between them, but their eyes spoke volumes. Finally, Nakima let go and turned his horse, leading it into a trot to catch up with the small group of braves that had accompanied him. Grandpa watched until the group disappeared into the street crowds.

Charlie saw the corners of Grandpa's mouth twitch just for a second as the old man's eyes followed his friend, but then Grandpa turned and looked at him.

"You just saw a piece of American history, Charlie," he said fervently. "A piece of history that, I'm afraid, will soon be lost forever. When we get home, and I share some of my story with you, that man right there will be a big part of it. He and I go back a long way."

Charlie looked back down the street, but the Indians were gone.

The two turned their horses and started back up the street in silence, but it didn't take long before Charlie was enjoying the sights and sounds of the city once again. They saw other Indians, but Grandpa didn't stop to speak to any of them.

Everywhere women bustled from store to store, often with unruly children in tow as they searched for that one last item before scurrying home. They too were wearing every clothing style imaginable. Some wore dresses that had come straight from the fashionable studios of Europe, while others wore the threadbare garments of the poorest homesteader or gold prospector. There were even women standing high up on the balconies of a few saloons, who barely wore anything at all. Charlie stared in disbelief for a second and then turned quickly, his face hot with embarrassment.

"Pay no mind to them," warned Grandpa.

Charlie was still blushing. "Don't worry, Grandpa, they aren't my type."

Grandpa chuckled. They both knew the boy had never really courted a girl, so neither was certain of just what his type was, but Grandpa was pleased to know that these wouldn't even be considered.

"I don't judge them for what they do," he replied. "Only God can do that, but I'll be judged for what *I* do, and it's those actions I have to mind."

"Well, I reckon they're *my* type," interjected McQueen,

who was riding ahead of Grandpa. "Me and Peterson'll stop here and meet back up with you borin' saints come mornin'."

"Suit yourselves," said Sarge, "you're on your own time now, but come sunrise, you're back on my clock, so don't be late getting back to the herd!"

The two soldiers stopped their mounts and stared upward at two women beckoning to them from an upstairs window. After a few minutes of mumbling to each other, they eventually tied their horses to the hitching post in front of the brothel and went in.

The rest of the men moved on. "Let's head on over to The Gold Rush Hotel," said Grandpa. "We'll get settled in for the night and then we'll find us a place to eat some real food."

Charlie smiled. Anything besides gritty beans sounded awfully good to him.

They found a livery stable on Larimer Street and turned their horses over to the owner. Grandpa paid for several days of boarding and a little extra for some sweet mix for Bessie. She'd done exceptionally well keeping up with the soldiers and Grandpa felt he owed the old gal for it. Charlie led Star into a stable where he stripped the saddle and tack from him and gave him a quick rub down. Pulling a cube of sugar from his pocket, he held it up to Star's mouth and the big animal gently took it from his palm then brushed his tongue across Charlie's hand as if to say, "Thank-you."

"I take a few cubes of sugar for my coffee," Charlie whispered to Star as he stroked the horse's long neck, "but I don't use 'em all." The horse nodded and whinnied.

"Rest well," said Charlie. "I'll come get you in the

mornin'." Charlie left Star and ran to catch up with Grandpa and the others.

Just down the street from the livery was The Gold Rush Hotel. It wasn't as fancy as other hotels a little farther down the road, but it was clean and orderly. It would do fine. After checking in and getting settled in their rooms, they found their wash basins and cleaned up enough to make themselves presentable. Couldn't be any worse than some of the ranch hands they had seen earlier as they were coming into town.

They found Sarge in the lobby, where some fancy-dressed Mississippi gambler was inviting him to join a "friendly" game of cards in the hotel parlor. Sarge passed on dining out with his crew and hung back with the tinhorn.

Grandpa, Charlie, Miller, and LeFaye went down Larimer Street, peering through windows and reading signs. "Pueblo doesn't have half as much stuff," said Charlie excitedly. "In fact, we've got only one mercantile and it can't hold near what one of these stores has." He pushed his face against a large store window. "Look, Grandpa. This one sells nothin' but candy."

Row after row of wooden barrels were filled to the brim with every imaginable kind of sweet. The woman behind the counter flashed a pleasant smile and motioned for the men to come in, but Grandpa nudged Charlie along, while smiling and tipping his hat to the lady inside.

"Ruin your appetite it will, so we'll keep movin," he muttered, barely moving his lips as he spoke.

Down the way, they found another store that sold men's clothing, sporting very smart suits in its showcase window.

The men pressed their noses against the glass to see the colors and styles. Shielding the sides of their faces with their hands to block the reflections cast from the gas lamps behind them, they were able to see farther back into the store.

Then, like a thief sneaking up behind, the teasing aroma of fried chicken tickled their nostrils. Instantly their mouths watered. Forgetting the store and its fancy suits, the men spun on their heels and searched the street for anything that looked like a restaurant. They spread out and moved down the street on a mission and the goal was to find the origin of that smell. They only had to walk a couple of blocks when Grandpa found it. Dark red letters were painted across the window: *Dixie's Southern Fried Chicken.* He inhaled deeply and patted his stomach.

"Ahh, now this is the mother lode."

The four men removed their hats and walked into the establishment, surprised to find the place homey and comfortable. Unlike the dimly lit, ramshackled tents down by the rivers that served as diners for those who had nuggets to spare, this restaurant was clean and bright. Pressed red and white checked cloths covered the tables, a pot-bellied stove sat in the corner and offered a welcoming fire, and the smells escaping from the kitchen invited the potential guest to sit and stay a while. The foursome found an empty table and made themselves comfortable.

A few minutes later, a young girl came out of the kitchen and spotted the newcomers. Approaching their table, she pulled a tablet and pencil from her apron pocket. Her long, blonde pigtails swished from side to side. She greeted the men with a warm smile and Charlie noticed that the tiny freckles that dotted the bridge of her upturned nose spilled lavishly over onto her pink cheeks. She reminded him of a younger Mary Lou.

"Well, howdy, little Miss," said Miller, trying to get her attention. She glanced round the table, blushing when her eyes met Charlie's.

"Howdy, sir," she replied pleasantly, casting a look at Miller, and then looking down at her pencil and pad. "Do ya know what ya wanta eat or do ya need a few more minutes?"

"I think we're ready, little Miss," Miller said with enthusiasm.

Without looking up from the pad, she sighed. "Rebecca," she said, sounding agitated. "My name is Rebecca. I just turnt eleven years old and am almost growd up. I'm just short for my age."

Miller twisted his lips as if to keep from laughing. He placed his hand over his heart and bowed his head. "My apologies," he said sincerely. "I think we're ready, Rebecca."

Charlie cleared his throat and LeFaye chuckled under his breath. Grandpa threw them both a warning glance, abruptly ending what could have been a torrent of teasing for Miller. Behaving themselves, the men placed their orders then sat back and took stock of their surroundings.

"We sure don't have restaurants like this in Pueblo," said Charlie. "I wonder if—"

Grandpa never heard the rest of Charlie's question. For just then, the kitchen door swung open and a handsome woman stepped into the dining room.

Her silver hair, though still streaked with blonde, was arranged into a fashionable bun. A neatly starched pinafore covered her green and gold plaid dress. And she, just like the establishment, looked as sharp as a pin. Her blue eyes danced as she scanned the room, looking eager to greet each onlooker. Glancing over at their table, her eyes met Grandpa's and she smiled. He returned the smile and tipped his head. A soft pink flooded her cheeks and she quickly turned to welcome her other patrons.

Grandpa's eyes followed her, and Charlie's followed his, as she went from table to table and spoke with folks who had either finished their meal or were somewhere in the middle of it, introducing herself and inquiring about the food. Before the men knew it, she was standing at their table. Grandpa stood to his over six-foot tall height, then the others followed his lead, the feet of their chairs sliding noisily on the wooden floor.

"Please gentlemen, be seated," she said with a soft, southern drawl. "Welcome to Dixie's."

Charlie, LeFaye and Miller took their seats, but Grandpa remained standing, looking dignified. "And do I have the privilege of being in Miss Dixie's company?" he asked.

The woman smiled warmly. "Yes, you do," she answered softly. "My name is Dixie Graham and I own this establishment."

"It's a pleasure to meet you, ma'am," replied Grandpa, absentmindedly turning his hat in his hand. "My name is Stuart Smith." Pointing his hat at each man in turn, he made the introductions.

"This here is my grandson, Charlie, and our friends Scout Miller and Phillip LeFaye, both of the U.S. military stationed up in Fort Collins."

Dixie nodded and smiled pleasantly to each of them. "Well, thank you for choosing our restaurant to dine in this evening. I hope you'll find the food and the atmosphere satisfying and enjoyable."

Grandpa kept turning his hat in his hands. "So far, everythins' been great."

Charlie's mouth fell open. He'd never seen Grandpa put on the charm.

Dixie looked up at him, her cheeks glowing pink. "Thank you," she drawled.

Heads turned when Rebecca pushed the kitchen door open with her shoulder and presented them with a large tray of food.

"Well, I see Rebecca is ready to serve your meals, so please enjoy. But don't hesitate to let us know if we can be of further assistance," said Dixie.

"Thank you, ma'am," replied Grandpa, his eyes twinkling.

Dixie went on to another table as Rebecca sat plates piled high with crispy, golden chicken, fluffy mashed potatoes, thick white gravy, green beans, and flaky buttermilk biscuits. "I know y'all are gonna love this," she said cheerfully. "Best food in the world."

Charlie couldn't respond; his mouth was watering too much. LeFaye just nodded, his eyes glued to the plates of food. Miller smiled at the young lady and said, "We're gonna give it our best shot, Rebecca."

As she skipped to the kitchen with the empty tray, she glanced over her shoulder and chirped, "Let me know if ya need anythin' else."

Grandpa was still standing, his eyes following Dixie around the room. Charlie tugged at the old man's shirt sleeve. "Okay, you can sit now."

Grandpa looked down at his grandson. "What?"

Charlie laughed out loud. "Sit, Grandpa. Our food is getting cold."

"Oh. Forgot about the food."

Charlie chuckled. "Well, we didn't." He looked at LeFaye and Miller. "I'll ask the blessing since Grandpa would probably forget what he needed to pray for and we'd have to wait until he remembered."

Grandpa elbowed him in the ribs. They all laughed, then bowed their heads.

Not much was said during the meal; they were too busy eating. It wasn't until after the last crumb of cherry pie had disappeared that LeFaye spoke up.

"I'll be more than happy to spread the word about this restaurant while I'm here," he said, wiping his mouth with a cloth napkin.

"Well, you better do what you can tonight, 'cause we move out before sunrise tomorrow morning," said Miller.

"Oh, yeah," replied LeFaye. "I guess we'll have to leave the advertising to you, Mr. Smith."

Grandpa smiled and laid his napkin across his empty plate. "I'll be happy to do my part, boys."

Standing out on the boardwalk, the three younger men groaned and patted their full stomachs. They made their leisurely way back towards the hotel while still savoring the aroma of fried chicken.

LeFaye straightened his hat. "Well, I guess starting tomorrow, it's good-bye cherry pie, hello cow pie." Charlie and Miller burst out laughing.

Lingering, Grandpa turned and looked back at the brightly lit windows of the little restaurant, knowing he'd visit it again during his stay in Denver. Yet, although the food was especially delicious, his return wouldn't be entirely because of the menu.

15

THE FOURSOME STOPPED AT THE CORNER
of Larimer and First Streets, in front of the hotel, and
watched a group of boisterous cowboys come up the street
toward the saloon. "Looks like they've had enough to drink
already," mumbled Grandpa.

Charlie nodded in agreement. LeFaye didn't seem to
notice or care. He stretched and yawned.

"How about we go in and play a game of pool before
retiring for the night?" asked Miller.

LeFaye nodded. "Sounds good to me. I have to do
something to let this food settle before I head off to bed."

"You boys go on," said Grandpa. "Charlie and I need to
find a certain business before we go back into the hotel. I
want to make sure I know where to head come mornin'."

"Okay," said Miller. "We'll catch up with you two later."

Grandpa and Charlie passed the saloon, turned the
corner, and found themselves on Holladay Street, about a
half block south of the judge's office. Charlie was glad to
see that the judge's office was fairly close to the hotel. He
noticed a large brass plaque hanging above the two large
wooden doors and was about to approach them when one
door opened. The bright glow from the lights inside spilled
out onto the boardwalk, revealing the slim silhouette of a

young woman standing on the threshold.

Her cheerful voice echoed into the night air as she turned and said good-bye to someone inside. She then stepped out onto the boardwalk and, shutting the door behind her, started towards the two men as she pulled a pair of gloves from her bag. The light from the gas lamps flickered on her face and hair.

Charlie was awestruck at the sight of her. He didn't understand why, but his heart raced in his chest.

Good grief, he thought, *she's headin' right towards me. What'll I do?* He stood frozen to the walkway with drops of sweat rolling down his forehead. Charlie gasped for air.

Grandpa glanced at his grandson. He wrapped his fingers around Charlie's arm and pulled him off to the side and under the lamp, out of the shadows.

Suddenly aware of two strange men standing on the boardwalk, the young lady slowed down as she approached them.

Charlie didn't expect that either. *Is she gonna say somethin'?* he fretted to himself.

Grandpa tipped the rim of his hat to her. "Evenin', Miss," he said warmly.

She looked at Grandpa and then at Charlie and smiled. "Good evening, gentlemen," she softly replied.

Charlie stood there with his mouth hanging open, not able to articulate one intelligent word, not even "Hello."

Before he could blink, she had stepped past them and walked gracefully down the boardwalk; but her perfume lingered in the air. Charlie inhaled deeply and closed his eyes as he normally did when he tried to add a memory. He wanted to remember the smell of her light floral fragrance, the image of the auburn ringlets that flowed from beneath her hat and down her slender shoulders, her rose-colored cheeks, and her soft green eyes.

He watched as she disappeared into the darkness. Her long skirt swished and her heels clicked on the boards until, from somewhere within the darkness, a man's voice greeted her. Then the sounds faded into the night.

Grandpa slapped him on the back. "Get bit by the bug, did ya, son?" He chuckled.

Charlie realized he'd been standing in the same spot with his mouth wide open. He closed it and turned around.

Grandpa laughed again. "Gotta watch them love bugs," he teased. "They'll getcha when you aren't lookin'."

The young cowboy cleared his throat. "Probably the same one that bit you, back in the restaurant."

Grandpa's eyes widened with surprise. "Who, me? Mr. Hard Hearted? No way, no how. Already had the love of my life."

"I know, Grandpa, you're a man of iron," Charlie teased. "Let's get back to the business at hand then, shall we," he said, trying to sound mature and in control. "This is where you come tomorrow to see the judge. It's not far from the hotel, so you ought to be just fine."

"I know I'll be fine." The old man snickered and his eyes danced in the lamp light. "But I don't know if you will be."

The two broke into laughter and turned back down the boardwalk. Glancing once more at the large doors, Charlie said, "Just remember to find out who she is when you're in there tomorrow, will you?"

Enjoying their comeraderie, the two took their time walking back to the hotel, the sidewalks emptying by this time. They paused once in a while to peek into darkened store windows. Rounding the corner onto Larimer Street, the hotel with its welcoming glow was just ahead.

Without warning, the swinging doors of the saloon flew open and a tall, dark-haired cowhand stumbled out onto the boardwalk in front of them. Charlie didn't have time to stop himself from walking right into the stranger's chest. The wrangler turned on his heels and almost fell over, but caught himself on a porch pole. Staggering, he pointed a meaty finger in the boy's face.

"Hey, pup," he slurred, spit flying in all directions, "you better watch wair yer goin' or I'll beat da tar outta you."

He was taller than Charlie, with big arms and broad shoulders, and he reeked of liquor. The boy jumped back and planted his feet firmly beneath him. He didn't want to look threatening to the older cowboy, but readying himself for anything the wrangler might try to do, he assumed the fighting stance Grandpa had taught him years earlier.

Grandpa was silent.

Almost nose to nose, the cowboy's putrid breath made Charlie gasp, but he didn't bat an eye. "My apologies, sir," he said sternly. "You came out of the saloon so fast, I—"

Spit splattered Charlie's face. "I don't care," yelled the wrangler. "You sass me agin, and I'll shoot ya dead on the spot."

Charlie's fingers twitched.

Grandpa stepped between the two. He locked eyes with the stranger while he spoke to his grandson.

"Let's go, Charlie," he said firmly, "this here ain't nothin' but trouble. Wouldn't be a fair fight anyway."

"Why not?" slurred the man. "'Cause he ain't nothin' but a weak, dumb pup?"

"Nope," answered Grandpa, "'cause you're drunker than a skunk and Charlie'd have you down for the count before you knew what hit you, that's why. I think the boy should wait till you sober up some first, so you'd at least remember some of the lickin' you got."

A crowd of miners and ranch hands had gathered in the street, but Charlie didn't turn to look. He knew Grandpa's remark would warrant a response from the large man. It didn't take long.

As expected, the wrangler's eyes grew wide with contempt and he clumsily reached for Grandpa's shirt collar, but before he touched cloth, Charlie was holding his wrist and letting his eyes do the talking.

"You know who I am?" yelled the man. "Do you know who yer messin' wit?"

Charlie looked into the bloodshot eyes.

"I really don't care."

The dark, red eyes grew wider. "Why you . . ." he growled.

Just then, a red-haired Irishman in a uniform stepped out from the shadows and put his arm around the wrangler's shoulders. He threw a warning glance at Charlie and then turned back to his friend.

"Let 'im be, Big T," muttered McQueen. "Now ain't the time."

The wrangler hesitated, then nodded. "I'll wait this

time." He staggered backward. "But if I see that pup again, I'll kill 'im. . . . You too, old man."

McQueen and Charlie glared at each other as Charlie slowly let go of the big man's wrist. Taking the wrangler by the arm, McQueen turned and guided him down the boardwalk.

"Okay. Next time, then," he told his friend, "when there ain't witnesses. We'll get 'em next time."

16

A THIN GOLD LINE ON THE EASTERN
horizon ripped through the darkness, separating the night
from the earth, and dawn began to fill the gap. Charlie took
his hat off the bed post and slid it on his head. Leaning
down toward the ear of the sleeping old man, he whispered,
"It's time for me to go, Grandpa."

Grandpa stirred and opened one eye, taking a second to
recognize the tall cowboy leaning over him. Sitting up, he
wiped the sleep from his eyes and reached for his shirt.

"Don't get up. Sleep a couple more hours. I just wanted
to say so long before I headed back to the herd."

Grandpa swung his feet to the floor and stretched.
Yawning, he tapped the bed beside him. "Sit," he mumbled.

Charlie sat down next to him. Both men stared at the
floor for a moment. They'd never said good-bye to each
other before.

Finally, Charlie pushed his hat back and leaned over,
kissing the old man on the head. "Don't you worry,
Grandpa. I'll be fine; you just concentrate on takin' care of
your business and gettin' home safe and sound. I'll be right
behind you."

Grandpa kept his eyes downcast. "I know, boy," he
whispered hoarsely. "I just hate bein' separated from you."

Charlie put his arm around the tall, old man's broad shoulders, feeling the once-muscular arms that now barely filled the sleeves of his undershirt. "I'll be with you every step of the way, Grandpa," he said softly, as he smoothed the unruly gray hair. "Just think of me, and I'll be right there."

Grandpa sniffled and nodded his head. He pushed himself slowly up off the bed and shuffled in his stocking feet across the cold wooden floor to the water basin. He splashed water on his face.

Charlie broke into a smile. "You be mindful of how many times you visit that fried chicken place, Grandpa, or some silver-haired lady might trick you into marryin' her."

Grandpa chuckled. "Hush, boy." He dabbed his face with a hand towel. "There's only one thing on my mind right now, and it doesn't involve fried chicken or a silver-haired lady."

Charlie stood up and straightened his pant legs over his boots. "Well, you're the one who said we can find good things in the most unusual places, so if you're not thinkin' about fried chicken, what is it?"

Turning to face him, Grandpa grew solemn. "You, boy. You said if I think about you, you'd be with me, so it's you I have on my mind." His voice cracked and he looked away so Charlie couldn't see him wipe a tear. "We'll both be home before we know it," he said with forced confidence.

Charlie nodded his head and swallowed hard.

"Oh. Here, son . . . I almost forgot."

Grandpa squared his shoulders, took a deep breath, then turned to the bureau. From the top drawer he drew out a bundle wrapped in soft cowhide. His hands shook slightly as he handed the heavy package to Charlie.

"You need to take this with you."

"What is it?"

"Open it and see."

Charlie untied the string and pulled back the folds of soft leather.

"A Smith and Wesson," he whispered.

"Yep," replied Grandpa, "a pistol of your very own."

"But Grandpa—"

"It's okay, son. Your great uncle sent that to me awhile back. I didn't have much use for it, preferrin' Big Blue to any other gun, so I saved it back for you. But you're a man now. You're ready for it. You know the rules. I taught you well."

Staring at the gun, Charlie whispered, "Yes, sir, you did."

Charlie picked up the Model 1 Smith and Wesson and ran his fingers down the blue barrel, remembering all the shooting lessons Grandpa had given him over the years.

At the same time, Grandpa was recalling the things he had taught the boy about proper use of a gun—and how surprised he had been at the natural skills Charlie displayed. Yes, his boy knew how to handle and care for a gun. And he was fast on the draw—one of the fastest Grandpa had ever seen, and he'd seen plenty. But the truth is, that fact bothered Grandpa a little; he didn't want to encourage quickness above other skills.

"Respect this gun, son, and it will serve you well. Use it only when you have to, in self-defense, whether against man or beast, or if you need food. And though you're one of the fastest draws I've ever seen, don't ever tempt another man to pull his gun."

Charlie laid the gun back on the table. He picked up the belt and buckled it around his waist then carefully slid the pistol into the holster. "Is it loaded?" he asked as he tied the leather strap to his leg.

"Yessir," responded Grandpa. "And I slid an extra box of cartridges into your saddlebag last night."

Standing up straight, trying to make himself as tall as his grandfather, Charlie looked into the old man's eyes. "I don't know what to say."

"Say nothin', son, just take care of yourself."

"I will, Grandpa."

When Charlie walked out of the warm hotel into the cold morning air, he found the street empty except for Star, who was waiting for him at the hitching post where he'd left him earlier. Slipping a boot into the stirrup, the cowboy heaved himself up and slid into the saddle with ease. He and the horse were a natural fit. Grandpa seemed to know it would be that way.

He gathered the reins and glanced up at the hotel window. Grandpa stood there watching him, obviously forcing a smile. Tipping his hat, Charlie smiled back, then turned his horse. He touched Star's ribs with the heel of his boot and headed down the dirt street towards the outskirts of town.

By the time Charlie reached the Platte River, he knew everything had changed. His life was different now. He was alone, on his own, facing a world that was proving to be more complex and forbidding than he had ever imagined.

Grandpa had taught him all he knew about life. Now, the cattle drive, the horse, and the gun were a right of passage. He was no longer a boy wanting desperately to be a man. He was a man. Grandpa considered him to be one, and that was all the confidence he needed.

The wind rolled across the prairie and swayed the tall trees along the river banks. Charlie stopped and buttoned his slicker. He stood for a moment to watch the peaceful dance of the cottonwood and willow branches.

He searched the Colorado sky until he found the last star of the night, just before it disappeared behind a curtain of light.

"I know you'll take care of him, Jess."

17

GRANDPA STOOD ON THE BOARDWALK AND looked up at the modern, two-story, red brick building. He couldn't recollect seeing anything quite like it before. White framed windows stood about eight feet apart and encircled the entire building like clear sentries guarding a post. Those on the top floor mirrored the lower level, with the exception of the limestone arch and the center keystone that crowned each frame. Limestone keys offset each other as they climbed the four corners of the building. Above the familiar mahogany doors, a gold plaque announced the name of the business and its proprietor:

Probate Office
The Honorable Randolph P. Walker

He pushed the door open and saw instantly that the grandeur of the building's exterior didn't hold a candle to what was displayed inside. The marble floor shone like glass and reflected the fine objects exhibited in the grand entry hall. Elegant rugs softened the brilliance of the stone floor and beautiful artwork lined the walls. Thick tapestry drapes adorned each window, and off to the left in a parlor, large leather chairs stood on either side of an oversized fireplace

128

that was encased in the same red brick seen on the outside of the building. At the far end of the hall was a mahogany desk; behind it sat the beautiful young lady that had stunned his grandson the night before. Grandpa removed his hat and quietly approached her desk, catching a faint scent of lavender as he got closer.

She didn't hear him come in. She kept writing feverishly in her notebook, while he stared at the top of her auburn head.

"Excuse me, Miss."

She jumped slightly. Holding a hand to her chest, she looked up from her writing and smiled, a hint of recognition dancing in her green, fluid eyes. "My apologies, sir, I didn't hear you come in. May I help you?"

Warmed by her smile, he stepped closer to the desk. "Yes, ma'am. Didn't mean to startle you. I've come to see the judge."

"Oh," she mumbled, a bit flustered. "I didn't realize the judge had any appointments this morning." She turned back to her notebook. "May I ask your name, sir?"

Grandpa shuffled nervously from one foot to the other. "Mr. Stuart Smith."

The young lady's manner abruptly changed. She stood to her feet and extended her hand. "Welcome to Denver, Mr. Smith," she said with polite deference.

He accepted her hand and acknowledged her hospitality with a gentle shake. "Thank you, Miss." Looking around, he motioned with his hat, "It's quite a place you have here."

The young lady glanced around the large room and blushed. "Thank you. I haven't worked here long and it can be a bit overwhelming at times." Motioning to the chair in front of her desk, she said, "Would you please have a seat, Mr. Smith."

They took their respective seats and she turned her attention back to her black book. As she flipped through the pages, she became visibly nervous. "I'm sorry, what time was your appointment, Mr. Smith?"

"Oh, I'm sorry," replied Grandpa. "I don't have an appointment. You see, I responded to a telegram a couple months ago, tellin' the judge I'd be here late September or early October. When the time came, I jumped on my horse and headed north. I didn't know I needed an appointment."

The young lady slowly sat back into her chair, never taking her eyes off of the old man. He pulled an envelope from his vest pocket and handed it to her.

"I received this here telegram from the judge earlier this year telling me of my cousin's death, his debt, and a plot of land he left me somewheres out by Saint Louie. The judge asked if I would come to Denver to settle some matters as soon as I could. So, when I could, I just packed up a few things and headed north. I did let him know I would be comin' sometime this month, but wasn't sure of a date, with drivin' cattle bein' so unpredictable and all."

She raised her eyebrows, her green eyes shining brightly.

"That's how I came up here, with a small group of soldiers takin' a herd to Fort Collins."

The young lady sat motionless for a second then smiled, a sudden sense of the situation reflecting in her eyes. She gestured towards the large leather chairs in the parlor. "I understand now, Mr. Smith. Would you mind taking a seat in the waiting area while I go talk to Judge Walker?"

"Not a'tall, Miss. I hope I didn't cause any harm by not makin' an appointment."

"It will be fine, sir," she said pleasantly.

Then she disappeared behind a set of doors in the rear of the room with his telegram in hand. Grandpa took the opportunity to look closer at his surroundings. The *Rocky Mountain News* lay on a table next to his chair, so he picked it up and skimmed through a few articles.

One with the heading "Railroad Director finds Site for New Town" immediately caught his attention. He laughed quietly to himself as he read about the beginnings of Colorado Springs, information which Mr. Dooley had already told him and Charlie back on the trail. Another article announced the arrival of Dr. and Mrs. Buchtel to Denver. Seems the doctor was a war hero, a recipient of the Medal of Honor after the Civil War. He and his new wife decided to move out west and set up shop here in the city. Grandpa found it interesting that his wife was a Barnum, of the Barnum and Bailey circus. He was reading about the killer heat wave and the ensuing drought that was drying up the mid-west all the way from the flatlands of the Colorado Territory to the Appalachian Mountains in Tennessee, when the young woman stepped back into the room. She sat down at her desk and began to fumble with her black book. Grandpa folded the newspaper. Placing it back down on the table, he waited patiently for her signal.

After a few moments, she finally looked at him and waved him over to her desk. "Mr. Smith, Judge Walker asked that I clear a few things from Friday's docket so he can meet with you to discuss the matters surrounding your cousin's death. Would you prefer a morning or afternoon appointment?"

Grandpa raised his bushy eyebrows. "Friday?" he asked. "Doesn't he have anythin' sooner?"

The young lady remained calm. "Mr. Smith, if the judge hadn't made this exception, you wouldn't be seeing him until . . ." Flipping through the black book again, she finally stopped and looked up, "until October 29th at 4:30 p.m."

Grandpa whistled and shook his head. "Holy smokes," he said under his breath. "It's Wednesday, September 27th now. You mean I'd have to wait over a month to see the judge if'n he didn't make this exception?"

"Yes, sir." Her green eyes gazed up at him, unblinking.

"Well then, Friday doesn't look so bad after all." He chuckled. "If possible, I'd like to see the judge early in the day so I can discuss our business and head on home."

Again, she started to scribble something in her black book. "I'll make your appointment for 9:30 a.m. on Friday, Mr. Smith. Does that meet your approval?"

"Yep, it does, Miss. Please thank the judge for his consideration."

"I will, Mr. Smith. And please, call me Amelia."

It took him a second to place the name. Then a smile inched across his lips. "You mean Amelia Taylor?"

"Why, yes." She giggled as if amused at his inquiry.

"Well, I'll be." Grandpa studied her and shook his head.

She tilted her head and waited for him to explain.

"I beg your pardon, Amelia. You just don't look like I pictured you, that's all."

132

"Have we corresponded before, Mr. Smith?"

"Briefly. It was you who sent me that telegram a few months back expressing the judge's utmost desire to have me come to Denver as soon as possible."

"I'm sorry, sir. I don't remember. I send so many—"

"It's okay, Amelia. I'm glad I got to meet you in person. Cleared away a lot of suspicions on my part."

She nodded, but was obviously confused by his remark.

Grandpa grinned. "Not to worry, young lady. I'll be here promptly at 9:30 Friday morning." He gallantly tipped his hat and headed for the doors. *I was wrong 'bout that one*, he thought. *Definitely not an old bitty.*

The heavy doors closed behind him and he stepped out into the fresh Rocky Mountain morning.

"Now, what to do with myself for two days," he muttered as he stood on the walkway, looking up and down the street.

Out of the blue, the name Dixie scurried across his mind, and he smiled.

18

*T*IRED, *HOT*, AND *GRITTY* WERE THE WORDS
to describe a normal day on the trail. Some cowboys used
other words, but Charlie wouldn't repeat those. They had
to put up with sweat stinging their eyes, flies biting their
horses, and dust invading everything. There was grit in their
food and grit in their water; everything was covered with
a layer of gray.

Then there were the smells. Charlie could make out two
distinct smells when they made it past the fine powder that
constantly caked his nostrils and phlegmed his throat: camp
smoke that saturated everything, even his Bible cover; and
the smell of the cattle droppings. Even when the dust didn't
threaten to choke the life out of him, he'd tie his wildrag
around his face just so he could smell the camp smoke
instead of the herd's byproduct.

Just two days outside of Denver everyone was ready
for the drive to be over. None of them were cow punchers
by trade and they were all ready to resume their normal
lives, whatever those entailed. The soldiers pushed the cows
harder after they left Denver. Fort Collins was seventy miles
north of Denver, two days closer than Pueblo.

Charlie thought the little cabin back near Pueblo that he
once felt closing in on him didn't sound so bad now.

Lost in thought, Charlie didn't notice that Miller had brought his horse up alongside Star, until he spoke.

Without taking his eyes off the cattle ahead, Miller said, "See you're sportin' a new pistol there, cowpoke."

Charlie glanced at the scout from the corner of his eye. "Yeah," he replied casually. "Grandpa gave it to me before I left Denver."

The horses plodded along lazily beside the herd. "See you have it tied down. That sends a signal to folks who might be lookin' for trouble, ya know."

Charlie shrugged his shoulders. "I'm just more comfortable with it tied to my leg than floppin' around, that's all."

"Do you know how to use it?"

Charlie glanced over at the scout again. "Yep," he replied with confidence. "I do."

Miller sighed. "Not that I'm doubtin' you, but you seem mighty young to be so sure."

Charlie stared straight ahead, silent for a moment, and then he slid his level gaze back to the scout, his jaw muscles taut and flexing. "All it takes is a bad case of loneliness and an attack from a mama grizzly to make a person want to learn how to shoot a gun and shoot it fast 'n straight."

Miller gave a short whistle. "A grizzly," he said, rounding on Charlie, his eyes wide with surprise. "When did that happen?"

Charlie shifted in the saddle. He didn't want to recollect the incident, but the memory rose to the surface. A cold sweat formed across his brow.

"It was almost eight years ago, but it seems like yesterday," he said. "She came out of nowhere and I really thought

I was dead. I woulda been, too, if it weren't for a clump of aspen trees."

Again, his mind wandered back in time, but before he let it get the better of him, he turned and looked at Miller.

"Anyway, I lived through it, but once I healed, I was determined never to have to go through anything like that again, so when Grandpa was able, he taught me how to shoot. Not just how to hunt, but how to shoot. He says I'm the fastest natural draw he's ever seen, but I don't take that into much account, since I don't know how many gunfights he's actually seen. I just know I'm more confident now, and I believe I can take care of myself if the need arises."

"Well, wear it safely," said the scout. "Some men have noticed the change. One day a man isn't wearin' a gun and the next he has one tied down to his leg. For some reason they take it as a challenge; a perfect time to test the waters, if you know what I mean."

"I know," responded Charlie, "but I doubt if I'll ever see that ranch hand again, so I'm not too worried."

Miller raised an eyebrow. "I was talkin' more about McQueen. I suggest you cut a wide berth between the two of you."

"Why?"

"Let's just say he and his buddy had too much to drink the other night and he's been sayin' some stuff about you and your grandpa that you might not like."

"I reckon Grandpa shouldn't have said what he did to the wrangler, but he was irked by the whole situation. I tried to apologize, but that cowboy was too drunk to accept it. Just kept spittin' in my face and callin' me a pup. It all just got on

Grandpa's nerves, I guess. Anyway, nothin' they say bothers me. Men like that are usually just full of hot air."

Miller snickered. "Big T, better known as Trevor Cassidy by folks who aren't considered his friends, is the son of a wealthy rancher and he's a troublemaker. He's never been in trouble with the law, but he's come awfully close at times. He's usually just talk, loud talk, but he's a drinker and one day, the combination will get him into trouble."

"That's all it was the other night," mumbled Charlie. "Just loud talk."

"Well, it may turn into a bit more now," said Miller. "It seems Big T took your grandpa's words as a challenge and now the man is wantin' to fight you. Seems the old man wounded his pride in front of his men and now he's got to get it back."

"Well, I'm not gonna go searchin' for them, but both of 'em know where to find me if they want me bad enough."

"Just be careful, Charlie. I don't trust either one, so I'd watch my back if I were you. I have a hunch McQueen's a bad man and plays dirty. In fact, I think it's him that's eggin' this whole thing on, wantin' there to be a fight."

"Why?"

"For a couple of reasons."

"And they are?"

"You sure ask a lot of questions," said the scout.

"And I'd appreciate some honest answers," said Charlie. "I don't like unexpected surprises, in any form."

Miller nodded. "I can appreciate that. So here are the reasons. First, way back a couple of weeks or so ago when you worked point for the first time, you missed one of my signals and we ended up camping about two miles from where I originally planned on bedding for the night."

Charlie's eyes widened.

"It turned out to be okay, 'cause it rained that night, so there was plenty of water for the cattle, but if it hadn't rained, we woulda had to go the extra miles to water before we made camp."

"But I, I—"

"Listen Charlie, it's alright. Everyone misses a sign once in awhile. Sometimes we end up a little off base because of it, but we learn from it and move on. We learn to read sign better. And since that one time, that's what you've done. You've gotten better at point, so I never saw the need to bring up the one mistake."

Embarrassed, Charlie looked at the scout, "Then why bring it up now?"

"Because that is the first reason why McQueen has it out for you. He's mad at me for letting the lesson slide; thinks I'm too soft on you just because your grandpa and the colonel's pa are old friends. Personally, I think it's just a bad case of jealousy. I think he resents you for being so good."

"Okay, I learn fast; what's the second reason?"

Miller hesitated for a minute. "'Cause he knows you're a Christian and he hates you for it."

Charlie looked over at the scout. "Well, I am that. They can beat me to a pulp, but they can never change that. Why's he hate Christians so bad?"

Miller wiped the sweat from his face with the flap of his wildrag. "Well, seems his pa was a preacher back in Ireland, but only on Sundays. The rest of the week, he made life hell on earth for his family. He often beat McQueen and his brother—most of the time, just 'cause he was drunk and any little thing set him off. From what I hear, his pa almost beat his ma to death once, and would have if McQueen hadn't jumped him."

Charlie was flabbergasted. He couldn't imagine living like that. "Doesn't McQueen know we're not all like that? I mean, we're all human and we'll do dumb things sometimes, but some of us who profess to be Christians, really are."

"Don't reckon he plans on taking the chance to find out," said Miller.

Charlie nodded thoughtfully. "So that's why he doesn't believe in God. I was wonderin' what made him so adamant about that."

"That'd be why," Miller said with a stern look.

"I appreciate your warnings, Miller, and I'll keep my eyes open, but there is one thing that McQueen should know."

"What's that?"

"I'll try to keep the peace when I can, but I won't be pushed around. If the need arises, I'll defend myself."

"Fair enough," said the scout. Then, without another word, he clicked his tongue and disappeared into the dust cloud.

It was late September and the days were getting cooler, but Charlie could feel the heat of the sun penetrate his pants and burn his upper legs, except for where the holster lay tied securely around his right thigh.

It was Charlie's night to stand watch and Miller's warnings

still rang fresh and clear in his thoughts. Making a quick mental note of where McQueen had bedded down for the night, he pulled himself up onto Star and headed out to the herd. They never camped too close to each other, except when it rained and the weather forced all of them to sleep under the tent, but Charlie thought it best now to know folks' locations.

Darkness was closing down on them as he and Star made their way to the grazing herd. He could hear them lowing as he drew nearer, passing some that had already bedded down and were lazily chewing on their cud.

It was then that he saw Peterson walking back to camp. He waved. Peterson raised his hand and called Charlie over. The lanky southerner was dusty and tired, but instead of heading straight for the bedroll, he wanted to talk. Cautiously Charlie let Star approach him.

Peterson looked around nervously, then spoke. "Just want to tell you to be careful from now on, Charlie."

"Why? Something goin' on with the cows?"

"Well, they are a tad nervous, but I was talkin' more about keepin' an eye on McQueen. He's seen that gun yer sportin' and he was drinkin' on the trail today."

"Thanks for the warnin'. I'll keep my eyes and ears open."

"And Charlie, I don't think he is who he says he is."

"Whatta ya mean?"

"Well, when we was in town the other night, he got real drunk after the run-in he and that Big T feller had with you, and he started shootin' off at the mouth when we got back to the hotel. He said we ain't got no idea who he is or what he can do. Said somethin' about killin' a man in Kansas City a few years ago just 'cause he didn't like the way he looked at him. Changed his name and joined the ranks to keep the law off of his trail."

Charlie leaned on the saddle horn. "Have you told Sarge about this?"

"Naw, I haven't; and don't know if I should," answered Peterson. "He likes McQueen and probably won't believe me. He ain't like Sergeant Barlow. I think I'll keep my mouth shut till we get back to the fort. I'll brief the colonel when it's my turn to see 'im, but I thought you needed to know now."

"Thanks," whispered Charlie. "You get on into camp now. Some folks might think it's strange that you're not back yet and come lookin' for you."

Peterson nodded then disappeared into the darkness. Charlie's eyes trailed him until he couldn't see any sign of him, figuring he was back safe in the confines of the camp.

Charlie and Star circled the cattle slowly as the night grew darker. Thunder rumbled in the distance and clouds covered the stars, only allowing the moon to share its light with the open prairie for a few minutes at a time. The cattle were restless and stomped around as if uncertain where to stand. Something besides the storm was bothering them.

Suddenly, Star snorted and pricked up his ears. Charlie had no doubt now. There was someone or something out there in the darkness. *Maybe it's just one of the soldiers come out to relieve himself,* he thought.

"Who's there?" he called out.

The breeze carried the moans of the herd out to the empty grassland, offering the only reply to his question.

Everything else was quiet. He slowly moved his right hand to the butt of his revolver. Humming softly, he tried to keep the animals calm, but the tune was stopped short by the pop of a tree twig. Quietly, he slid off his horse and kept low to the ground, his eyes scanning the darkness.

"I'll ask again," yelled Charlie. "Who's out there?"

The intruder kept out of sight; out of the line of fire, but finally answered slow and sure.

"Trouble," came the sharp reply. "I know this accent of mine tells ye who it is out here, but that don't bother me," said McQueen. "Besides, I got a bead on ye right now that would silence yer screams before they reached air."

"Step out here like a man and let's talk, McQueen," replied Charlie, his keen eyes looking from tree to tree, shadow to shadow.

"Oh, I'm a man alright, boy," answered the Irishman. "I'm a bigger man than ye are, but there's no need for talkin'. I don't aim to kill ye. I expect Big T'll do that. I just want to warn ye that he's comin' for ye. Somewhere, sometime, when ye and yer grandpa don't expect it, he's gonna . . ."

Charlie didn't move. His eyes sought the form that would eventually be revealed by the very shadows in which it hid. He'd learned that from Grandpa a long time ago. "Finish it, McQueen," he yelled. "Don't stop now."

But nothing came back to him, except the sound of his own voice and the lowing of the cattle. McQueen was gone.

19

GRANDPA ENTERED THE RECEPTION AREA of the Probate Office at 9:25 a.m. Friday. Amelia greeted him, then announced his arrival to the judge. At 9:30 sharp, she escorted Grandpa through the doors behind her desk that he had seen her enter on Wednesday, up a flight of stairs, past a pair of mahogany doors with the word *PROBATE* etched on one and the word *COURT* on the other.

The judge was a short, round man of about fifty years, with a balding head and little ears that supported his round, gold-rim glasses. Like the rest of him, his cheeks were round and rosy, holding a friendly smile between them.

The judge stood and extended his hand. "Good morning, Mr. Smith. I'm Judge Randolph Walker, at your service."

Grandpa gave him a firm handshake. "Good mornin', sir."

The judge motioned him over to a large round table where they made themselves comfortable and then went straight to the business at hand.

"First, let me express my appreciation for the attention you've given this matter, Mr. Smith. It's good to have finally met you and I know, the sooner these legal issues are settled, the happier you will be."

"Yes, sir," replied Grandpa. "I have a hankerin' to be on my way home."

"And where exactly is home?" asked the judge.

"I figured you knew that, since you were the one to contact me first."

The judge smiled and his cheeks turned into little, plump cherries. "Let's just pretend I don't know a thing about you, Mr. Smith. I'm going to take notes for the file, and what you tell me will be used to confirm what we think we already know about you. As a matter of fact, what we discuss here today will be held in strictest confidence and kept just between you and me for the time being."

"I see," said Grandpa. "Well, we live about two weeks' ride from here, a day north of Pueblo. We're south of that new town down yonder that they call Colorado Springs."

The judge rubbed his chin. "Yes, I know of Pueblo and I've heard talk that a railroad man was starting a town called Colorado Springs. I've not had the pleasure of seeing your part of the territory, but I might have to take a trip down there once the railroad is in operation. If I recall, there is still ample room for growth in the southern regions of the territory."

"I reckon there is, but I'm quite happy with my little spread. My boy and I own about sixty acres and we do okay."

The judge had been scribbling notes on a yellow tablet. He lifted his head and raised his eyebrows.

"A boy you say? Do you have a son, sir?"

"I did once," explained Grandpa. "But he was killed years ago. The boy I am talkin' about now is *his* son, my grandson, Charlie. Best thing in my life, he is."

The judge looked back at his tablet and scribbled some more. "I'm sure he is, sir. And where is Charlie's mother?"

"She's gone too. Died givin' birth to Charlie."

The judge stopped taking notes and looked at the old man. "My sympathy, Mr. Smith."

The judge's sincerity surprised Grandpa. "Oh, oh, that's alright. It's just been me and Charlie now for so many years."

"So you raised him?"

"Since he was three."

"How old is he now?"

"He'd be almost eighteen years old now, Judge. He was born on Christmas day eighteen years ago. Becomin' quite the young man, too. I imagine he'll be wantin' to do somethin' here soon besides watchin' over his old grandpa. He's helpin' to drive a small herd of cattle up to Fort Collins right now, matter of fact. Gettin' a taste of some of the real world."

The judge kept scribbling and nodded his head.

Just thinking of Charlie made Grandpa's eyes tear up so he immediately turned his attention to the telegram that lay open on the table in front of them. Tapping it with a boney finger, he directed the conversation towards it.

"So, enough 'bout me and my boy, Judge. Your telegram said this business is urgent and that if neglected, it could impact my family. What business do I need to settle for my deceased cousin? God rest his soul!"

Laying his pen aside, the judge sat up and adjusted his glasses. "Mr. Smith, do you understand why you are here?"

"Well, by the sounds of the first telegram I got, seems

my cousin made some money, spent it all and got himself into debt, and now you want to sell whatever it is he left me in Saint Louie to pay off his creditors."

The judge smiled and sat back in his chair. "Mr. Smith, were you aware of your cousin's holdings?"

Grandpa shook his head. "No, sir. Don't have an inklin' what he did. I haven't seen ol' Ralph in over fifty years, since we were just young men. I knew he had drive and I figured he'd make somethin' of himself, but we didn't keep in touch."

The judge interlocked his short fingers and lay them over his round middle, smiling.

"Well, Mr. Smith, allow me to explain it to you."

Grandpa sat back into his chair. "Okay, Judge, I'm ready to hear what you have to say."

"Well," said the round man, "your cousin did alright for himself over the years. At a young age, he bought into a couple of the upcoming railroad companies, and as his income would allow, he continued to buy stock in each company. Eventually, the stock started making money for him, so he was able to purchase more stock. You are correct in saying that your cousin spent a lot of what he earned, which left some debt upon his death, but to make a long story short, Mr. Smith: At the time of your cousin's death, he was a very wealthy man."

"Well, I'll be," responded Grandpa.

"He did well, indeed, Mr. Smith. And as soon as his debts are settled, he will do alright by you as well."

Grandpa's eyes grew wide and his mouth fell open. "By me?" he asked. "What do you mean?"

The judge leaned forward and rested his hands on his knees. "Sir, your cousin made millions from the railroad. He chose wisely in that investment."

Sitting back in his chair, the judge went on, his eyes sparkling delightedly at Grandpa's reaction. "He made other choices that weren't so rewarding, and those will be settled later, but as I said, he died a very wealthy man. The real estate in St. Louis is yours to do with as you will; it actually has no bearing on the financial issues surrounding his death. His debts will be paid from his estate, not by the sale of that land. Whatever remains in the estate after his debts are settled will come to you as an inheritance."

Grandpa bolted upright. "Me?" he asked, his eyes growing wider. "But didn't he have a family? I'm sure he had a wife and children. What about them?"

The judge leaned forward again, staring Grandpa in the eye. "No, Mr. Smith. Your cousin had no family to inherit his fortune, and although it's been over fifty years since you've last spoken with him, you are the one to whom he felt the closest."

"He took a mighty big gamble on findin' me alive, don't ya think? I mean, I'm as old as he is . . . or was."

"He planned for that. Should you have preceded him in death, he willed his estate to your next of kin, whomever that might be; in this case, it's your grandson."

Grandpa shook his head and tugged nervously at his hat.

"We don't just leave things to chance, Mr. Smith. We investigated. We learned exactly who to contact once we received word of your cousin's death. That's how we knew where to send the initial telegram."

Grandpa grew pale. Slowly he turned his gaze from the judge to the window and stared into the blank space beyond, trying to digest all he'd just heard.

"Well, I'll be," he whispered.

The room grew still and quiet. The leather chair creaked as the heavy man leaned back and waited.

Outside, wagon wheels groaned as they rolled down the street and occasionally an hombre with a heavy step could be heard walking down the boardwalk. In the stillness, the old man's memory took him back to a far away place, slowly peeling back the years until he saw two young boys, Stuart and Ralph, romping through the thicket together, fishing in the creek, and wrestling in the grass. They were closer than brothers back then, but had since gone their separate ways. Shortly after Teddy was born, Stuart loaded his small family up in a wagon and headed west, but Ralph stayed in St. Louis, determined to find his fortune there. Now, after all these years, it was Ralph's death that brought them back together. Grandpa realized now how much he had missed by living so far away.

Solemnly, the old man turned and looked at the judge. "How does all of this affect my family?"

"Well, Mr. Smith, you and your grandson will soon be very wealthy people. That will be a bit different from what you're use to, I'm sure. It will affect your lifestyle, Charlie's education, where you live . . . those kinds of things. It will also mean you will have to be a little more discrete about who you socialize with and what you tell them about your personal matters."

"What do you mean?" asked Grandpa.

"Well, in this day and age, being wealthy can be risky. There are kidnappings, murders, and the like. People get stupid when it comes to money."

Grandpa's face creased with worry. "My boy is on a cattle drive as we speak. Could he be in some kind of danger?"

The judge smiled warmly. "I doubt it from this news, since no one but you and certain employees of this firm know about this situation to date. However, just to make sure, once I had an idea of when you'd be arriving, I hired a Pinkerton man. He's on the drive too."

Grandpa threw a quick glance at the judge. "Are you tellin' me one of them soldiers is a Pinkerton man?"

"Yes, sir, I am. And he's a mighty fine detective, too. He's been hired to not only protect Charlie if needed, but to find out as much about the folks who are on that drive, who might befriend him, who might only be a ship passing in the night, that sort of information."

Grandpa nodded. "But Charlie's alright?"

"Charlie is just fine," assured the judge.

Grandpa let out a long sigh of relief. "But how'd you know he'd be on this cattle drive?"

The judge smiled. "You told me."

Grandpa was surprised. "Yeah! Just a few minutes ago."

The judge patiently shook his head. "No, back in July when you sent me that rather interesting telegram telling me I'd have to wait until September to visit with you because that's when you'd be heading north with your grandson and the military with their last cattle drive to Fort Collins."

The old man snickered. "I guess I did say that. Amazin' how much information a person can give without even thinkin' about it."

"I advise you to take extra precaution now that you've come into some money, Mr. Smith. Your life will change."

"What'll I do now, Judge?"

The judge's voice softened. "There are some legal forms that will need your signature, Mr. Smith. Once those have been processed, we will settle your cousin's debts and have a check cut in the remaining amount to be deposited into your bank account."

"Bank account? But Judge, I don't have a bank account. Never had use for one. Keep all my extra money in a tin can atop my dresser at home."

The judge laughed. "A tin can won't do for this much money, Mr. Smith. But that's all right, you can remedy the situation easily enough. May I suggest you open an account immediately upon your arrival home, or, if Pueblo does not yet have a bank, I recommend you open an account here in Denver before your departure. Either way, Amelia will need the account information at some point in time so she can make the proper arrangements."

"Proper arrangements?" whispered Grandpa. Looking at the judge he admitted to himself that this was more than he was prepared to handle, either physically or mentally.

"Don't let all of this trouble you, Mr. Smith," said the judge, trying to reassure him. "My staff and I are here to make sure the process goes as smoothly as possible. I will assign an accountant and an attorney to manage your affairs and to ensure your transactions are handled with the utmost integrity. They will be at your service until you deem otherwise. I will have Amelia put the appropriate details in writing, so you will understand everything about this situation and about who is assisting you from this point on. We will leave nothing unanswered, but will handle your affairs in a professional manner and to your complete satisfaction."

Grandpa nodded. "Thank you, Judge," he whispered. "I appreciate your help."

The judge slid his pen into his vest pocket, gathered his tablet, and walked over to his desk, signaling that the discussion had come to a close. Then he turned and asked, "May I make another suggestion?"

"Yes, sir."

"Why don't you go somewhere quiet and think about our conversation. Come back at 2:00, and I will have Timothy Atkins, one of our attorneys, meet with you to walk you through the process and answer any questions you have."

Grandpa gave a weary smile. "I think I'll do that if'n you don't mind, Judge. This is more information than I was prepared to take in."

"Quite understandable, Mr. Smith. But after you've rested and talked with Mr. Atkins, I know you will feel much better about things."

"I reckon." Grandpa sighed. "Right now a cup of hot coffee does sound mighty good."

"Good! We'll meet back here at 2:00 then."

"2:00 it is," agreed Grandpa.

After shaking hands, Judge Walker called for Amelia to escort Grandpa to the front door.

As they left the chamber, she asked, "Are you alright, Mr. Smith? You look as if you're not feeling well."

Grandpa looked at her and smiled nervously. "I will be,

Miss Amelia. I surely will be."

She smiled courteously at him as he tipped his hat to her and walked out the door.

20

REBECCA STARED AS IF COUNTING WRINKLES in Grandpa's face, while he glanced needlessly at the menu.

"Are you going to be eating all your meals here, Mr. Smith?" she asked with interest.

Grandpa closed the menu and laid it on the table. Throwing a quizzical look at the girl, he said, "Well, Becky, I don't know. There's a place just down the street that serves up a mighty nice plate of liver 'n onions. Or I could go meet up with that cattle drive that Charlie's on. Their cook fixed up a swell pot of prickly beaver one night. Why, we even sat around the campfire later and picked the meat outta our teeth with its quills. That was some mighty tasty stuff."

The girl wrinkled her nose until little freckles melted into a brown mass. "Eeyoo, that's awful," she protested. "I don't see how anybody can eat liver, even if the nasty taste is covered up with onions. And what's a prickly beaver?"

Grandpa laughed. "I guess they're called porcupines now. Looks like a beaver, only one has fur and the other has sharp needles stickin' outta their hide." Grandpa picked up the menu again. "Hmmm, I don't see nothin' like that here on this menu."

"And you won't, either," said the girl sternly. "Grandma only makes fried chicken, and the best at that!"

"Come to think of it, neither liver nor prickly beaver sounds so appetizin' after all." He smiled at the girl. "Yeah, I guess your grandma's chicken is lots better."

"You bet it is. So, what will you have for lunch?"

"Right now, I'll just have a cup of your grandma's delicious coffee."

"Want a piece of pie to go with it?"

"Naw, sweetie. I gotta watch my figure."

Rebecca looked at him and wrinkled her nose again. "What figure?" she asked innocently.

Grandpa tossed his head back and laughed. Becky shrugged her shoulders and ran to the kitchen, her pigtail swinging behind her. A few minutes later, Dixie came out from the kitchen carrying two cups of coffee and made her way over to Grandpa's table.

"I was wondering if you were ever going to come in at a time when we could talk," she said.

Grandpa stood up and motioned to the empty chair on the other side of the small table. "I, I . . ." he stuttered.

She sat down and handed a cup over to him. "Relax, Mr. Smith, please."

He carefully took the cup from her hand. "Thank you, ma'am. I just didn't expect the pleasure of your company. And please call me Stuart." He felt like a silly school boy.

Her keen blue eyes sparkled when she smiled. "Okay, then relax, Stuart. And you're welcome. Please call me Dixie."

"Is that your real name?"

"Yes, it's my real name. And I'm straight from Atlanta, Georgia, too."

"Ah, a real southern belle."

She wrapped her fingers around the warm cup and blew into the rising steam. "No, just a southern girl."

Grandpa looked at her over the rim of the cup as he sipped his coffee. "How long've you been in Denver, Dixie?"

She stirred the sugar into her coffee and added a little cream. "Just a few months. Becky and I moved here to start anew."

"I see, so do you plan on stayin' here?"

"For as long we can. There's nothing left for us in Georgia. General Sherman made sure of that."

Grandpa had heard of the atrocities inflicted in Georgia by the general during his march to the sea and had some idea of the reason for the pain in the woman's voice. "I'm sorry, Dixie. I didn't mean to drudge up difficult memories."

The soft features of her face enchanted him. Her eyes were the lightest shade of blue he'd ever seen and her silver hair still showed traces of blonde. He had no idea how old she was and her smooth skin revealed no secrets.

"It's alright, Stuart." She smiled warmly. "Becky and I have learned to accept things as they are now, but at first there were too many memories and too much loss, especially after President Lincoln was assassinated. The south was in ruins, still is basically, and there is little leadership to guide the reconstruction. So here we are. Running a restaurant is hard business, but cooking is what I know best; and so far I've been able to provide a living for the two of us."

Grandpa took another swallow of coffee. "May I ask where Mr. Graham is?"

Her gaze drifted towards the window and the busy street beyond. "He's dead," she said coldly. "Sherman made sure of that too, along with my son, Luke. He was Becky's pa. They died fighting. Becky's ma died of pure shock."

Grandpa shook his head. "Again, I'm sorry, Dixie. I think I better stop askin' questions, 'cause I can't seem to ask the right ones."

Still looking out the window, she softly replied, "Time heals all wounds, as does the grace of God." She looked back at Grandpa and her warm smile reappeared. "Despite our loss, God has been good to Becky and me and I believe He'll continue to take care of us."

Grandpa smiled. He finally found a subject that he could breach without opening up old wounds. He and Dixie sat and talked about the Scriptures until Dixie had to prepare the kitchen for the lunch crowd that would soon find its way through the doors.

She gathered the cups. "Come back soon, Stuart. I haven't enjoyed a conversation like that in such a long time."

Grandpa stood to his full height and smiled broadly. "I will, Dixie. In fact, you'll probably see me tonight."

She returned the smile. "I hope I will."

In his hotel room, Grandpa pulled the lace curtains back and stared out the window at the city below. The chest pains that had started that morning were becoming progressively worse. Although he desperately wanted to, the pain wouldn't allow him to lie down and rest before his meeting, so he stood there watching the hustle and bustle of the street below, praying that God would remember their deal.

"I've got other matters to give my attention to, Lord,"

he said aloud. "Once I've taken care of the legal matters and I know Charlie is cared for, I won't mind if you cash in on your part of our bargain, but please not before then."

He buttoned his jacket and grabbed his hat. Before meeting with Mr. Atkins, he needed to go to the bank and establish an account, then find a doctor's office. He pulled the little brown bottle from his pants pocket and reluctantly twisted off the cap. Throwing his head back, he swallowed the last of the sweet, thick liquid. He smacked his lips and shivered. The sweetness was almost nauseating.

Chuckling softly, he admitted that he shouldn't help close the deal between himself and God so fast. He probably needed to eat something else besides fried chicken.

Grandpa stepped out of the bank and slowly made his way down the boardwalk, searching the signs for one in particular and it didn't take long for him to find it: *Richard Taylor, M.D.* He pushed the door open and entered the small waiting room.

It was dimly lit by an oil lamp and the sunlight that found its way in through the front window. A white curtain hung on the back wall. There were a couple of old chairs underneath the window, and across from them sat an elderly woman behind a tiny desk. She greeted him with a cheerful smile. Her starched, white nurse's bonnet sat stiffly on top of her starch-white hair.

"Is there something I can help you with, sir?" she asked.

Taking the brown bottle from his pocket, he approached her. "I'd like to give this bottle to the doctor," he said.

She took it and held it close to the oil lamp. "Are you wanting a refill? If so, you'll have to speak to the doctor first."

Grandpa shook his head. "Naw, I'm not lookin' to refill it. Don't care for anything that can become habit formin'. I just know these bottles can be hard to come by and thought the doc might be able to use it for someone else."

"But—" She looked at the label again. "—but Mr. Smith, this was given to you for heart complications. I think you should talk to the doctor about refilling the medicine."

Grandpa smiled. "Don't need no refill, ma'am. I just thought the doc could use the bottle."

Grandpa turned and walked out the door.

≈ 21 ≈

GRANDPA STOOD IN FRONT OF THE OFFICE building and pulled his watch from his vest pocket. It was three minutes until two. Right on time! He pushed past the mahogany door and walked into the grand hall. Although he'd seen it a couple of times before, he was still awestruck by its beauty.

Amelia met him and led him upstairs, past the judge's office, and down the hall to a smaller office. The attorney's office door was made of mahogany, just like the judge's, but right in the center, in frosted glass, was the name: *Timothy D. Atkins, Esquire.*

Mr. Atkins was a polite young man, about thirty. He was neatly dressed in a blue suit and his hair was meticulously combed so that every hair fell into place. His dark eyes shimmered and his handshake was firm, but friendly. His mannerisms set Grandpa at ease.

His office wasn't as large as the judge's, but it was clean and orderly. The books on the shelves were aligned by height. His desk was bare, except for a yellow tablet of paper, an ink pen, and the documents which the judge had referred to earlier. There wasn't a speck of dust in the place.

After making sure Grandpa was comfortable, Amelia excused herself and Mr. Atkins dove into the situation, explaining in detail what every document was, what it meant, and what it would or would not allow, per the law. It was a lot of information, and took a couple of hours to explain, but when the meeting was over, Grandpa knew that the inheritance he was passing on to Charlie was sound and secure, no matter what happened to Grandpa.

When the last document was signed, Grandpa pulled his watch from his pocket. It read 4:00 p.m. He had completed his business with Judge Randolph P. Walker and the probate office for now. Amelia had his bank account information from the Bank of Denver and Mr. Atkins had his signature on the appropriate documents. Everything was in order and Grandpa was free to go home.

Stopping at the front desk, he removed his hat. "It was a pleasure doing business with you, Miss Amelia," he said. "I hope we'll see each other again real soon."

Looking up from her work, she smiled. "I do too," she said softly as she stood and walked round the desk, taking his large hand in hers. She looked deep into his faded brown eyes and murmured, "Take care, Mr. Smith. I pray the Lord and His angels guide and protect you on your way home."

"Thank you, Miss Amelia. I know He will."

Grandpa gazed into her lovely face. Her eyes were soft green and seemed to drill into the depths of his heart. Swallowing the lump in his throat, he slowly raised his hand and gripped the rim of his hat, tipped it slightly, then turned and walked out the door.

It was too late to start out that evening, so he stopped at the General Store and bought a few things for his trip home. He only needed a few essential items like coffee and jerky; and he wanted sugar cubes for Bessie. He paid for his purchases and stepped out onto the boardwalk. The coolness of the evening swept across the dirt street and pushed the sun's rays westward.

He finally felt at peace. All the legal matters had been settled. Sure, he'd have to come back to Denver in a few months to sign the final papers once Ralph's matters had been legally settled, but for now, things were in order and Charlie's future was secure.

He carried the supplies up to his hotel room and packed his saddlebags. After a good night's sleep, it would be time to go home; but right now, he'd have his last meal at the little restaurant around the corner.

He whistled happily as he combed his hair in front of the dresser mirror. "Guess it's time to head on over to Dixie's and say so long to her and Becky," he said as he slicked his hair back. Looking at his reflection, he shook his head and chuckled. "I'm her best customer. I hope she can make a decent livin' when I'm gone."

Miller rode up alongside Charlie, his nose and mouth covered with a kerchief to keep from choking on the dust. "Heard you had a visitor a couple of nights ago while on watch," he mumbled.

Charlie pushed his hat back so he could see Miller. "Yeah. Seems McQueen wanted to chat."

"Say anything interesting?"

Charlie shook his head. "Nope. He just wanted to visit for awhile. He did get a little rude, though."

"Why do you say that?"

"Well, he was right in the middle of giving me some vital information and then he just stopped talkin'. No 'Excuse me, I got to go,' or 'We'll talk more later.' His talkin' just stopped, and he was gone."

"Maybe he saw something that scared him and decided to go back to camp."

Charlie laughed quietly. "Oh, I'm sure that's exactly what it was."

"What d'you think it was?" asked the scout.

"More like *who*."

"Okay, *who* then?"

Charlie snickered. "I'd bet *you*."

"Me?" Miller raised his eyebrows. "Why would I be out in the cold and dark when it wasn't my time to pull watch?"

"Well, I'm not sure of your reasons, but I know it was you. I circled the area and I found where McQueen was standing, and off to the west a bit, I found another set of boot prints."

"What makes you think they were mine?"

"It isn't that hard to figure out," said Charlie with a smirk.

"Your grandpa taught you well!

Charlie threw a glance at him from the corner of his eye. "Like an Indian," he stated emphatically.

"Well, at least you know someone is watching your back."

"And I appreciate it, but don't put yourself in harm's way 'cause of me. I've got friends in high places who watch over me all the time."

"How do you know I'm not one of them?" Miller laughed.

"Well, maybe you are."

"I'm not sure what high places you're referring to, but I would like you to consider me a friend."

"Done."

The short wrinkles at the corners of Miller's eyes indicated a grin must be hiding beneath the kerchief that covered his face. He turned and tapped his horse with his knees.

Charlie watched till Miller was gone, then said, "Who is he? And why didn't he know about the other set of boot prints that were out there? He, McQueen, and I weren't the only hombres out there, but he acted like he didn't know there was someone else—and he's a scout. Guess I'll have to keep a better eye on him too."

22

LATER, AOUND THE CAMPFIRE, MILLER, LeFaye, and Charlie read from the Bible and talked while the others gambled. McQueen had been drinking. That was against the rules, but Sarge was as tired as the rest of the crew and some things were going unnoticed.

"Ever think about going back to France, LeFaye?" asked Charlie.

"No," came the sharp answer. "I don't have anyone left there. America is my home now."

"I'm sorry, friend," responded Charlie. "I didn't mean to bring up bad memories."

LeFaye lowered his eyes. "It's okay, Charlie," he murmured. "My mother, little sister, and I came over together a couple of years ago, but things got too bad when we were on the boat. They both died of pneumonia shortly after we arrived. I didn't have anyone after their deaths, and I knew there was nothing left for me in France, so I headed west. It didn't take me long to realize I didn't know how to handle the wildness of the country, so I joined the military to give myself a chance to become accustomed to it all. I only have a few more months left to serve and then I'll be discharged. I didn't mean to be so defensive. I love my native land, but there's nothing there for me now."

Charlie stared into the fire. "I understand. I don't know what I'd do if I lost Grandpa."

Just then, in the distance, the lonely call of a coyote echoed across the prairie. The three sat in silence for a long while, mulling over their own memories, or fears, whatever each kept buried just beneath the surface.

McQueen's warning from the other night rushed into Charlie's memory. *Somewhere, sometime, when you and your grandpa don't expect it* . . . Charlie looked around and spotted the red-haired soldier leaning against his saddle. A cigarette butt dangled between his lips and five cards fanned across his meaty hand. Occasionally, a slurred curse word slipped through his clenched teeth as he fumbled with the cards.

Charlie had a sudden urge to jump on Star and head home. Something was wrong; he could feel it. Where would Grandpa be right now? Still in Denver? Somewhere on the trail home? He wouldn't expect to run into Big T, so he wouldn't be ready for him. Gripped by a sudden panic, Charlie sat up and reached for his hat, but a still, small voice stopped him.

Do you believe I have everything under control, Charlie?

Reluctantly, Charlie eased back against his saddle. He couldn't just go running off into the night. *Yes, Lord, I do. I don't know what's troublin' me, but you do. Tell me what I'm supposed to do, Lord. What do you want me to do?*

Be still, came the soft reply.

LeFaye reached for his saddlebag. "Well, now, I think we need something to keep our thoughts from drifting. How 'bout a game of dominoes?"

Miller had been watching Charlie, but turned to

LeFaye. "I'm not familiar with the game," he said. "Is it hard to learn?"

"Oh, it isn't hard. But it helps pass time. In my country it is a gambling game, but we don't have to play that way."

Charlie gazed into the darkness of the prairie.

"Let it go for now, Charlie," whispered Miller.

Charlie turned to the scout. "Let what go?"

"Whatever it is that has you spooked," said the scout. "Nothing you can do tonight, so you might as well try to relax. Besides, aren't you the one who always says God has everything under control?"

Funny how the question came up again. "I am," he answered. "I do believe that. It's just that back on the farm—"

"You aren't on the farm, Charlie. This is the world, where bad men live among good men, but where sometimes it appears there's more bad than good. This is where faith is tested and love doesn't always conquer. This is where you will make up your mind exactly what you will or will not believe."

Charlie sat up and their eyes locked. "I already know what I believe, Miller," he answered sharply. "My surroundings have changed, but my faith hasn't. I know my faith will be tested, but I'll just keep telling myself that's exactly what it is, a test. And when it's over, whatever it is, I'll have learned and grown in my faith. But if I'm supposed to be somewhere else right now, if my gut tells me something's wrong, then I'll have to believe it's the right thing for me to do."

"Fair enough. But make sure God is telling you to go,

Charlie, and not just your gut. Read the signs right."

Agitated, Charlie took a deep breath. "I've got lookout in a couple of hours. I hope this game doesn't take too long."

LeFaye laughed. "It won't take that long, my friend."

As he laid out the rectangular wooden tiles, the Frenchman said to Charlie, "Why don't we trade watch times? I'm not tired, but I'm the last one on watch. I'd rather do it early and get it over with instead of sleeping too lightly, worrying about the time, and not getting any rest at all."

Charlie shrugged. "You go at ten, then, and I'll go at four."

"Great," said Miller, a hint of sarcasm in his tone, "good to have that settled. Now teach me this game."

LeFaye chuckled. "Okay, my friends, this is how you play dominoes."

23

GRANDPA TRIED NOT TO PUSH BESSIE HARD. But he was anxious to get home. A week seemed forever, but they had put some miles between them and Denver. They were getting closer, only a couple more days. He didn't know where Charlie was right then, but he'd feel closer to him at home. There was so much to tell him. He hadn't been this excited since the day his son was born years ago.

During the long ride home, he felt like he would burst if he didn't talk about all that had taken place in Denver, so he talked to Bessie. He talked so much in fact, he was sure she could recite the whole story to Charlie herself or at least fill in anything Grandpa forgot to tell him.

When he wasn't talking, the old man was sleeping in the saddle. He wanted to cover as much ground as they could in the daylight, so he would ease back in the saddle and surrender to the gentle rocking motion of the old mare. It was when she began to slow down that he awakened from his slumber.

Grandpa opened one eye and looked out at the horizon bobbing up and down between Bessie's ears. She was cautiously approaching a deep crevice that slithered across the prairie like a giant, black snake. Carefully, she stopped at the edge and looked down the steep embankment. Grandpa

shook the cobwebs from his head and stood up in the
stirrups, trying to sight measure its length.

"It'd be a dried up river bed. Dern thing could be this
deep from here to Timbuktu." He rubbed his chin. "I wish
I'd kept note of where we crossed on our way to Denver.
Don't remember it bein' so steep when we crossed it before."

They were still heading south; the mountains were on
his right. But this territory didn't look familiar. Standing up
in the stirrups again, he took a second look over the edge.
"Well Bessie, the good news is we're still headin' south, just
off course a bit. The bad news is, I'm not of a mind to double
back to find the trail. So we're goin' for it ol' gal."

He sat back down and folded his hands across the
pommel, "Well, if we aren't sore now, we will be later.
Mighty glad we happened upon this in the daylight. It
woulda surprised us both to be walkin' in the dark and all of
a sudden disappear into a giant hole in the ground." Bessie
snorted and tossed her head, but Grandpa knew she wasn't
amused. They had traveled many a mile in the dark.

Without his coaxing, Bessie slowly started down the side
of the steep gully. With each step, she tested her footing
before putting her weight down on the earth beneath.
As she descended, small rocks and clumps of dirt rolled
from beneath her hooves and down into the snake's belly.
Grandpa sat straight and balanced in the saddle, letting
Bessie manage the terrain. It took a while, but she succeeded
in getting them both safely to the bottom.

When they reached the wide bottom, Grandpa slid off
the horse and stretched his aching muscles. Patting Bessie's
head, he leaned towards her ear and whispered, "Good job,

girl. We'll rest a spell before we try climbin' up the other side. Not for long though; don't want to get caught in this thing if it starts to rain." Then he pulled a sugar cube from his pocket and she quickly nibbled it from his hand.

Obviously the river had been dry a long time, but the riverbed could fill up in minutes and turn into a raging death trap if a good rain fell, which could happen without warning.

Dozens of old tree stumps poked up from the cracked earth, white from years in the sun. Clumps of dried grass dotted the hard river floor every few feet and small bushes of sage brush grew thick across the steep banks. Grandpa tried to imagine the spot as it would have looked years ago. The trees would have been tall and strong, covered with green foliage, shading the area from the hot sun and providing shelter for birds, squirrels, and other critters. The river obviously would have been deep and full of fish, good for the eating.

It's a shame. Woulda been a nice place to build a cabin.

Bessie nibbled on grassy remnants while Grandpa pulled out some beef jerky and hobbled to a shaded rock to rest a spell. After finishing off the jerky, he pulled the bandana from his pocket and wiped his forehead and neck. It was tempting to stay in the shelter of the tree for the rest of the afternoon, but he decided it would be best to press on.

Bessie's wet nose tapped Grandpa's cheek and he opened his eyes. He had fallen asleep on the rock. He snapped his head up and looked skyward. The sun had moved across the sky considerably. He jumped up and grabbed the reins that Bessie had been dragging, scraping the dirt floor as she walked from grass clump to grass clump, but now, it was time to go. Grabbing the saddle horn, he put a foot in the stirrup and swung the other up over the horse, leather creaking.

"Okay, girl, now for the climb up." He turned the horse toward the hill. "Just take your time and be just as sure-footed as you were comin' down, and we'll be fine."

As they started the slow climb upward, the crack of a rifle split the air. Bessie jumped and bucked. Grandpa, not expecting her sudden movement, shifted in the saddle and lost his balance, but didn't fall. He fought to right himself as she stumbled in the hard dirt of the riverbed. Another bullet whizzed past his ear. Bessie reared to her hind legs, throwing Grandpa to the ground with a heavy thud. Unable to move, he fought to catch his breath. Then, as if in slow motion, he watched Bessie fumble and crash down on top of him.

The horse struggled to get up, but couldn't find her footing. She fought hard, rocking back and forth with every try. Unknowingly, her efforts were crushing the old legs that lay pinned beneath her. Falling back, pushing upward, falling back, pushing upward, she broke bones with every thrust. Exhausted, she finally gave up and rolled over onto her side, screaming in agony as she surrendered the fight

Who would be out here shooting at me? And why? Panic gripped him. Sprawled in the open riverbed, they were sitting ducks.

He tried to move to get a better look at Bessie, but he couldn't budge. His head felt like it was going to split in two, he had no sensation at all from the waist down, and his lungs refused to take in air. He lay his head back down and rested a minute, gasping, then tried to raise up to gauge the damage to his legs. The left leg was starting to tingle. *At least I can feel somethin'*, he thought. But his right leg was numb. He couldn't feel it, nor could he see the splintered bones beneath the skin.

Disappointed, he lay his head back onto the dirt and listened to Bessie's heavy rasping breath while he tried to control his own. He didn't know the extent of her injuries and couldn't get up to find out. Talking low and soft, he tried to calm her and let her know he didn't blame her.

He tried to convince himself to stay calm too, but it was hard with the sky spinning and twirling above him. His eyes darted from the clouds overhead to the hill above him, in search of anything that would come into focus, anything that looked familiar. He felt sick to his stomach. He was sweating but shivering from cold. He knew he and Bessie would die one way or the other if he didn't get help, so he had to try.

"I gotta get home. I gotta see Charlie."

Cold beads of sweat rolled down his face and stung his eyes. Hot searing pain tore at his ribs. His head pounded like it was being beaten with a giant hammer, someone bent on trying to crack his skull, but he continued to struggle up onto his elbows. Waves of nausea rolled over him as he lifted his chest in a final attempt.

"Gotta get home. Gotta get to Charlie."

Then he heard approaching footsteps. *So this is it*, he thought. *This is how it'll end. Not a heart attack, but an ambush.* Unable to see, he closed his eyes and sucked in as much air as his lungs would hold.

"I ain't got much money on me, but take what you will," he whispered.

There was no reply, just the comforting sensation of warm hands dabbing at his forehead before laying him gently back on the ground.

Trying to sit up again, Grandpa struggled to see. Squinting, he still couldn't focus. "Who are you?" he whispered.

A warm hand lay across his chest and gently pushed him back to the ground. "Lie down," whispered the familiar-sounding voice. "I'm here to help you, not to rob you. Everything will be okay, you just lie—"

"Charlie, boy, is that you?" cried the old man, becoming delirious.

The comforting voice replied, "Shhh. You're going to be okay, Grandpa."

The old whiskered chin quivered as tears spilled down his wrinkled cheeks. "Sounds like Charlie," he whimpered.

"Easy now, don't struggle anymore," the rescuer said. "Rest a while, and I'll get you and Bessie out of here."

With no more fight in him, Grandpa let go. Slowly, day faded into night.

24

CHARLIE SANK DOWN AGAINST HIS SADDLE and stared into the fire, listening to the murmur of the surrounding conversations which to him was meaningless chatter that mingled with the ghostly wisps of campfire smoke and floated into the cloudless night sky. He closed his eyes against the pain in his buzzing head.

Why? he thought, *What happened?* He wondered if the answer would ever be clear.

Rubbing his eyes with his palms, he sighed. He wanted to figure it out, understand everything, but at the moment nothing made sense. Charlie laid his head back against the wagon wheel as his mind ran through the night's events as he remembered them: LeFaye was getting ready to teach him and Miller a game called Dominoes. As they were setting up the tiles, he and LeFaye discussed switching their guard duty times for the night. LeFaye would go out to watch the cattle in the late night, while Charlie would take LeFaye's turn in the early morning hours. It was common practice among the men to swap times. No one would even notice. Apparently no one did. Someone had expected Charlie to be out with the cattle around ten o'clock and had thought they were sneaking up on him. They'd wanted to hurt him, maybe even kill him.

But it wasn't Charlie who was out by the herd for the ten o'clock watch. It was LeFaye, the innocent Frenchman. Charlie could imagine LeFaye standing on the hillside overlooking the herd, dreaming of making a home in Colorado. He had told Charlie about his desire for a home with a wife and children, land to call his own, and a few head of cattle.

But now two hoodlums had cut his dream short. He had carried no weapon to defend himself, so the thugs had attacked him violently, half killing him before they realized they had the wrong man. He had received the beating that was meant for Charlie. Charlie's heart sank as a hard knot of guilt fell into his chest. How could he ever forgive himself?

The sound of his name pulled Charlie back to the fire and the conversations that were being whispered around its flames. Looking around, he hoped to find the one who had called him, but no one was seeking him out. Their eyes turned away from him, only looking at each other and mumbling words barely audible over the crackle of the fire.

Miller was to Charlie's right, his head propped against his saddle and his feet close to the fire, whispering something to Sarge about the attack on LeFaye. The sergeant and Peterson were spread out across from him, their eyes glowing in the firelight but the rest of their faces hidden in the shadows beyond the fire's reach. Cook was behind him at the chuck wagon, slapping a knife across a leather strap. He appeared to be lost in his own thoughts. Even Jess seemed to be gone.

He heard the cattle low in a nearby meadow. They'd be chewing their cud or sleeping in the tall grass under the large, translucent moon. Sarge hadn't assigned anyone to watch them. He had said he didn't want to risk losing another man, with Big T Cassidy roaming in the darkness.

Bleary-eyed, Charlie watched the three men whisper about what had happened to LeFaye while on guard duty, Charlie's guard duty. A cold dread lay heavy in the pit of his stomach. Each man averted his eyes, intensifying Charlie's loneliness and shame.

It had been hard enough to watch Sarge and Miller carry his friend's broken body into camp earlier. But to sit and listen to the men talk about the ordeal over and over again was almost more than Charlie could handle.

Nothin' like this ever happened back home, he thought to himself. *There were farmin' accidents and all, but no one deliberately went huntin' another man just to hurt him.*

He scanned the dark prairie beyond the campfire. It would be so easy to run, to just get up and disappear into the darkness. But he couldn't; not yet. His friend was broken and battered, fighting for his life, and although he was sure LeFaye wouldn't want to see him ever again, Charlie felt he had to talk to him, just one more time.

The shrill call of a coyote echoed from the hills and a chill ran down Charlie's spine. He pulled his blanket tighter around his shoulders. "I never would have switched times with LeFaye if I'd had a clue what McQueen was planning," he whispered to anyone who might be listening. But no one was listening. They weren't even looking at him.

Suddenly, and with great animation, Peterson decided to lead just one conversation among the men. Heads popped up all around—even Cook's—and looked at Peterson.

"Never saw nothin' like it in my life," Peterson said loudly. "He's just one big mess. I hope we can get him to Fort Collins all right, but I don't know. His face is pretty smashed in. Might even have lost an eye. The boy didn't have a chance. Found his gun sittin' off aways with his hat and slicker. Don't know why he didn't keep it on him. Always supposed to keep it on. How many bones do you reckon McQueen and his partner broke, Sarge?"

Sarge rubbed his large hand across his tired eyes and down his stubby jaws, sighing heavily. "Too many," he answered quietly. "LeFaye's face isn't going to be the same, and like you said, there's the possibility of losing sight in one eye. He's got a few ribs that will need to mend, and an arm that is broken in a couple of places. They just about beat him to death, that's for sure." He leaned forward and stirred the fire with a stick. "He wouldn't have made it if you hadn't come along when you did, Peterson."

Charlie's heart thumped hard against his chest, pounding molten anger through his veins with every beat. He brought his knees up to his chest, folded his arms across his knees, and buried his head in his arms.

"If LeFaye dies . . ." he whispered. He stared at the campfire then closed his eyes and the image of the flames burned against the inside of his eyelids. The sergeant's voice became muddled, fading from Charlie's consciousness as he tried to fit together the pieces of this puzzling evening.

Let's see. The way I understand it, around ten o'clock, while I was fast asleep beside the fire, my friend LeFaye went out to sit with the cattle. Unbeknownst to him—or the rest of the crew—two men were prowling in the darkness, ready to kill the man whom they thought was going on watch at that hour, the one they were out to get—me! The scum didn't even take the time to realize their mistake before they made their move.

Charlie was startled back to the circle by Miller's voice cracking through the darkness. "Where's McQueen now?" he asked Peterson.

"Over yonder, tied to a tree," drawled Peterson, tilting his head over his shoulder. Everyone's eyes followed the motion, looking out into the darkness, wondering if the prisoner was still there. Peterson glanced around at them, reading the expressions on their faces.

"He isn't goin' anywhere," he said with a smirk. "Have you ever been hog tied?" He didn't wait for anyone to answer. "When I was a kid, we used to tie hogs up so we could take them over to the butcher. They'd fuss and squirm, tryin' to get outta their ropes, but they'd only make the ropes tighter every time they moved. Eventually they'd give in. McQueen did the same thing. I figure he's got himself plumb tuckered out right about now. Too bad I couldn't catch both him and his partner, though," he added, spitting on the ground with a little more force than usual. "Seems like they were huntin' the old man, too, accordin' to what LeFaye was mumblin', so the trouble may not be over."

Charlie's head was between his knees, and he didn't see Sarge throw a warning look at Peterson then glance over at Charlie, but his ears were listening to every word.

Peterson shook his head. "I just can't believe the boy lived through that beatin'; but what's been eatin' at me is, why'd they do that to LeFaye? He's always stuck to himself and minded his own business. I don't understand it."

Charlie snapped his head up. "Because they thought it was me," he growled. "The cowards were after me and didn't realize they had the wrong man until it was almost too late. Didn't even give LeFaye a chance to identify himself. McQueen wanted so badly for me to have a taste of what his so-called Christian pa gave him when he was growin' up, that he didn't even give LeFaye the chance . . ." Glaring at each man, his body shook as he cut himself off so he could swallow the angry words he so desperately wanted to yell out loud. Frustrated, he slumped back against his saddle, drooping his shoulders so low that his blanket rolled down his back and fell onto the grass. "I didn't know," he mumbled helplessly. "I didn't know."

Charlie felt a hand gently grab his shoulder. He looked up and saw it was Miller.

"No one is blaming you, Charlie," Miller said softly. "We all know the truth and we certainly know you didn't cause this to happen."

"Miller's right!" agreed Sarge. "If anyone's to blame, I am. The colonel's going to hold me responsible, you can bet on that, but I'll deal with that later."

Charlie shuddered. He thought he heard thunder pound across the prairie miles away, but listened harder when he heard the noise again; a low and mournful groan rose from the back of the chuck wagon. Charlie quickly wiped his face on the back of his sleeve, hoping no one saw, then jumped up and ran to LeFaye, praying his friend was awake enough to answer a couple of questions.

25

"**Y**OU DON'T *KNOW* SOMEONE'S AFTER YOUR grandfather, Charlie," said Miller. "What happened to LeFaye may have been meant for you, but that doesn't mean your grandpa's in danger."

"Yes, it does," argued Charlie. "McQueen warned me the other night, and then LeFaye said they yelled something about Grandpa being in danger even while they thought they were beating me."

"LeFaye was in no shape to be thinking clearly."

Charlie's jaw muscles flexed as he stared out across the prairie. "I'm still goin', Miller."

Miller looked at the young man for several long seconds then reluctantly let go of the reins and took a step back from the horse. "I see there's no stopping you," he said. "Go on, then. I hope you're wrong."

"Me too. Tell Phillip I'll be praying he gets better, and I'm sorry it was him. I'm sorry I—"

"I'll tell him. He'll be fine."

Charlie tipped his hat to his friend. "Take care, Miller."

"You too, Charlie."

Turning Star southward, Charlie pressed his heels against the horse's ribs. "He-yaw," he yelled. The horse leapt into a gallop.

*   *   *

Charlie pushed Star hard, but the horse didn't falter. He was born for running on trails, twisting and turning, and jumping over fast flowing creeks or fallen branches.

Charlie made sure they bedded down late and rose early, and without cattle to slow them down, it didn't take long to cover the miles from Fort Collins to Denver. Before they knew it, Charlie had reined Star up in front of The Gold Rush Hotel.

Leaping from the saddle, he threw the reins around the hitching post, bounded up the wooden stairs and through the front doors, straight up to the front desk. A middle-aged man appeared from behind a heavy tapestry that hung behind the polished counter and approached Charlie, over the rim of his glasses scanning the trail-worn cowboy.

"Would you like a room, sir?" he asked dully.

Out of breath, Charlie shook his head. "No, but I need to find out when someone checked out of one. His name is Stuart Smith. Can you tell me when he checked out?"

"When did he check in?" droned the clerk.

Charlie rolled his eyes. "I don't know," he grumbled, "a week or so ago."

The man pulled the register around so it faced him right side up, and licked his thumb. Turning the pages backwards, he mumbled the names slowly as his eyes scanned the list. "Tucker . . . Franklin . . . Creek . . . Is Mr. Smith a friend of yours?"

"What?" asked Charlie.

The clerk stopped his search and looked over the rim of

his glasses again. "I said, is Mr. Smith a friend of yours?"

"No. I mean, yes." Charlie took another deep breath. "Mr. Smith is my grandfather. He stayed here for a couple of days. I need to know when he left."

The clerk turned his attention back to the names. "Johnson ... Walker ... McCabe ... Smith. Yes, here it is: Stuart Smith. He checked out on Saturday, September 30th."

Charlie slapped the counter. "Thank you."

As he turned to leave, the clerk said, "Mr. Smith, I do have something here for your grandfather, if you wouldn't mind giving it to him."

Charlie turned back to the counter. "What is it?"

The man pulled a little brown bag out from beneath the counter and handed it to Charlie. "It's from Doc Taylor," said the clerk. "He refilled it and hoped he could get it to your grandfather before his next attack."

Charlie stared blankly at the man behind the counter.

"I, I'm sorry, Mr. Smith," stammered the clerk. "I thought you knew of your grandfather's condition."

Dumbfounded, Charlie took the bag and opened it, pulling out the little brown bottle of thick serum. He carefully read the label, the directions written in the doctor's own handwriting and then slowly placed the bottle back into the bag and folded down the sides. "Are you sure the doctor didn't mean some other S. Smith?" asked Charlie, handing the bag back to the clerk.

"Well, he said his daughter told him there was a guest here by that name and when he described your grandfather to me, it sounded like the same gentleman."

"Well, I don't think it is," said Charlie. "Grandpa

would've told me. He wouldn't have suffered through heart attacks without my knowing it. So keep this here. I'm sure it was meant for someone else."

Puzzled, the clerk took the bag and placed it back under the counter.

Charlie thanked him and left the hotel. Stepping off the stairs, he quickly forgot about the medicine and started some mental calculations. *It's October 7th now. If all is well, Grandpa should be safe at home, or real close to it. Two or three days out at the most, depending on how fast he and Bessie traveled.*

Untying the reins from the hitching post, his attention was drawn to voices somewhere behind him.

"No, really, I can manage by myself," a young woman said nervously.

Charlie froze. Another voice, gruff and cold, made his pulse beat faster for some reason.

"Come on, Millie," persisted a man's voice, "just let me walk you home. A pretty little thing like you shouldn't be without an escort."

"I'm fine, really . . . "

Charlie turned from the post and looked across the street. Two people, a man and a woman were huddled close together on the boardwalk. The large man's frame blocked her from his view, but she had sounded distraught. Did she not want to walk with him? Then, the big man moved and Charlie recognized the young woman as the one he had seen coming out of the judge's office several evenings ago.

And the man? Who was he? He stared a few seconds longer, hoping to get a better look at the face. When the man cocked his head to the side Charlie recognized him in an instant. He quickly tied Star back to the post, jogged across the dirt road, and hopped onto the boardwalk, the thud from his boots causing the big man and the young woman to look up in surprise.

It took a second, but the wrangler's bloodshot eyes soon recognized the young cowboy; then they narrowed, reflecting a deep, cold anger. Grudgingly, he let go of the lady's arm and turned to face Charlie.

Charlie looked into the cold blue eyes and tipped his hat. "Nice to see you again, um, Trevor," he said, a smile curling the ends of his mouth. "I do believe that's what the folks you don't consider to be your friends call you, isn't it?"

"What are you doin' *here?*" growled the wrangler.

Charlie ignored the question, peering over the wrangler's large shoulder at the beautiful young woman instead. He smiled and tipped his hat again. Her face was pale, a trace of horror still shining in her eyes. Charlie thought she was way too pretty to look so scared.

Charlie turned his attention back to Trevor. "Aren't you going to introduce me to the lady?" he asked innocently, stepping aside to let a couple pass by, their faces shadowed with curiosity.

Big T stepped forward and positioned his large frame squarely between Charlie and the girl. "This ain't none of your business, Smith," he snarled.

Charlie stood on his tiptoes and glanced over the man's shoulder again, addressing the woman warmly. "I heard this brute call you Millie. Is that your name?"

She nodded nervously and stuttered, "A . . . Amelia."

"Hello, Amelia. My name is Charlie."

Trevor nudged Charlie in the chest, pushing him a couple steps back.

Charlie gathered his composure and stayed cool. "If you prefer to go on about your business, Miss, I'm sure Mr. Cassidy won't mind. He and I may be tied up in a conversation for awhile, since we have a lot to catch up on, and we certainly wouldn't want you to be late for an appointment or anything, so please, feel free to go."

Amelia managed a weak smile before gathering her long skirt and escaping down the stairs. Charlie and Big T watched as she scampered across the street and down the opposite walkway, but the expressions on their respective faces differed like night and day.

Trevor Cassidy didn't watch her long enough to see her duck into the sheriff's office, nor did he see the sheriff come out of the jail house and lean against the door frame. Trevor didn't see because he'd turned his scowling face back at Charlie.

Over the wrangler's shoulder, Charlie watched the lawman roll a cigarette and nonchalantly throw a long look up and down the street. The sheriff was acting cool, but Charlie knew he had the two of them in his sights.

Big T grabbed Charlie by the shirt collar and pulled his face up close to his. The big man reeked of alcohol.

The sheriff stood up straight and checked his gun.

Holding up a finger, Charlie tried to signal him to back off for just one more minute.

"What are you doin' back in my town?" growled Big T, his face red with rage.

Charlie blinked a couple of times, but he couldn't turn his head. He held Trevor's gaze and slowly moved his hand upward until it rested on the big fist pushing against his throat. Charlie stared into the big man's eyes, deliberately pushed the hand away, and stepped back.

"I thought I was in Denver," he said coolly. "Am I in a different town?"

The wrangler snickered coldly. "Go ahead and try to be cute, pup. But you won't think you're so cute when you find your old grandpa dead and gone."

Charlie's face turned white. "What about my grandfather?" he snarled.

A dark scowl clouded Big T's face. "See? Ain't so cute now, are you?"

In one fluid motion, Charlie stepped forward and grabbed the wrangler by the collar with one hand and shoved his pistol into the man's solid abdomen with the other. Big T never saw it coming.

"You almost killed my friend, which alone gives me cause to put a bullet in you," Charlie whispered through gritted teeth. "But if I find one hair on my grandfather's head out of place, you'd better run, big man. Do you understand?"

His nose almost touched the wrangler's as he stared into his large blue eyes. Pushing the gun barrel deeper into Cassidy's stomach, Charlie growled, "I said, do you understand?"

Sweat slid down Big T's forehead and dripped onto the tip of Charlie's nose.

"Anything I can do for you, gentlemen?" asked the

sheriff, who had decided it was time to cross the street. He was standing close, stoney-faced, with his gun drawn. On his leather vest glinted a tin star.

Big T turned his head slightly, trying to look at the sheriff. Charlie didn't take his eyes off the wrangler.

"I was just trying to ask Amelia Taylor if I could walk her home, minding my own business and the like, when this dirty cowpoke barged over. He scared her half to death and has been threatening me ever since."

Charlie chuckled low and cold. "You're just a little girl."

A threatening scowl formed across Big T's face.

"You don't scare me," whispered Charlie. "I see what you're made of now."

"Let him go, Mr. Smith," commanded the sheriff.

Charlie stared into the cold blue eyes a second longer, then slowly released his grip on the man's shirt. It took a second longer for him to holster his gun.

Toe to toe with Trevor Cassidy, the sheriff stood several inches taller. "I think it best you head on back to the ranch now, Mr. Cassidy," he said calmly. "This conversation is over."

Big T took a couple steps back and smoothed his shirt.

"Aren't you gonna arrest him, sheriff? After all, you were witness that he attacked me."

Sheriff Bingham's face colored. "You just go on your way, as I said." Aggravation rose in his voice. "I'll take care of Mr. Smith."

Big T threw a menacing glace at Charlie. "You better," he growled, "or one of these days, someone else will."

Charlie stiffened. "Go, now," ordered the sheriff.

Big T turned with a huff and headed down the boardwalk.

The sheriff and Charlie watched him until he disappeared round a corner. Then the sheriff looked at Charlie. "Mind steppin' into my office, Mr. Smith?" he asked.

"Not at all, sir, but how'd you know my name?"

The sheriff flashed a toothy grin. "Well, I can't claim to be an expert mind reader, or investigator for that matter. I confess, Miss Taylor told me."

The two men crossed the street to the office that Amelia Taylor had entered earlier. She wasn't there now, but Charlie noticed the scent of her perfume. Taking a seat across from the sheriff, her name suddenly hit him.

Amelia Taylor. She's the one grandpa thought was an old bitty. The thought almost made him laugh out loud, but he held himself in check, not wanting to give the sheriff the wrong impression.

Bingham walked round the desk and sat down in his chair. "What are you doing back in Denver, Charlie? I thought you were headin' up to Fort Collins with that small herd."

"I was. But there's been a change in plans." Charlie told the sheriff about how he and Big T first met, McQueen's warning the night he was on watch, LeFaye's beating, and Cassidy's recent threat about Grandpa.

"Did your friend, LeFaye, see Cassidy during the altercation?" asked the sheriff.

"No. He was punched in the face the minute he turned around, but he heard McQueen say his name."

"Where is this McQueen now?"

"In the stockade up at Fort Collins, waiting for a court-martial, I suppose. You may want to check him out, though. You might find he's a wanted man, using an alias."

The sheriff grabbed a tablet and pen out of his top drawer and started jotting down notes. "Where's your grandfather, Charlie?"

"I'm hopin' he's at home, but I'm not sure. That's why I'm here, checkin' on dates 'n things."

"Amelia told me he met with the judge on the 29th and lit out on the 30th. Would he have had enough time to make it home by now?"

"It depends," said Charlie, thumping his knee nervously. "He's part Indian and knows how to travel, but I don't know how fast he and Bessie were moving. I don't think he'd push her too hard, so he could still be about two days out. I just don't know."

"Do you think Cassidy may have done something stupid?"

Charlie chuckled. "That's a loaded question, sheriff."

The sheriff smirked. "To your grandfather, I mean."

Charlie stopped laughing. His dark eyes met the sheriff's. "For his sake, I certainly hope not," he answered coldly.

The sheriff shook his head. "I just don't know how Cassidy could've had time to get from the northern part of the territory, to down south of Denver, almost to Pueblo, to hurt your grandfather, and then be back here to butt heads with you."

Charlie stared out the office window. "I don't know, either. Does Cassidy have any brothers who would do his dirty work?"

"No, he's a lone child, but there are plenty of tough cow hands on his father's ranch that might oblige him."

"I think it's something you should look into, sheriff."

"Well, right now I don't have reason to. It's your word against his. I mean, we don't know if anything's gone awry or not; but I'll keep my ear to the ground. What do you plan on doing now?"

"Once we're done here, I'm ridin' out towards home."

"Your horse looks done in. I suggest you get a room at the hotel, eat a hot meal, let your horse rest, and start out in the morning."

Charlie started to shake his head, but the sheriff interjected, "Might be a good time to call on Miss Taylor, to thank her for stopping in here when she did. Don't know how long you mighta been laid up in the doc's office if she hadn't."

Charlie threw a look at the sheriff.

"He's mean, Charlie. He's as big as an ox and clumsy too, so he's not too good with a gun, but he's blazin' fire with those fists. He's almost killed a couple of men with 'em, including your friend, but I've never had enough grounds to arrest him. Folks are too scared of him and his friends. The men he's beaten always end up takin' the blame for the fight and won't press charges."

Charlie stood up. "I do thank Miss Taylor for her quick thinkin', but I better be ridin' out."

Just then Amelia stepped into the office. "Excuse me, Mr. Smith. Judge Walker was wondering if you would mind having dinner with him this evening over at the Palace Hotel?"

At the sound of her voice his heart raced. Turning slowly, he didn't respond immediately, but studied her, standing there in the doorframe. Her auburn hair, glistening in the afternoon sun, cascaded gently over her small shoulders and her green eyes smiled as she nervously looked away then back again at Charlie. She blushed.

And mysteriously, he could feel his own cheeks turning red as he stood there, barely breathing.

26

POT ROAST? *WHEN DID I GET HOME?* SLOWLY
Grandpa opened his eyes. The aroma of beef cooking in the
pot certainly filled the room. But he wasn't home. He tossed
a quick glance around. The furnishings weren't his. He didn't
know where he was, but he did know two things: the bed
was soft and the food smelled good.

He tried to sit up, but the agonizing truth of the accident flooded back. He eased himself back onto the pillow. *I
wonder,* he thought. Carefully, Grandpa lifted the bed covers
and looked down at his right leg. To his relief, it was still
there. He thought for sure he'd lost it. But it was bandaged
nice and neat and still a part of his body. He ached from
head to toe, but he was alive, he had his legs, he could feel
pain; and coming from the next room, he heard voices.

"Well, there you are," said an old woman who shuffled
into the room. She brushed a lock of white hair out of her
face. "I thought you were going to sleep another day away."

In the light of the oil lamp, she looked small and frail,
and her face had more wrinkles than a shriveled prune. She
pulled her shawl tightly around her shoulders and held the
ends close to her chest with long, thin fingers of one hand,
as she bent and felt Grandpa's forehead with the back of the
other boney hand.

She looked tired. Her white hair was pulled up. Once in a while, a soft wisp fell around her face, and she poked at it with her translucent fingers, to secure it with a pin on top of her head.

Grandpa watched her scurry round the bed, pulling the bedding up to his chest and tucking him in tightly.

"I beg your pardon, ma'am. How long have I been out?"

Sitting down beside Grandpa, she took his large, but now thin, hand in hers and gently massaged it. "About three days."

"Three days! I coulda been home by now."

"You could have, but you're here. Reminds me of the flood of '24. Took everything else and left us stranded."

"I don't remember a flood in '24," mumbled Grandpa.

"Well, you ain't of a mind to remember much of anything right now, young man. Bein' all beat up like you are."

"My head hurts," Grandpa said, squeezing his eyes shut.

"I see you've met my husband, Gill."

Grandpa opened one eye and looked at her. She was standing beside the bed staring at him, her hands on her hips and her bottom lip sticking out.

"No," he mumbled. "I haven't."

"Oh, I thought you had. He always says his head hurts too, whenever I say somethin'."

Grandpa closed his eyes and swallowed hard to keep from laughing. "I'm grateful for all you've done, ma'am."

She patted Grandpa's hand. "It'll be alright, son. You just wait and see. We're just glad you're here."

"I'm thankful for that too, but where is *here*?"

Pressing a cold rag onto Grandpa's forehead, she

laughed. "Oh, I guess you wouldn't know, would you? Well, you're right here at the home of Gill and Orpha Dobson. I'm Orpha."

"Nice to make your acquaintance. I'm Stuart Smith."

"Nice to have finally made your acquaintance too, Stuart. Micah, he's our grandson, found you layin' out there half dead, so he and Gill brought you home and we've been takin' care of you ever since."

"Sorry to have been such a bother, ma'am. Soon as I'm able, me and Bessie'll head on home."

As he spoke, the fog lifted from his memory. "Bessie was hurt real bad. I don't think she . . ." Grandpa's voice cracked and he turned towards the window.

"She's fine, Mr. Smith. Her leg was sprained pretty bad, but with splints and a lot of rest, she's pullin' through, too."

Grandpa's eyes widened. "But that can't be. It woulda taken a miracle to save her."

"Well, miracles happen, Stuart. She's in the corral. But the two of you won't be going anywhere anytime soon. You both still have a heap of healin' to do."

Grandpa closed his eyes and let the pillow cradle his head. He was so tired.

"Most important, you're alright," she whispered. "Jess says it's not time yet; you're still needed here for a season."

Grandpa fell into a light sleep, mumbling to himself. "Yes, Charlie. I'm still here for a reason. And I'm glad you're with me." Grandpa squeezed her hand.

Orpha leaned towards his ear. "Are you hungry?"

"As a pig!" Grandpa mumbled.

"Good, I'll go fix you up a plate."

"Sounds wonderful, son. I'll take a heapin' of everythin'."

He was snoring lightly as she shuffled across the wooden floor and into the kitchen. Turning slightly, she looked back at the old, worn out body. "Sleep well, Grandpa," she whispered.

Heavy breathing. Heavy nasal breathing. That's what he heard. Slowly, Grandpa opened his eyes. To his surprise, he found a very old man leaning over the bed and staring into his face, breathing heavily out of his nose.

"May I help you?" asked Grandpa.

The old man's ancient eyes bore deep into Grandpa's. He didn't say a word, just kept breathing heavily through his nose.

After several minutes, the stranger moved away from the bed, but he didn't stand straight. Grandpa had thought he was leaning over him, but that must have been as straight as he could get. Must have ruined his back by years of heavy lifting.

"Gill," the older man said firmly. "Name's Gill Dobson."

Grandpa tried to sit up.

"Wouldn't do that if I were you," said the ancient one. "Orpha'd come down on you like rain on a wheat field if she knew you was in here movin' all over the place. Apt to mess up her nice bandage work."

Thankful he could skip the niceties, Grandpa fell back down into the soft bed and tried to catch his breath.

"Yes, siree," continued Gill. "She'd be madder'n a teased rattlesnake."

"Don't want that," whispered Grandpa.

"Nope, ya don't! . . . I didn't catch yer name."

Grandpa looked up at the old man and snickered. "Sorry, was just havin' a bit trouble breathin', that's all," he muttered.

"Oh, not a problem, ol' timer."

Who's he callin' an ol' timer? thought Grandpa. *He's gotta be older'n dirt!* Then out loud he mumbled, "Stuart, Stuart Smith."

"Nice to make yer acquaintance, Smithy."

Gill shuffled to the end of the bed and threw the bedcovers off Grandpa's legs. "Let's see what I need to do here."

"What do you mean?" asked Grandpa, more alert.

"Well, this right leg is mangled up pretty bad. I think I should cut it off and make a cane out of the bone fer ya."

Grandpa blinked his panic-stricken eyes. "Cut it off," he stammered. "I don't think you'll—"

Gill cackled with laughter, which led to a coughing fit. Grandpa lay his head back down into the pillows and prayed the old man would catch his breath soon.

Orpha's shrill voice called from the other room. "Gill Dobson, are you tormenting that man?"

"What?" he yelled between hacking coughs. "Am I tillin' up the land? Land sakes, woman. How am I supposed to do that when I'm in the house? Besides, it's wintertime."

Orpha appeared in the bedroom doorway. "That's not what I said, Gill, and you know it. Now leave him alone." She shook her wooden spoon and stormed back into the kitchen.

Gill got control of the hacking cough and stuck his head out of the bedroom door. "I ain't botherin' him. Just joshin' with this young whipper snapper."

"Well, you let him be. He needs his rest."

Gill looked down at Grandpa like a child who'd just been scolded. "Well, we'll talk more later, Smithy." He grunted. "I'd best go work on that cane."

Grandpa smiled and nodded. "Thanks," he whispered. "Mind puttin' the covers back over my leg?"

Gill didn't hear him, or didn't seem to. Grandpa was sure it was because the old man was too busy trying to breathe.

Then Grandpa heard a different pair of footsteps coming toward his room. A young man carried in a tray of food.

"Charlie," he whispered. "Charlie, I knew you were here."

The boy sat on the side of the bed and smiled. "I've got some food for you."

Grandpa tried to rise to his elbows, but the young man shook his head. "Lay back down, Grandpa. I'll feed you."

Grandpa obliged willingly. Everything hurt; he was in no mood to argue. His head was pounding. He had so many questions: How did he get here? Where was Bessie?

Then he smelled what lay on the tray and his mouth began to water profusely. He was hungry!

The boy offered him small spoonfulls of mashed potatoes and gravy. Grandpa smacked his lips after every bite. "Best food I've had in a long time," he said between gulps.

"Nice 'n slow," said the boy. "There's plenty where this came from."

Grandpa nodded and opened his mouth.

"My name is Micah."

Grandpa glanced at him warily. "Micah!? Your name's Charlie."

The boy winked mischievously. "No," he said, his eyes gleaming. "It's Micah."

It took Grandpa a second and then he arched his eyebrows and smiled. "Oh," he said softly. "The old folks call you Micah, so to keep them from thinkin' I got a loose marble, you want me to call you Micah too."

"That sounds as good a reason as any," said the young man. He held up a glass of cold milk. "Thirsty?"

After finishing his meal, Grandpa threw the covers off his other leg. "Mind helpin' me to the outhouse?"

Micah placed a hand on Grandpa's shoulder and stopped him from moving any further. "It'll be awhile before you can go that far, Grandpa. Let's try things one step at a time."

"Okay," said the old man. "What do ya have in mind?"

Micah pointed to a corner where Gill had rigged up a stool and bucket. "This is as far as you go for now, Grandpa."

Grandpa stared at the contraption. He was now more determined than ever to get better.

≈ 27 ≈

"I DON'T HAVE ANY CLEAN CLOTHES," SAID
Charlie, his eyes on Amelia's beautiful face.

She smiled and his heart skipped a beat.

"It's all right, Mr. Smith. You have an expense account at
Jackson's Mercantile down the street."

"Expense account? Why would I—"

"Trust me, Mr. Smith, everything is fine regarding
expenses." Amelia nervously fingered the silk cord of her
small handbag. "All you have to do is go in, and Mr. Jackson,
the proprietor, will assist you with anything you want or
need. The judge has prearranged everything."

Charlie turned back to the sheriff and searched his face
for approval or permission, something to assure him that if
he stayed, he'd be doing the right thing. The sheriff nodded.

"You're travelin' on a hunch about your grandpa, Charlie.
Just a gut feelin'," said the sheriff. "If I were you, I'd take the
judge up on his offer; see what business he has with you. . . .
And your horse needs a rest, too."

Charlie's eyes found Amelia's again and he nodded, as
if in a trance. "Alright, tell the judge that I'll meet him at
The Palace Hotel this evening. What time does he expect
me?"

Amelia smiled, clearly delighted by his decision. "Oh,

he'll meet you in the grand lobby of the hotel at 7 p.m. You won't have far to go; he's booked a suite for you there."

Charlie directed his next question to the sheriff. "How'd he know I'd stay?"

When he turned back to Amelia, she was gone.

"How'd he know I'd stay?" repeated Charlie, his voice rising to a higher pitch.

"I guess he had a gut feelin', too," said the sheriff. "Now I'm sure Mr. Jackson's expectin' you at the mercantile."

Charlie scratched his head as he walked out the door. He turned and looked at the sheriff, who smiled and pointed to the left. Charlie shrugged and walked south. There was the mercantile sign a couple blocks down the street.

Although well dressed, Judge Walker looked nothing like Charlie expected; but Amelia looked exactly like he thought she would, absolutely stunning. The green silk bodice gently rolled from her shoulders and revealed her slender neck, adorned with an string of pearls. The bodice of her dress held her form elegantly, all the way down to her small waist, where it connected to a matching skirt by a petite cummerbund. From there, the skirt flowed gracefully to the floor. Her green eyes, framed by auburn curls, reflected the light of the crystal chandeliers. She was lovely. Charlie could hardly take his eyes from her when she introduced him to the judge.

She made formal introductions and then turned and looked up into the tanned face of the young cowboy. He wasn't sure, but he thought she had to catch her breath a couple of times before she could speak.

His new brown, pin-striped suit complemented his brown hair and eyes. A chocolate ascot was tucked perfectly into the neck of his white shirt and was held firmly in place by a small gold nugget. Charlie would have made Grandpa proud, having taken the time for a hot bath, a hair trim, and a face shave before getting dressed in these fine clothes. It felt odd to dress so fancy. But next to Amelia, he felt like he was in rags.

Their eyes met again. Amelia spoke softly. "Mr. Smith, before I leave, I want to thank you for intervening this afternoon. Mr. Cassidy is not a gentleman, and although I've tried many times to thwart his advances, he aggressively persists. I don't want to cause a scene, so most times, I dash into a store or attach myself to a lady friend. But this afternoon, being a Sunday, I was alone and hadn't a clue as to what I could do until you came along."

Charlie cleared his throat, trying to conceal his nervousness. "First of all, please call me Charlie. My grandfather has always been known as Mr. Smith and I don't deserve that title yet. Second, you're certainly welcome. Mr. Cassidy is a brute. The sheriff's on to him now, but don't ever hesitate to yell out, stomp on his foot, anything to get him away if you want him away. Never hesitate to make a scene, if you feel you need to. And third, won't you please stay and join us for dinner?"

Amelia giggled and smiled enchantingly, but shook her head. "I sincerely appreciate the offer, Mr.—Charlie, but I dare not. I respect the judge's time with his clients, and I do have other plans for the evening. If I don't see you before you leave, my best to you and your grandfather."

She glanced at the judge, then back at Charlie. Her cheeks flushed red. She smiled, then quietly turned and left their company. Charlie watched her leave. When she reached the front door, a young man stood up from one of the guest chairs and greeted her warmly. He took her hand and gently placed it around his arm and together they walked out the door.

Charlie was overcome by a strange feeling; like something had just been taken from him. It wasn't the same sadness he felt when Mary Lou walked away, but more of an emptiness, a void. He didn't want Amelia to leave. He didn't want her to belong to someone else. He'd never felt like that before. He didn't like the feeling.

The judge interrupted the silence. "Please, have a seat young man," he said jovially. "We've a good bit to talk about."

Charlie buttoned his shirt and from the hotel window watched the morning traffic on the street below. A new sun had just started its journey over the horizon, streams of red and gold shooting their way across a retreating black sky.

A new day, a new beginning for Grandpa, he thought. A wave of excitement surged through him. He couldn't believe what the judge had told him the night before. Grandpa was going to come into a little money. He had no clue how much, but it should be enough to take care of his grandfather until the good Lord called him home. Imagine that! And none too soon, either, since he wasn't sure where their cattle business was going with the closing of the Fort. Charlie grabbed his hat off the bed. *Well, no one deserves it more*, he thought.

He tucked the packages that held his new suit and old clothes under his arm and left the room for the front desk where he'd have the clerk send everything to Pueblo. He'd pick them up from Wilbur later.

While he stood at the counter, he heard a weary male voice speak his name.

"Charlie."

Charlie turned and scanned the room. Just opposite the counter, in front of a large velvet-draped window, sat two guest chairs, and in one slumped a haggard-looking man. The mud-encrusted buttons on his shirt bore the distinguishing marks of a uniform, but that was all that was familiar. It took Charlie a minute to recognize the dirty, weathered face.

"Sarge?" he whispered. "Sergeant Wilkins, is that you?"

The man could barely pull a smile across his face, but managed and signaled for the boy to come take a seat.

"I can't believe I found you," he said, his voice cracking as Charlie sat across from him. "The colonel made me high tail it outta there right after we pulled in. Said if I didn't find you and report back that you were safe and sound, he'd hang me himself."

"He made you leave as soon as you got there?"

The sergeant nodded. "I've been ridin' day and night. He only give me a week, so I prayed you'd still be in Denver." The sergeant went into a coughing fit.

Charlie waved a young woman over. "May I have a glass

of water for the sergeant, here?"

"Certainly, sir. I'll be right back."

She walked briskly through a swinging door in the parlor and soon returned with a pitcher and a clean glass. "Will there be anything else, Mr. Smith?"

Charlie was about to ask, but decided it didn't matter how she knew his name.

"Actually, there is," he replied. "Would you please reserve a room for the sergeant? He'll be staying a couple of nights."

"Yes, sir. Is that all?"

"One more thing; is there a telegraph office nearby?"

"The hotel clerk, Mr. Stiles, can help you with that."

"Thank you kindly, Miss."

She turned and hurried to the front desk, mumbling something to the clerk, who Charlie assumed was Mr. Stiles. The two huddled over the open register, then glanced at the worn soldier. The clerk found his pen and began scribbling.

The sergeant gulped eagerly at the cold water. His hand trembled as he lifted the pitcher and filled his glass again, spilling droplets onto the oak table.

"When you can, tell me everything," Charlie said eagerly, sitting on the edge of his chair. "How's LeFaye?"

Sarge cleared his throat, took another gulp of water from his glass, then sat back and let his head rest against a wing. He stared at nothing in particular, his eyes slightly unfocused.

"Well," he started, "LeFaye's quite the fighter. He hung on and made it to Fort Collins where I'm sure they're caring for him properly. Miller got him comfortable in the infirmary and then took off, even before I did. Don't know where he was goin' in such a hurry."

The sergeant shifted in the chair and grunted, then grinned sheepishly. "Sorry, a bit saddle sore." When he had found a comfortable spot, he continued. "Don't know much more about LeFaye's condition. Like I said, I didn't spend much time at the Fort."

Charlie winced at the thought of the sergeant having to mount back up and head off to find him without having the chance to rest or visit with family.

The sergeant turned his rump in the seat again. "Colonel Humphries was in one raw mood by the time I hit his office door. He loves his Cubans."

A look of confusion crossed Charlie's face.

"Ya know, cigars. He loves to smoke stogies in the evenings while he sits on the bench outside his office door and watches the sun go down. But when he gets mad or upset, he smokes like a chimney. One right after the other. Smoke so thick, a man can hardly breathe. By the time I got to his office, I thought I was gonna die for lack of oxygen. I could hardly see the colonel in all that smoke; but he was puffin' and pacin' the floor like a wild animal. The floor boards were squeakin' as he walked back 'n forth behind his desk."

Charlie fought the urge to laugh. He poured another glass of water, while the sergeant rubbed his eyes.

"Anyway," said Sarge, stretching his legs and stifling the rest of his sentence with a wide yawn before he could stop himself. Giving a quick shake of the head, he continued.

"After lettin' me have it, verbally that is, he gave me fifteen minutes to get some clean gear, whatever grub I could find, and a fresh horse before settin' out to find you. To be honest, I just wanted out of there. He was madder than a rolled polecat and there wasn't enough room in that office for the both of us."

Charlie couldn't suppress a chuckle as he envisioned the scene. Sergeant Wilkins was a big, rotund man, but Charlie could imagine him squirming under the glare of Colonel Humphries, a tall muscular man, with steel gray eyes and a long, bushy mustache to match. The colonel's father was a close friend of Grandpa's; that's how Charlie was able to finally go on this cattle drive in the first place. And Colonel Humphries was a man of his word; when he swore that his men would take good care of Charlie and that he would personally be responsible for Charlie's health while on the trip, he meant it. So, once it was brought to the colonel's attention that the sergeant had let Charlie slip away from the group and out on his own, not only was he angry because Charlie's welfare was in jeopardy, but his own reputation and respectable career were now on the line.

Charlie's heart was sinking. "I didn't mean for—"

"You didn't do nothin', Charlie," the sergeant waved away the comment. "I knew the colonel was gonna be angry and all, and bein' the sergeant, I'd get the brunt of that anger. To be honest, I didn't expect him to send me right out after you, but he did, and now we're here. You're safe and sound, and I can rest a spell, knowing I don't have a date with the gallows."

"Well, before I leave town, I'll send a telegraph to the colonel myself and let him know I'm okay and I'll let him know that you'll be staying here for a couple of days before you head back to Fort Collins. I'm no longer your responsibility, Sarge; don't worry about me from now on."

The sergeant's eyes drooped sleepily and he nodded.

Charlie pulled the heavy velvet curtain back from the window and glanced outside. The sergeant's horse was tied to the hitching post, all lathered up and done in.

"I'll take care of your horse too," he whispered.

Charlie got the room key from Mr. Stiles, then helped the soldier up the stairs. In the room, Sarge stripped to his long johns and settled into bed. He was snoring before Charlie hit the door to go back down to the desk. He ordered a quick breakfast of biscuits and bacon for the sergeant, with enough to pack in his own saddlebags to last him for a few days.

"Did you wish to send a telegram, sir?" asked the clerk. "Emma mentioned earlier that you intended to do so."

Charlie signed Sergeant Wilkins' name to the register. "Yes, I do," he said looking up at Mr. Stiles.

"And may we assist you with those packages?"

Charlie looked at the brown wrappings under his arm. "I've got to send these to the post office in Pueblo."

Mr. Stiles nodded. "We can accommodate, sir, if you wish."

"That'd be great," said Charlie. "It'll save me some time."

"Not a problem, sir. Just fill out these forms and sign them. We'll take care of the rest."

"I appreciate your help, Mr. Stiles." He handed the bundles and forms to the clerk.

"We aim to please, sir."

"And you have, but the name is Charlie."

Mr. Stiles smiled. "Thank you for choosing the Palace Hotel, Charlie, and we look forward to seeing you again soon. Have a safe trip."

Charlie wrote out the telegram message for the colonel and left it with the clerk, who promised he'd send it off immediately. After paying for everything, Charlie stepped outside and headed to the judge's office.

28

CHARLIE STOOD ON THE BOARDWALK AND stared at the large mahogany doors. He swiped at a bead of sweat rolling down the side of his face.

This is the right thing to do, he assured himself. He turned the knob and stepped inside.

He didn't notice the beautiful surroundings, the handmade rugs, the marble floor, or the large brick fireplace. He saw only Amelia, sitting behind her desk, busy at work.

He removed his hat quietly and approached the desk.

Without raising her head, she said, "Please have a seat, I'll be with you in just a moment."

Charlie was too nervous to move. He stood frozen to the floor, his heart pounding in his ears. Could she hear it too? Finally she looked up from her work and her eyes met his. Her pink cheeks turned crimson as she recognized the young cowboy standing in front of her.

"Mr. Smith," she whispered. "I didn't expect—"

"Charlie, please. Mr. Smith should be home by now."

She stood up and smoothed out the skirt of her dress, her fingers shaking slightly. "Charlie. I'm sorry, I'm so used to having to address people by their proper names, that I—"

"I was hoping you were just pleasantly surprised and didn't know what to say."

Her eyes sparkled. "I am . . . I don't," she stammered.

He tapped a knuckle on the desk top. "Well, I'm headin' home. Wanted to stop and say good-bye before leavin' town."

She walked round the desk and held out her hand.

"I'm sure we'll see you again," she said with professional confidence. "We will be handling your grandfather's affairs."

He took her hand in his and gazed at her fingers. The small, thin, well manicured fingers, as soft as down, felt warm inside his large calloused hand. Mary Lou's words echoed in his mind: *Someday you're going to meet a girl and fall in love with her, but if you hesitate too long, you'll find her in the arms of another.*

Still looking at her fingers, he whispered softly, "I started wanting something new the first time I saw you."

"I'm sorry, Charlie, did you say something?"

He looked into her fluid eyes. Not deterring his gaze, he slowly raised her hand to his lips and kissed it. Lost in a sea of green, he felt a tremble, but didn't know if it was from himself or her. "I'm not going to say good-bye, Amelia," he whispered. "I'll be back. I'm not sure when, but I'll be back."

She didn't move. Her eyes searched his for just a second. Before lifting her fingers, she gently caressed the palm of his hand. "I'll be right here."

The sergeant's horse was covered in lather. White, airy froth dripped from its mouth as it rested its muzzle on the cross bar of the hitching post. His winter coat was thick and unruly. Charlie looked at the sad animal and shook his head.

He carefully untied the reins and led the horse to the livery. It followed close behind, trudging along with head hung low and nose almost scraping the dirt, stumbling across the ruts in the road. For the sake of the worn gelding, Charlie walked as slowly as possible, but couldn't help but wonder whether the animal was going to drop dead right in the middle of the street. To his relief, they made it to the stable.

Charlie led the horse into the barn expecting to meet the proprietor, but instead found Big T leaning against a rail, pulling on a cigarette. Just the sight of him aggravated Charlie. He hated unexpected surprises. His first instinct was to pull iron, but he didn't want trouble now. He wanted to head home.

"Don't you know it's dangerous smokin' in a barn?" he mumbled as he stepped round the man toward an empty stall.

"I don't want to fuss on such a beautiful mornin', Charlie," growled T. "I just stopped by to wish you safe travels. I'd hate to think of somethin' happenin' to you, or your grandpa."

Charlie ignored the comment and pulled the saddle off the sorrel and threw it across the stall rails, then grabbed a brush and started to wipe down the horse. He thought he heard the animal start to snore.

"But wait a minute," continued T. "I guess it would be too late to wish that for the old man though, wouldn't it?"

Charlie froze at the remark. His temper flared and he reached slowly for his gun; but a strong hand gripped Charlie's shoulder.

"Be still, Charlie." Jess's voice was clear and strong.

"Anger won't settle this. Don't cross the line with that gun, son. Use the sword instead, the book I gave you. Remember the big plan, the mission, even when you don't like the circumstances."

Laying his head against the sorrel's ribs. "I can't help it," he whispered. "He tries to irk me, get under my skin, and he knows nothin'll get to me faster than to make threats about Grandpa."

"Believe me, I understand," said Jess, "but sometimes you just have to turn a deaf ear. Do you still believe God's powerful enough to have everything in control?"

Charlie nodded.

"Then trust me, son. Even when it comes to Grandpa."

"I do trust you, but I'm not as strong as you and I never will be." Charlie turned in closer to the horse. "Sometimes a man hasta fight, Jess, especially when he knows he's right. I didn't do nothin' to this guy. I tried to apologize to him, but he won't let go; so maybe we should just have it out, once and for all. Get it over with and—"

"Charlie."

The boy swallowed hard and nodded again. "You're right," he whispered. "I'm sorry."

"Charlie, do you know what I want you to do?"

Charlie looked up into Jess's eyes. "Yes, sir, I do."

"Then waste no more time fightin' it, son."

Charlie threw some clean hay into the trough for the horse and filled a feed bag with fresh oats. The sorrel was as comfortable as he could make him, so he found Star and saddled him up.

"Guess you'll understand once you get home to an

empty cabin," jeered T. "From what I heard, he went down pretty hard. He and that old mare of his."

Charlie clenched his teeth and cinched the strap.

"Probably won't find his body, though. Heard it happened in a riverbed, so they probably floated away by now."

Charlie secured the reins to the bridle and led Star out of the stall, straight up to the tough wrangler.

Big T, still leaning on the rail, waited for him to get close enough, then blew cigarette smoke into his face. Charlie closed his eyes and waited for the smoke to clear, then looked deep into the hard eyes of Trevor Cassidy.

"This is just the start of it, Trevor," he whispered.

Big T smirked and snarled, "I'm ready."

"No, I don't mean a fight. I mean the start of a pursuit. You thought you were after me, but now I'm after you."

Trevor raised his eyebrows and snickered.

"I'm after your soul. So I'll make you this promise. From now on, there will never be a day or a night that I don't mention your name in prayer. It was my grandpa who said sometimes you can find something good in an unusual place. I won't think an unkind thought about you, but will look for the good in you. I will not buckle to your threats or be tempted to fight you needlessly; but don't be fooled in thinking I won't defend myself if I have to. Eventually my plan is to kill you."

Trevor stepped forward. The knuckles of his balled fists were white.

Charlie threw a hand up. "With kindness, Trevor," he continued. "I will kill you with kindness."

Trevor stepped up into Charlie's face and leaned in close.

"You say that now, pup, but you ain't lived without your grandpa yet. You ain't seen what was done to him."

Charlie closed his eyes and inhaled deeply, quietly praying for strength. When he opened his eyes, he squared himself with the wrangler and looked him in the eye. "No, I don't know what's happened," he muttered. "But God does, and He'll take care of my grandpa. He'll take care of all of us."

The snicker disappeared and Trevor's large round face looked pale and drawn. "Don't you be preachin' me no—"

"I'm not preachin' anything, Trevor. You can ignore preachin'. I'm gonna be prayin' for you. You can't control that. As for what comes of it, that'll be up to you and God, but I'm gonna do my part in making sure He has His eye on you every minute of every day."

Charlie pulled some money from his pocket and peeled out a couple of bills, handing them to Trevor. "Please give this to the proprietor for me and tell him I'm obliged for the service. Sergeant Wilkins' horse is in the stall to the right. And part of that should cover his stay as well."

Trevor looked at the money and looked back at Charlie. "How do you know I just won't keep this?"

Charlie flashed a smile. "'Cause you know I'm prayin' for you," he said evenly. "And since you'll be in God's sights, I reckon you won't want Him to see you stealin', will you?"

Cassidy's mouth fell open. Then he closed it again. Looking perplexed, he stared at the money, opened his mouth to say something, and then closed it again.

Charlie eased himself into his saddle and tipped his hat. "Be seein' ya, Big T."

29

CHARLIE SLID OFF STAR AND KNELT BESIDE the creek. A cold wind blew through the oak leaves above, sending a shower of red and gold down around his shoulders. Shivering, he pulled his slicker tighter around his body and fastened the top buttons.

The horse had already plunged his muzzle into the cold liquid when Charlie bent down to wet his parched mouth and slake his thirst. He and Star had traveled fast and hard the past few days, covering about twenty miles a day. He was already out of food; but home was just a day away. Right now, berries and water suited him fine.

Then Star raised his head and pricked up his ears. He heard something. Not wanting any sudden surprises, Charlie slowly lowered his hand toward his holster.

"It's just me, Charlie," someone yelled. "Don't shoot."

It was Miller's voice.

Still holding Star's reins, he stood and waited. Miller and his horse came through the trees. "Mind if I join ya?"

"What are you doin' way out here?" asked Charlie.

"Foller'n you, which isn't easy," said Miller with a laugh.

"I thought you had business with the army or somethin'."

Miller slid from the saddle and knelt beside the water's

edge. "Not anymore. And let me show you how this is done."

Scooping a handful of water, Miller brought it up to his face instead of putting his face to the water. "That way," he said, "no one can sneak up on you and take you by surprise. If you have your face down by the water, you can't see or hear. Won't know anyone's around until it's too late, probably when they're drownin' ya, or shootin' ya in the back."

Charlie knelt beside the scout and followed his lead. "Thanks," he said between gulps.

They drank their fill of the sweet, cold water then mounted their horses and headed back to the trail in silence. They were a mile down the road when Charlie looked over at Miller. "Still don't know why you're way out here."

Miller shrugged his shoulders. "Just thought I'd tag along in case you need the help."

"Well, suit yourself. . . . I've been followin' what's left of Bessie's tracks. I lose them once in awhile, but pick them back up after a bit. Mr. Dooley, the man back at the Log Cabin, said he saw them pass by late one afternoon awhile back. Seems Bessie and Grandpa are headin' straight home."

"How much farther?" asked Miller.

"For us, if we keep the same pace, about a day. Two, if we slow down any. Grandpa should already be there."

"Well, let's keep goin' and see where they lead us," said Miller.

They led their horses into a fast walk. Riding in silence, they scanned the prairie in search of tracks.

Finally, Charlie spoke. "How's LeFaye?"

Miller stared at the prairie floor. "He was beat up pretty

bad, as you know. They'd a killed him if they hadn't been stopped in time. But he'll be fine with some rest."

"Did he have anymore questions about God?"

"When I talked to him last, he still had lots of questions. You know he was stuck on the 'If God is so good, how come such bad things happen' question, and then that happened to him. He was wondering where God was when he was gettin' beat up."

Charlie looked up. "I could ask the same question," he said coldly.

Miller glanced over at the boy. "But you know God is here, don't you Charlie? You know He sees where your grandpa is at this very minute."

"Then why doesn't He tell me everything's alright?"

"He will when He's ready."

Charlie stopped his horse. It dawned on him that he still didn't know anything about this man, except that he believed in God. "How do you know what God's plan is for me, Miller?" he asked angrily.

Miller turned his horse so he could face Charlie. "Because God always has a plan, Charlie. Remember what I told LeFaye the first time we talked to him about God? Sometimes it's through our pain and suffering that God draws us closer to Him. He's trying to teach you something, Charlie. You just need to stop and listen."

"What can I learn from this?"

"Faith, maybe. Trust, submission, the chance to examine where your dedication really lies."

Charlie threw a confused look at the scout.

"Your grandfather is the dearest person to you, Charlie,

and that's okay; but maybe God wants to be even dearer
to you than Grandpa is. Maybe God is asking you to learn
to love *Him*."

"But I do love God."

"More than anyone, Charlie?"

Charlie grew quiet as he mulled the question over in his
head. Right then, he didn't like the answer.

Moments later, Miller pointed to the ground. "Your
grandfather got way off the trail. Still headin' south, but
east at the same time. Musta been asleep in the saddle for
awhile."

Charlie didn't like the looks of things. Grandpa was
better than this, or at least he was when he was younger.

A couple hours later they rode up to the dry riverbed.
Both men stood in the stirrups and looked up and down the
wide chasm that split the earth for miles.

Charlie walked Star westward, along the edge of the
steep bank about half a mile, then he turned her back.
Almost a quarter of a mile past Miller to the east, he yelled,
"I found 'em! I found where Bessie and Grandpa crossed."

Miller spurred his horse up to Charlie and looked down
into the ravine, his gaze following the tracks. "Then we cross
here," he said.

The two men eased their horses down the chasm walls,
taking their time with every step. Eventually, they reached
the bottom and saw where Grandpa and Bessie had rested.

"This riverbed hasn't had any water in it for years," said
Miller, pointing to sun-bleached stumps and cracked earth.

Charlie grunted in reply. He followed the tracks that
led to the spot where Grandpa dismounted, the stump

where he rested, then where he remounted Bessie. Although windswept, the tracks were clear. He could see where Bessie had jumped, and then where they both fell.

"This isn't good," he mumbled. "Somethin' *did* happen. Right where Cassidy said it happened."

Charlie told Miller of Cassidy's taunting in the Denver livery. "He said it happened in a riverbed, and he thought the bodies would be gone because of rain water flooding the area. But that didn't happen." He looked up at the scout with questioning eyes. "If it hasn't rained, then where are they?"

Miller walked to the spot where Grandpa had fallen. Sitting back on his haunches, he studied the tracks. "His horse was spooked," he said solemnly.

Charlie walked up beside him and stared at the torn up ground. "How do you know?"

"See, here she was walkin' nice and steady, on solid ground. But there, for some reason, she jumped off to the side, and she was scrambling to stay up. See how deep her prints are? You can see where she jumped and then started to struggle, then eventually fell, landing on your grandpa. Here is where she rolled off of him."

Charlie followed Miller's finger as he pointed to the spot where Grandpa and Bessie had lain, injured, possibly dead. "What spooked her?"

Miller shook his head. "Anything could've," he stated, looking around. "I didn't see any other tracks, did you?"

Charlie shook his head and started pacing.

"I'm sure they're fine, Charlie. Maybe it was a bad tumble, but they were able to get up and move on after awhile."

Charlie walked the tracks again. "I can see where they went down," he muttered as his eyes surveyed the terrain. "But I don't see anything showin' that they got back up." A strange look came over his face. "There're no tracks leading out of here. Water didn't carry Grandpa and Bessie away, or all the tracks would be wiped out. If they didn't climb out, then what happened?"

"Maybe wind blew those tracks away—?" offered Miller.

Charlie was already in the saddle. He tapped Star with his heel and headed him up the embankment. At the top, he let Star open up and fly.

Miller had a hard time keeping up.

Late afternoon the cabin came into view and Charlie drew up on the reins. They'd traveled all night and he was tired. His raw nerves were on edge, but he wasn't finished. His eyes searched for movement, a sign of life; but other than the few cows grazing in the pasture, there was none. No smoke rose from the chimney. The cabin was dark and almost hidden by the wild grass that had grown tall and thick around it. Behind the house, leaves fell from the trees like rain. Obviously, Grandpa had never reached home.

When Miller drew up beside him, Charlie asked, "Where could they be?"

"Seems they should be somewhere between here and the riverbed, but I didn't see another place where they coulda holed up. Maybe he went to town for supplies."

Charlie clicked his tongue and Star ran down the hill, then around the house to the back where Grandpa stored the wagon. To Charlie's dismay, it was there under the oak tree, nestled beside the barn where Grandpa always parked it. Prairie grass had grown tall around the wheels and the bed had filled with brown leaves.

He slid off his horse and dropped the reins. Star strolled over to the water trough and, rooting his muzzle through the soaked leaves that had covered the surface, sipped on the little water that was left at the bottom. Miller's horse ambled over and joined him.

Charlie ran to the back door and threw it open. The cabin was cold, dark, and empty. Everything was just as he and Grandpa had left it. He pulled a chair from the table and sat down, rubbing his face with his hands. To Miller he said, "I just don't know where he could be."

"Listen," said the scout. "I know Grandpa is somewhere safe and could come down the hill any moment. Maybe you should stay busy by getting the cabin cleaned up and ready for him."

Charlie slowly got up and walked over to the wood bin. In a few minutes, he had a warm fire blazing on the grate. Outside he led Star into the barn where he stripped off the dirty gear and rubbed him down. Miller followed in silence.

Charlie ran down into the root cellar and grabbed a chunk of smoked bacon and a small wheel of cheese. That was dinner. While they ate in silence, he decided he'd let his horse rest the next day; but come the morning after, he was going to Pueblo.

30

MILLER AGREED TO STAY WHILE CHARLIE
went to Pueblo. As Charlie and Star left, Miller waved and
called out, "God be with you, Charlie."

"You too," Charlie yelled.

"He always is."

Charlie barely heard those words of Miller's. And he
just caught the knowing smile on the scout's face before he
and Star were galloping down the wagon road toward the
Tuttle's farm.

When he arrived, Charlie pulled up at the cabin door
just as Mrs. Tuttle swung it open, grinning from ear to ear.

"Why, Charlie Smith, you get down from that horse and
come give me a big hug," she ordered. "We haven't seen you
in weeks. Look how tall you've grown. Why, I wouldn't have
recognized you if I passed you on the street."

Charlie blushed as Mrs. Tuttle threw her arms around
him, reaching high to grab his neck and pull his face down
for a kiss on the cheek. He chuckled and pecked her cheek.

"Come on in for some breakfast," she said in her same
cheerful manner.

"Ah, no, no I can't, Mrs. Tuttle. I'd love to, but I'm
headin' for Pueblo. I just stopped by to see if you wanted me
to take anything to Wilbur."

"Why on earth are you headin' to Pueblo?" said Mr. Tuttle, who had just walked up from the barn.

Charlie told them about Grandpa's mysterious disappearace. They listened intently.

"Well, I never," said Mrs. Tuttle, dabbing her eyes with a corner of her apron.

"Mind if we pray with you before you head out, son?" asked Mr. Tuttle.

Charlie had no objections. The three bowed their heads and Mr. Tuttle asked for God's mercy on Charlie as he searched for his grandfather. He commited his friend, Stuart, to the Lord's care. Then he walked Charlie to the edge of the yard.

"There isn't anything to send to Wilbur this trip Charlie, but thanks for checkin'. I would like to mention something to you. I know this may not be the appropriate time for an invitation, but we hardly see you and I want to make sure you know."

"It's alright, sir. What is it?"

"Well," he began. He hesitated, glanced at Charlie, then started again. "Mary Lou will be coming home for the holidays soon."

"Yes, sir," he said politely, although his mind had been on others things besides the holidays and Mary Lou.

Mr. Tuttle reached down and picked up a fallen apple and slid it into his jacket pocket. Star took note and rooted until he found it.

Mr. Tuttle chuckled and patted the horse's thick black neck. "I'm happy as a man can be that my daughter will be home soon and able to stay till after the first of the new year.

But she's bringing a male friend with her, too."

Charlie just smiled. He knew how Mr. Tuttle felt about his only daughter, and that any beau of Mary Lou's would find her father a challenge.

Mr. Tuttle sighed. "Yep, bringin' a male friend home already." His brow furrowed as he stared out into the vastness of the open prairie. Finally, he slapped his leg. "Well, anyway, the missus is already plannin' a dinner for them. Won't be home for a few weeks, but she wants to get word out to folks so they include the dinner in their holiday plans. I guess she wants to show 'im off a bit." He sighed again. "Personally, I'd rather show 'im to the door."

Charlie laughed out loud.

Mr. Tuttle grinned. "I'd like for you to plan on joinin' us, if you can."

Charlie shoved his hands into his pockets and kicked at the ground with the point of his boot. "I appreciate the invitation, Mr. Tuttle, but I don't know; I'll have to see what happens. I might need to stay around the house, just in case." He didn't say it out loud, but he wasn't looking forward to the holidays, or his birthday, either, for that matter. He would find it hard to celebrate any occasion under the present circumstances.

Mr. Tuttle nodded. "I understand, son. But tuck it in the back of your mind."

"Thank you, sir. I will . . . and I'm sorry I haven't made the effort to come out more since Wilbur left, but I've—"

The older man placed a big hand on Charlie's shoulder. "It's okay, son." Their eyes met and Charlie knew this man really did understand. "I'm here if you need me."

Charlie pulled himself into the saddle and headed down the road. For some reason, the knowledge that Mary Lou was coming home made him want to see Amelia.

Ben Jacobs rested an elbow on the gate of the corral as he listened to Charlie explain his grandfather's disappearance. Shaking his head and mopping his forehead with the back of his sleeve, he said, "No, I haven't seen him. I hope nothin' serious has happened to him."

Charlie tried not to look disappointed. "If you don't mind, Mr. Jacobs, I'd appreciate it if you'd hold onto Nellie for a few more days. I'd like to search around a bit longer for Grandpa."

"Not a problem, Charlie," answered the old neighbor. He removed his hat and scratched his head. "It's not like your grandpa to go off without tellin' anyone."

"No, it's not. But I aim to find 'im."

"Don't worry 'bout ol' Nellie; she ain't no trouble."

"Thank you, sir. I'll be back in a couple of days."

Charlie turned his horse and headed towards Pueblo. If nothing else, he would send word to Sheriff Bingham in Denver and to Colonel Humphries in Fort Collins that Grandpa was missing. Cassidy and McQueen should be held and questioned.

The trip to Pueblo produced the packages Charlie had sent from the hotel in Denver and a telegram from Peterson informing him of McQueen's extradition to Texas to stand trial there for murder. The military would hold a court-martial before they gave the disgraced soldier a dishonorable discharge; so it looked like he'd be held in Fort Collins for a while before being sent back to San Antoine. He was also wanted in Kansas City, but Charlie knew he'd never make it there. The jury in Texas would see to that. There was no word from Denver.

While Charlie read his mail, Wilbur was huddled over the telegraph machine, frantically tapping out a message.

Charlie folded his telegram and shoved it into the pocket of his jeans. He watched as Wilbur pounded out another response. He was impressed by Wilbur's knowledge of Morse code and fascinated with how fast Wilbur could respond, until he became aware of the change in his friend with each in-coming message. Sweat dripped from the young man's forehead and his eyes darted wildly as he tapped out his replies.

"Wilbur, what is it? You look like death is knockin' on your door."

Wilbur ignored the question and tapped again. After several volleys of questions and answers, Wilbur finally let his hands fall to his lap and sat back on his stool. He looked defeated as he stared out the post office window and listened to the machine tap out the last of the series of messages. Then the room grew quiet. Wilbur didn't move; he just stared, his eyes glassy.

"Wilbur, what is it?" Fear gripped Charlie. "Did you hear somethin' about Grandpa?"

Slowly Wilbur shook his head and turned to Charlie. His distorted face was eerily white. He appeared to be desperately trying to maintain his composure, biting his trembling lower lip. He avoided Charlie's eyes and finally slumped over his desk and buried his face in his hands and sobbed.

Charlie didn't know what to do. He glanced across the small office, wanting help, yet thankful there was no one there to see his friend so emotionally distraught. He knew Wilbur. He knew he wouldn't show such emotion unless the news was extremely devastating. But he didn't know what to say, so he just stood there with a hand on Wilbur's shoulder.

After a few minutes, Wilbur lifted his head. Between sobs, he strained to tell his friend what was wrong. Wiping his now-crimson face with the back of his sleeve, he said almost inaudibly, "A . . . a barn caught fire a few nights ago . . . "

Charlie waited patiently for more information.

Wilbur pulled his visor off and threw it onto the work bench. He ran his trembling fingers through his hair. His body shuddered. "Chicago is gone," he mumbled.

"Gone? Wilbur, you're not makin' any sense. What do you mean Chicago is gone?"

Wilbur rested his head in his hands. His elbows pressed against his work bench. He sighed heavily a couple of times then looked at Charlie again. "A barn caught fire on the outskirts of Chicago a few nights ago. Because of the draught this summer and the high winds off Lake Michigan, it spread fast and nearly destroyed the whole city."

"But aren't there rivers there to stop it?" sputtered Charlie.

Wilbur shook his head. "They didn't stop it. Witnesses

say the fire grew so big, it jumped a river and burned all of downtown. Thousands of people homeless, hundreds dead."

Charlie whistled low.

"Ch . . . Charlie . . ." Wilbur trembled.

"What else, Wilbur? What is it?"

"Mary Lou is one of them."

Charlie felt like someone had punched him in the stomach; he almost fell backward from the blow. His head swam. His mouth went dry so fast he could hardly utter the question. "Dead?" He closed his eyes and grabbed the side of the work bench to steady himself. "Mary Lou can't be dead," he said in disbelief. "She's comin' home in just a few weeks. Your pa said she was bringin' a beau with her."

Wilbur nodded, burying his face again.

The postmaster stepped up to the desk. "Wilbur, what's going on, here?"

Charlie blinked his brown eyes hard and grabbed Wilbur's elbow and gently pulled him up off the stool. "I'm taking Wilbur home, sir," he said to the postmaster with a conviction that even surprised himself. "Wilbur just received some very bad news and needs to go home."

The elderly man was about to object when the telegraph machine started tapping again. He turned his ear towards the apparatus and listened for a moment, then wearied by what he heard, sat down on the stool. "Oh my," he whispered as he continued to decode the message. "Chicago . . ." He grabbed a pencil and paper, jotting notes as fast as he could. He threw a glance up at the boys and nodded. "Take him home young man. I understand."

Neither Charlie nor Wilbur said a word, even as they broke from the trail and made camp for the night. They built a small fire, then shared a simple meal of biscuits and jerky.

The coffee pot simmered on the small campfire. Charlie leaned back on his saddle to watch the sun set behind the Rockies and count the first stars as they glistened from within their pale gray blanket. He would search out the North Star, and he would pray.

As night approached, Charlie didn't push Wilbur to talk. He had a million questions running through his own mind, leaving him feeling numb and exhausted; so he could only imagine how Wilbur was feeling right then. He knew his friend would talk when he was ready.

Wilbur lay against his saddle, his blanket pulled tight around him. The warm glow of the campfire revealed the dark circles that hung underneath his eyes. His breathing was slow and deep, interrupted occasionally with heavy shudders that bore no tears. "I can't believe she's gone, Charlie."

Charlie kept searching the darkening sky for his star. "I can't either," he said softly. "Mary Lou was just always there."

Wilbur chuckled. "Even when you didn't want her to be. Do you remember when we—?" He stopped short, turned his head, then sniffled. "I'm sorry, Charlie."

"It's okay, buddy. And yes, I do remember."

The two stared up at the stars. "How can you be sure she was among the dead? The place must be in chaos."

Wilbur swallowed a few times before answering.

"Because she didn't die in the fires, she died at the hospital. All the girls got out of the school all right, but the streets were so crowded that she and a classmate decided to run through the alleyways towards the river. When she reached the end of an alley, she didn't stop running, but bolted right out into a main street. Right in front of an oncoming fire wagon. It happened so fast. The driver couldn't stop the horses in time."

Charlie sat up on one elbow and stared. He couldn't believe his ears. "Are you saying she escaped the fire, but was trampled to death?"

Wilbur nodded.

Charlie fell back down onto his bedroll and shook his head. "I can't believe it," he muttered. "How'd she get to the hospital?"

"As fate would have it, that very wagon had a few injured folks on it and was headin' to the hospital when it hit Mary Lou. The waterhouse had already burnt to the ground; so when the tanks ran empty and couldn't be refilled, they used the wagons to gather up the wounded. A fireman on the wagon saw what happened and jumped off to help her. He picked her up and loaded her on board along with her friend. They left them at the hospital before going out to find more victims. Her friend identified her and gave them Mary Lou's name and such."

Charlie rolled onto his side. "I can't believe it," he whispered again. Tears slid down his face as he watched the small flames of fire leap into the night air. "It's hard to imagine." He closed his eyes tightly.

"Charlie?"

"Yeah, Wilbur."

"How do I tell Ma and Pa?"

The two lay silent for a moment.

"Mind if I pray?" asked Charlie.

"No," came the solemn reply.

Charlie gazed at his star and tried to still his brain. He tried to gather his thoughts and start, but when he opened his mouth, all he could mutter was, "Lord, help us understand . . ." At that moment his heart broke. He didn't understand. He didn't understand any of it. First Grandpa; now Mary Lou. He buried his face in his blanket and wept.

Charlie and Star stood under one of the old oak trees that adorned the Tuttle property. Its brilliant leaves swirled to the ground as Charlie watched Wilbur approach his father and mother.

The Tuttles had seen the two boys coming, and had stepped out of the cabin to greet them. They looked surprised and jubilant to see their son, but Charlie watched as the sad story unfolded from Wilbur's lips and their expressions changed from joy to concern to despair.

He instinctively lurched forward when Mrs. Tuttle's knees buckled and she slumped toward the ground, but he stood back when Mr. Tuttle caught her up in his arms. Then, instead of carrying her into the cabin, the man gently cradled his wife and they sank to their knees together. Sobbing, Mr. Tuttle buried his face in his wife's hair. Wilbur knelt beside them and hid his face in his father's shoulder.

With his own tears streaming down his face, Charlie

quietly turned Star and headed towards home.

The ride back to the cabin was long and depressing. At times there were so many questions running through Charlie's head, he thought it would burst. Other times he wanted to yell at something, maybe even at God.

It took a while before he realized he and Star had company. The tall, broad mountain man and his large Belgian horse had silently come alongside Charlie and Star. They rode a while together, then finally Jess spoke soft and low.

"I know what you're thinking, Charlie."

Charlie didn't answer. He kept his head down and his eyes to the ground.

"You're asking yourself the same question your friend Phillip asked when you were on the cow trail. You're asking, 'If God is so good and so loving, then why all this?'"

"Yes, I am!" he said angrily. "I *am* asking why. None of this makes any sense. I know you're gonna tell me it's all in His plan, but I don't get it."

"Just because you don't understand the plan doesn't mean there isn't one," answered Jess. "He's only asked you to do one thing ever, Charlie. Can you remember what that is, son?"

A chilly gust of autumn wind brushed past them.

"Do you remember, Charlie?"

"Yes, I remember," he snapped. "All He's ever asked is that I trust Him."

"That a boy!"

"But it's like walkin' blind," muttered Charlie. "It's like bein' in the dark, and walkin' with your arms stretched out so you don't run into anything."

232

"That's only because you're not trusting Him," answered Jess. "He can see everything just fine. He can see the beginning, the ending, and everything in between. He doesn't ask that you try to see the situation, or understand it; He only asks that you trust Him on the journey."

"So I'm supposed to believe that Mary Lou's death is a good thing?"

"No. God weeps when his children suffer. But good can come out of the bad, Charlie. You know that."

Charlie nodded. "Yes, yes I do," he said with a heavy sigh.

A cold wind whipped through the branches overhead. "Trust Him, son," Jess whispered. "When you don't understand, trust Him. Lean on the Father for understanding, Charlie."

31

FALL SOON DISPLAYED CHARACTERISTICS OF winter. Dark gray skies escorted in winds from the north that often scourged the hills and outlying prairie with frost that chilled a man to the bone. Miller, who seemed in no hurry to leave, helped Charlie get ready for the onslaught of winter, to which the boy, in his grief, hadn't given much thought.

Charlie was taking one day at a time, staying busy with daily farm chores, praying that he would hear or see something from Grandpa, and hoping that time would heal the wounds he harbored deep inside.

It was a comfort to have Miller there, making it his mission, despite spats of snow or drizzles of rain, to cut and bind grass from the untamed prairie and collect kindling from the large trees for winter's coming blast of deep freeze.

Meanwhile, Charlie kept wondering: Would he hear anything positive back from Denver or Fort Collins? Cassidy might deny the allegations and there'd be no proof to hold him. McQueen could say he was only involved in mistaking LeFaye for Smith, and nothing more.

Late one afternoon, Miller stood at the back window and watched storm clouds roll down the mountains, showing signs of freezing rain. He wrapped himself up and went to work.

Charlie stayed in and fixed supper while a cold wind howled round the corners of the cabin, throwing handfuls of sleet against the windows. He stoked the fire and let the flames burn hot and bright. Soon the warmth chased the chill from the room.

As he pulled the kettle out of the fireplace, Charlie thought he heard a rap at the door. Surprised that anyone would be out in this weather, he tossed his pot holder onto the counter and opened the door just a crack. There stood a man—half frozen, yet smiling through his chattering teeth.

"Phillip!" Charlie shouted. "What are you doing here?"

LeFaye shuddered against the wind. "Would you mind if I came in and stood by the fire?"

Charlie laughed and stepped back. "I'm sorry, of course you can; come on in. I didn't expect to see *you* at my door."

LeFaye nodded and hurried past his friend to the fireplace. Miller came in through the back door and stopped abruptly. It took him a second to recognize the Frenchman.

"LeFaye!" He grabbed the young man's hand. "Where'd you come from?"

Charlie set another place at the table.

LeFaye let his woolen scarf and coat slide to the floor as he thrust his hands towards the fire. "I came from Fort Collins by Denver." His teeth chattered. "I've been in the saddle for days."

"Are you hungry?" asked Charlie.

"Starving, my friend."

Charlie ladled the stew while Miller gathered LeFaye's garments and hung them on the pegs beside the door. The Frenchman stood as close to the fire as he dared, soaking in the warmth. "Thank you, Miller," he stammered.

"You are very welcome. Stand there as long as you need to. Do I need to go out and put your horse up?"

LeFaye shook his head. "No. I put him in that old lean-to by the barn. I've rubbed him down and given him water. After supper, I'll give him some oats and hay."

"Well, I can see nothin' much has changed." Charlie chuckled. "You're not on time for much, but you're always on time for supper."

The three friends laughed as they made themselves comfortable around the small table and bowed their heads. Charlie thanked the Lord for the food and for the blessing of having two friends with him.

Charlie took the bread basket from LeFaye and passed it to Miller. "I'm surprised you remembered the way here."

LeFaye slathered butter across a warm slice of bread.

Miller chuckled. "Yeah, it's not exactly a beaten path."

LeFaye took a big bite of bread, trying to catch the golden liquid before it dripped to the table. "Actually, I remembered quite a bit of the trail, although some of the markers look different with the change of seasons. So, just to make sure I was still on course, once in awhile I asked folks if they could direct me to the Smith cabin. It wasn't hard," he said chewing. He grinned at Miller and swallowed. "After all, I may not have been a scout in the military, but I was a soldier all the same and can navigate my way around if need be."

"Touché," said Miller, smiling.

"I'm sure that is the limit of your French, Miller," Charlie teased.

"Miller stopped his spoon mid-way to his mouth. "Well, actually—"

"Before Miller launches into an explanation of his knowledge of the world's languages, I want to hear what you're doin' in these parts," Charlie said over the rim of his cup.

LeFaye swallowed. "Well, it's quite simple, really," he said. "I was honorably discharged from the army, as most of the men in our small regiment were, and I had nowhere to go. Since you're the closest thing to family I have now, I figured I'd find you and go from there."

Charlie smiled at his friend. "Well then, welcome home."

"You're lookin' good," added Miller. "Last time I saw you, you were in pretty bad shape."

"I'm feeling fine," answered LeFaye, "but I never fully recovered from the beating. My left eye is ruined, almost blind. That's why I had to be discharged a few weeks early."

Charlie set his spoon aside. "I'm sorry, Phillip. I truly am. If I'd gone on my watch like I was supposed to, this wouldn't have happened to you."

LeFaye patted Charlie's shoulder. "It's all right, my friend. If I hadn't gone through this, I wouldn't have finally surrendered my heart to Christ. Miller laid it on the line with me before he left to find you. Gave me plenty to think about while lying in the infirmary. So you see, it all worked out for the best."

"You've accepted Christ?" Charlie asked.

"With all my heart," answered LeFaye.

Charlie stood up so fast his chair fell backwards. Miller

and LeFaye followed, and all exchanged hugs and back slaps.

"So it was worth it," said LeFaye as they settled down to their supper again.

LeFaye passed the water jug to Charlie. "You'll never guess what we found out about one of the men on the drive," he said passively.

Charlie filled his cup and asked nonchalantly, "Who?"

Miller, who had just taken a big bite of bread, exclaimed, "What?" Crumbs sprayed across the table.

Charlie pounded Miller on the back. "Calm down, old man, before you hurt yourself."

Miller waved him off with a calloused hand. Then to LeFaye he said, "Go on, go on."

Charlie had little interest in trail gossip. He'd seen the men on the trail, though, whose attitude was that of Miller's now; they seemed to think their lives depended on what they heard sitting around the evening fires.

The Frenchman sat upright in his chair. "Well, on with the exciting tale, then, shall we?" He took on the air of one telling a ghost story to children. "It seems there was a detective amongst us on the cattle drive."

Miller pushed back from the table and folded his arms across his chest. Charlie raised his eyebrows. "A detective?"

"Ah." LeFaye's eyes narrowed and his accent thickened. "Not jest any detecteeve, but a Pinkerton man."

"Cut it out, LeFaye," said Charlie.

Miller grunted. "Yeah, why would he be on the drive?"

"Oh, but you should know, shouldn't you, Mr. Miller?"

"Me? Why should I know anything?"

LeFaye half closed his eyes and smiled. "Because you are the great scout. Because you live among man and beast and come out unscathed. Because you can track—"

"Wait a minute," said Miller. "Before you go and get your boots on backwards, let's get one thing clear: I'm no Pinkerton man. I've got scars aplenty on this old body, and I've earned the title of 'scout,' so whatever you've heard, it's wrong."

"No, sir," replied LeFaye warmly. "You misunderstand. I haven't heard wrong. I was not implying you were the detective, only that you are an exceptional scout and surely would have figured out who he was long before we knew."

Miller turned red and eased back into his chair. "I see."

"Okay," said Charlie. "So, if there was a Pinkerton man, there are two questions: Who? and Why?"

"Patience is a virtue, my friend," said the Frenchman.

Miller picked up his spoon and resumed eating. The logs crackled in the fireplace.

"So, guess," said LeFaye with a sharp clap of his hands.

"*What?*" Miller sprayed crumbs across the table again.

"Make this fast, LeFaye, I've got work to do," said Charlie.

LeFaye nodded. Play time was over. "He was on the drive to watch *you*, Charlie."

"Me?"

"Yes, you. That's all I could find out."

"Do you know who it was?"

"No."

Miller looked at them. "Well, if it isn't LeFaye or me, who does that leave? Sarge? Peterson? McQueen? Cook?"

"I don't know."

"Not McQueen," said Miller. "He's in the stockade."

"Wait a minute." Charlie sat upright. "I did run into Sarge in Denver, before riding back here. I wonder if—"

"You've run into the both of us again, too," said LeFaye.

Charlie looked at Miller, then at LeFaye, then back at Miller. He grinned. "No, not enough money in it for you."

His friends laughed. LeFaye looked around the cabin and then at Charlie. "You can say that again, my friend."

"God does work in mysterious ways," mumbled Miller. "But let's figure this out. We know it's not either one of us," he added with a nod to LeFaye.

"How do you know it was not I?" asked LeFaye, putting on an air of importance.

"Because you were laid up in the infirmary so long," answered Miller. "What kind of spy work could you have done from a hospital bed?"

"And with one eye?" teased Charlie.

"All right, all right," LeFaye surrendered. "I'm not the man."

"Who's left?" asked Charlie.

Miller held up five fingers, each representing a man on the cattle drive: "One, Sarge. It's not him, 'cause he's been there since Sergeant Barlow, and all he's ever been known to do is cook. Three, McQueen. We know it's not him! Four, LeFaye. Already ruled him out. And Five, Peterson."

Charlie raised his eyebrows. "Peterson?"

"Wait a minute," interjected LeFaye. "It couldn't be that tall, lanky southerner. Why, he couldn't even—"

"Exactly!" said Charlie. "It's because of what he couldn't

do that it all fits. He couldn't swim. He couldn't ride—not all that well, anyhow. He hadn't been at the fort long before the detail left to come down to the farm. He hardly left McQueen's side, and he warned me about McQueen." Excited, Charlie ran his fingers through his hair. "He's the one who sent me the telegram telling me about McQueen's extradition to Texas. It all makes perfect sense now."

"But why wouldn't he be here watching over you now?" asked LeFaye.

"Because he was hired to keep an eye on Charlie as long as he was on the cattle drive," Miller said almost too quickly.

Charlie and LeFaye stared at Miller.

Miller cleared his throat, cast his eyes down to the floor, and pulled his left ankle up to his right knee. It seemed to Charlie that he too-nonchalantly wiped his hand across the top of his boot.

"Well, that's what it seems like to me, anyway," Miller said.

They all sat silently a minute, then LeFaye changed the subject. "By the way, I ran into a young man by the name of Wilbur Tuttle. Said he was a good friend of yours."

"Like a brother."

LeFaye nodded. "He asked me to give you a message."

Charlie raised his eyebrows.

"It seems his parents would like to see you."

Charlie pushed his chair back from the table. He hadn't seen the Tuttles since he took Wilbur home a couple weeks ago and he was uncertain whether he wanted to see them now. He knew they were hurting, but he didn't know what he could say or do. He couldn't even help himself right now.

Miller cleared his throat. "Charlie, if it wasn't important,

Wilbur wouldn't have asked Phillip to say anything."

Charlie stood and cleared his dishes from the table. He hadn't had an appetite since he got home and found Grandpa missing. "I don't know—"

"I think you should go tomorrow," interrupted Miller.

"Tomorrow?"

"The sooner the better."

"But I have—"

"Nothin' I can't help with."

"Or me," interjected LeFaye.

Miller looked at the Frenchman. "I think it would be best if you went with Charlie. He could use the company."

"But I would hate to intrude on these folks," said LeFaye. "Being a perfect stranger and all."

"What intrusion?" asked Miller. "You're not movin' in with 'em; you'd just be with Charlie."

LeFaye and Charlie looked at each other. Charlie shrugged his shoulders. "Guess we're goin' to visit the Tuttle's tomorrow, LeFaye."

"If that's what you want, Charlie," said the Frenchman.

Miller stood and gathered his dishes. "It isn't necessarily what he wants," he said, as he walked to the basin. "But it's what he needs."

On the seven mile ride to the Tuttle's, Charlie explained the situation to LeFaye and the circumstances behind their request to see him. Charlie felt uneasy. What could he do or say to alleviate their pain?

LeFaye rode and listened in silence.

As the men rode into Mrs. Tuttle's yard, she was opening the cabin door to throw out the dishwater. She put the basin on the ground and ran to meet them.

Charlie reined Star to a stop and slid to the ground. Mrs. Tuttle threw her arms around his neck and wept on his chest.

Charlie handed the reins to LeFaye, then wrapped his arms around the dear woman. She was the closest thing he had to a mother while growing up in these wild parts—just him and Grandpa—and she'd brought a lot of warmth and tenderness into his life. He wished he could do something to comfort her now. But all he could do was stand there and kiss the top of her head as she cried.

She finally stepped back and wiped her face with her apron. "We didn't mean to neglect you, son, that day when Wilbur came home and told us about Mary Lou. In our own grief, we forgot you were there trying to deal with your own. Please forgive us."

Charlie was relieved to know they didn't expect anything from him. He didn't have to try to be strong for them. They just wanted him near.

"It's okay," he muttered. "I understood then and I understand now. It was a terrible shock to hear of Mary Lou." He wanted to go on, but he couldn't bring himself to talk more about her.

Glancing up at LeFaye and then back to Charlie, she motioned towards the cabin. "Come on in, both of you, and let's talk over some coffee."

Inside, Mr. Tuttle looked gaunt, almost sickly. He seemed to have aged twenty years. He welcomed Charlie with a bear hug. He greeted LeFaye with a strong hand-shake. After the introductions and settling down with their coffee, he pulled a letter from his shirt pocket.

"Me and the missus have been prayin' about how we could afford to go to Chicago and bring Mary Lou home." His lower lip quivered; he stopped for a moment to regain his composure, then continued. "Anyway, we've been prayin' the Lord would help us, show us what to do, and then we got this letter. It was delivered to us yesterday just before Wilbur headed back to Pueblo. I'd like to read it to you."

"Go ahead, sir," Charlie said.

Mr. Tuttle wiped the back of his sleeve across his eyes then unfolded the letter. He cleared his throat and began to read:

October 16, 1871

Dear Mr. and Mrs. Tuttle,

You don't know me. We've never been formally introduced, although Mary Lou had planned on doing so later this month. My name is George Conrad McCray. I am the friend that Mary Lou was to bring home with her to make your acquaintance.

Because of the sad and much different circum-stances that have befallen us of recent, I am writing to request that we continue with those introductions as planned. In summary, with your permission, I would like to bring Mary Lou home. My intentions are twofold: first, that Mary Lou's body rest in the land which she loved above all other; second, that I have the opportunity to meet you, her family, and share with you what your daughter meant to me.

We did not know each other long, but in that short time, she changed my future, yes, my very life. I had hoped to marry your daughter one day, but now, though she is gone, I hold a part of her in my heart that will remain with me forever, something that I most sincerely hope to share with you in person.

I patiently await your response.

Respectfully yours,
George C. McCray

Mr. Tuttle folded the paper and put it back in his vest. He looked at Charlie with raised eyebrows. Mrs. Tuttle wiped her eyes and blew her nose on the delicate hanky that her fingers had been fiddling with during the reading.

Charlie looked at the two of them. "Let him bring her home, Mr. Tuttle," he said softly. "God has provided, and the man has something to share with you."

Mr. Tuttle nodded. "I thought that's what you'd say, Charlie. Wilbur is going to send Mr. McCray a telegram."

"Is Wilbur gone already?" asked Charlie.

"Yep, left yesterday afternoon."

"Musta been where he was headin' when you saw him on the road," Charlie said to LeFaye.

LeFaye nodded.

"He's hopin' he won't be gone long," explained Mrs. Tuttle. "Just wanted to tie up some loose ends then come home. He'll be here for the funeral, and with us durin' the holidays."

"Will the post office be able to do without him during the holidays?" asked Charlie.

"Well, *I* cain't do without him *here*. I'll need his help on the farm until Ma and I pull out of this."

LeFaye, who had been quiet during the conversation, now spoke. "Maybe I can help. I know you just met me, but Charlie can vouch for my character. I hope to settle in these parts, and plan on staying around for awhile."

Mr. Tuttle smiled. "I appreciate the gesture, Mr. LeFaye."

"Phillip."

"I appreciate it, Phillip, but Wilbur'll be home soon."

"Well, just remember, sir. If for some reason it doesn't work out for your son, I'm here and willing to help."

Charlie stood and offered Mr. Tuttle his outstretched hand. "Let me know what I can do for you with Mr. McCray comin' and all."

Mr. Tuttle stood, and not noticing the extended hand, he threw his arms around Charlie.

"Thank you, son. And if you need help, just holler and I'll come runnin'."

Charlie nodded, but he knew there wasn't anything anyone could do, except God. Only He knew the answer to Grandpa's disappearance.

Mrs. Tuttle hugged Charlie good-bye. Then she took LeFaye's hand and told him he'd be welcomed back any time.

≈ 32 ≈

THE DAY OF THE FUNERAL WAS COLD AND gray. Mercifully, there was no wind, but a bitter and constant drizzle of rain mingled with the tears of the mourners. The large trees that separated the cemetery from the school yard stood barren and stark against the sky. They offered no leafy cover for the grieving family and friends paying their respects to the deceased on that dreary November morning.

Mr. and Mrs. Tuttle stood beside the box that held the lifeless body of their daughter, and they wept softly.

In one hand, Mrs. Tuttle held a white lace handkerchief that shook ever so slightly as she dabbed at her eyes. With the other hand, she pressed a small worn Bible to her chest.

Charlie, Wilbur, and his two brothers stood behind the elder Tuttles while folks of the small community gathered close. Miller and LeFaye stood in the distance. They hadn't known Mary Lou or her family; they were there for Charlie.

The casket lay on the ground beside a deep, gaping hole that would soon be its earthen tomb; a small puddle of water had formed in the bottom. Charlie watched thin rivulets of rain run across the lid and down the sides of the mahogany chest, some spilling over the brass handles and splattering into the grass. He imagined that it wasn't rain that dripped from the casket, but tears; for surely even the box that held

Mary Lou would weep over the loss. He was lowering his head and trying to discreetly wipe away a tear that had stolen the chance to run down his cheek, when Wilbur touched his arm.

George McCray had stepped up to the head of the casket. He was a handsome young man with dark brown hair and friendly eyes. Charlie figured he was a couple of years older than himself. He wore a fine woolen suit and his shoes were polished to a high gloss, yet it wasn't his clothes or mannerisms that revealed his wealth, but the casket in which he brought Mary Lou home. Most folks around these parts could only afford pinewood, and their guns and oil lamps were the only things they owned that contained brass.

McCray was obviously nervous, clearing his throat and looking around. His face showed recognition when he saw the young married couple who had offered him a place to sleep. And, of course, the Tuttles. His eyes were red and swollen, but he held his voice steady as he began to speak.

"I was hoping God would give us a beautiful morning to say our farewells to Mary Lou, but in his infinite wisdom, He thought better of it. Standing here, I realize how foolish that request was. We are not saying good-bye to Mary Lou. This is not just the end of her earthly life; it is the beginning of her heavenly life."

Several folks in the crowd nodded and whispered "Amen," while others dabbed their eyes.

"I wanted to share with you a bit of what Mary Lou meant to me. A few months ago, she and I were complete strangers, yet before she died I felt as if I'd known her most of my life. I met her in the library, which was housed

248

between our two schools. I was there reading a scientific work by Dr. Charles Darwin. To this day, I'm not sure why she was there; she wasn't studying, not seriously anyway. She and a classmate, who were sitting at a nearby table, got a bit noisy, so I let out a very loud, 'shh!' Mary Lou looked at me and crinkled up her nose and crossed her eyes."

Charlie heard a few giggles scurry among the crowd. He even caught himself smiling. That was the Mary Lou he knew.

Mr. McCray continued. "Well, I couldn't believe it. At first, I thought, *What a horrid little creature*. But then I almost burst out laughing. It was all I could do to keep my composure; but I couldn't let her know that.

"I watched her from the corner of my eye until she and her friend got up to leave. It was then I decided to leave too. To make a long story short, I was fascinated by this young woman who never seemed to feel awkward or have trouble expressing her opinion. More than once we got into a serious conversation about the origins of life, me being an evolutionist and she being a Christian believer."

The reference to evolution caused a stir. Mr. McCray smiled at the stunned faces and held his composure.

"Please, don't let the mention of Dr. Darwin's theory upset you. It didn't upset Mary Lou. In fact, she found it rather intriguing, and let me know in no uncertain terms that she admired the faith I held in such a theory."

His faint smile broadened as the conversation flashed across his memory. "She said she found my faith so strong and impressive, for surely one must have such a faith to actually believe this theory. For her, it was so much easier to believe in an almighty God as the Creator of all things. To believe in evolution, that the specific elements needed to create life derived accidently from nothing, was beyond her comprehension. She said I was an inspiration, and my faith shamed her simple Christianity. Needless to say, she left me speechless. I didn't know whether she was mocking me or was actually sincere in her comments; but I would soon find out.

"Because of my belief in evolution, Mary Lou refused to allow me to court her. She would only commit to being my friend. But we met often to discuss 'our faiths' and she would share with me and I with her. That sufficed for awhile, because honestly, I didn't care what we talked about; I just wanted to see her. Then one evening, I actually heard what she had to say. I started to listen more, talk less. Frankly, I had nothing else to say, but she would go on and on about the marvels in the Scriptures and how God answers prayers, and that even I was included in His wonderful plan.

George McCray stopped and looked down at the casket. He kissed his fingertips and then gently touched them to the lid. Inhaling deeply and straightening his shoulders, he looked back up at the crowd.

"I didn't come to know the Lord while Mary Lou was alive," he continued. "I came close a couple of times, but my pride got in the way. You see, I considered myself an educated man, an intellectual if you will, and thought religion was only a means to an end. People could believe whatever made them happy, as long as it didn't infringe on the happiness of others. For me, to believe in a heavenly Father who actually cared and interacted in the lives of mortal men seemed absurd to me, until one day after Mary Lou's passing.

"Not only did I lose my friend Mary Lou that horrible night, but when the fires were finally put out, most of Chicago was left in ruins. Friends were gone, our homes were gone, and our schools were gone. I was devastated by so much loss.

"I was sitting on a charred park bench one morning, resting my head in my hands and actually contemplating suicide. I had convinced myself that there was no hope in living and I was sinking lower with every passing minute, when I heard a man say, 'Mind if I sit here?'

"I didn't raise my head but opened my eyes and found myself looking at a pair of very large feet inside some very dark leather moccasins. I know moccasins aren't an unusual type of shoe in the west, but in Chicago they grab one's attention. I lifted my head and my eyes continued upward for quite a ways before they finally rested on the face of a very tall man." Mr. McCray chuckled. "I can see why such men are referred to as 'mountain men.'"

Again, giggles rippled through the crowd.

"He was dressed in buckskin from his head to his toes and he wore a coonskin cap. He had a graying black beard and the kindest eyes I've ever seen. I found myself answering his question with just a nod of my head."

Charlie's heart raced. *Could it have been?*

McCray continued. "The stranger sat beside me and didn't say anything at first, for which I was grateful. He just sat there and watched folks go by. Then he said, 'You know, it's hard to build somethin' from nothin' unless there is some kind of special power and plan behind it. These folks here, they're rebuildin'. They're buildin' on somethin' that was here once. It's gone now; but they have the know-how and fortitude to rebuild it. That's a lot different, though, than buildin' somethin' from nothin'.'

"I looked at him with, well, with what I can only guess to be a confused look on my face. He grinned and said, 'George, don't major on the minors so much that you lose focus on what really matters.' Before I could ask anything, he kept talking. He explained that, though it does matter how we believe the universe came into being, the major question doesn't lie with our origins, but with our ending. When we close our eyes in death, what happens then?

"Needless to say, I was astounded. He told me about Adam and Eve, man's sinful nature and how, because of it, we are doomed to be eternally separated from God; but because of a loving Savior, we have a way to exchange eternal death for eternal life. He alone can rebuild our lives.

"I hung onto every word he said, like my life depended on it; and looking back, I realize it did. It saddened me when he stood up, ready to leave. But before he did, he turned his gray eyes, bright and warm, on me. He said, 'George, Mary Lou is the happiest she's ever been; but she prayed for you with an earnest and sincere heart before she graduated; so I came to share with you one last time. What you do with what you've been told is now up to you.'

"I turned my head from his gaze for just a brief second. Then I saw a small Bible sitting on the bench beside me. I picked it up and said, 'Sir,' ready to tell him he'd forgotten his book, but he was gone. I jumped up from the bench and turned in every direction, but he was nowhere to be seen."

George McCray reached inside his jacket pocket and pulled out the small book, its brown leather cover new and unmarked. Although Charlie's was worn now, he recognized it immediately. George opened the cover. "If you'll allow me a couple more minutes, I'd like to share this inscription. It reads:

> To my friend George McCray,
>
> Only God can take a life worth nothing and make something beautiful. In your search for life, look to Him.
>
> Your friend,
> Jethro Ezekiel Samson Uriah Samuels

Charlie mouthed the name as George read it aloud.

The crowd looked stunned.

George continued.

"I wasn't looking for a way to begin my life when I met this man, I was looking for a way to end it. But he changed that in a few minutes. It wasn't until I read this inscription that I realized I had never introduced myself to him. I never told him my name or anything about Mary Lou, but he knew me. He knew my very heart." Tears streamed down the young man's face. "I now firmly believe that this man, whoever he was, was sent to me from God. He pointed me to Jesus and I now believe as Mary Lou believed. So you see, her death was not in vain. God used it to bring me to Life. Life in Him. And I know others will come to do the same."

He closed the small Bible and slid it back into his jacket. No one moved. He thanked the people for allowing him the opportunity to speak. Still, no one moved. Some heads were bowed; others were lifted towards the darkened sky. Looking unsure what to do, he stepped back into the crowd and lowered his head.

Mrs. Tuttle pulled away from her husband and went to the young stranger. She looked deeply into his eyes. Almost in a whisper she said, "I don't know how to thank you, Mr. McCray. Your words have eased my sorrow and have brought such peace to my heart." He looked at her and nodded, smiling through his tears. She then stood on her tiptoes and kissed his cheek.

Charlie wasn't sure who started the song, but from somewhere within the crowd a strong baritone voice rose above the soft whimpers of the mourners. "*Amazing grace! how sweet the sound, that saved a wretch like me!* . . ." The words resonated above the dampness of the soaked ground, above the starkness of the barren trees and the gloominess of the November sky. They rose slowly, almost gently, seeming to turn every sob into a note that, in turn, joined the baritone in unison and ascended upward. "*I once was lost, but now am found* . . ."

Eventually it looked as if everyone was singing. Charlie glanced around. A few folks had their eyes closed. Most were looking upward toward the ray of sunlight that had broken through the dense clouds and was shining brilliantly on the yonder hills. His eyes followed the tunnel of light as far as he could see. Just beyond the gray clouds was the sun and all its warmth; and just beyond this world, Heaven.

In that brief moment he understood. "This is just the beginning," he whispered. A chill of excitement ran down his spine.

". . . *Was blind, but now I see.*"

Charlie lifted his voice with the others.

> *When we've been there ten thousand years*
> *Bright, shining as the sun,*
> *We've no less days to sing God's praise*
> *Than when we'd first begun.*

33

ON A FROSTY NOVEMBER MORNING, CHARLIE watched Miller pack his bedroll and his few belongings. The farm had been prepped for winter—the garden produce stored, the corral rails checked and repaired, and enough prairie grass put in the shed to last till spring.

Now Miller was leaving.

As Charlie leaned in the front doorway and watched Miller tighten the cinch strap of his saddle, he felt the encroaching loneliness press in around him, like the shadows at end of day. Now he'd be alone waiting, waiting for a word, a clue, a return.

He wouldn't have Wilbur close by, either. Wilbur had had to stay in Pueblo after the funeral, and he wouldn't make it home before Christmas, after all. He had assured his parents he would leave his job in Pueblo after the New Year and come back to take over the farm. He said working longer would give him the chance to save up enough money to help buy whatever they needed for spring planting.

So Mr. Tuttle had taken Phillip LeFaye up on his offer of help. To keep from having to travel to and fro in the dark, LeFaye had taken up residence in one of the Tuttle's storage sheds. He said he didn't mind; Mr. Tuttle kept him busy,

Mrs. Tuttle kept him fed, and the small storage shed kept him warm enough.

Charlie would be alone with his thoughts. How long it would be before he heard something about Grandpa? Only God knew. He stomped his feet against the cold.

"Where'll you go?" Charlie asked Miller through chattering teeth.

Miller grabbed his saddle horn and gave it a good pull to make sure it was secure. "Don't know," he grunted. "I just know it's time to go."

"How do you know?" Charlie grumbled, his mouth barely moving. He thrust his hands into his pockets and looked out at the frozen prairie.

Miller cast a sideways glance at Charlie as he slid his boot into the stirrup and hoisted himself into the saddle.

"Let's just say it's on the wind, Charlie."

Charlie squinted and cocked his head. "The wind?"

Miller tipped his hat and smiled. "Yes. And stop fretting, son," he added. "You're never really alone."

With that, the scout turned his horse and led him into a fast walk up the road. When he reached the top of the hill, he turned in the saddle and looked back. He took off his hat and waved it in a wide sweeping arch. Charlie held up a hand and watched as the man disappeared over the crest of the hill. Charlie hoped he would see him again someday.

〰 34 〰

GRANDPA WAS LEARNING TO APPRECIATE the Dobsons, this fine old couple who had come west as a young married couple many years ago. They had built their cabin right where their wagon had broken down and they never left. At that time, it was a long distance from there to anywhere, but they grew most of what they ate, hand-made what they needed, and traded for the rest. Gill could make just about anything. He was quite the carpenter.

They had been married for over fifty years and knew each other like the back of their own hands. And, though Grandpa considered them a bit loco, they were pleasant hosts.

Grandpa learned to stay out of Orpha's way. He claimed the rocker as his seat and spent most of the time rocking to and fro, with one foot pushing and the other propped up on the hearth. From there, he could watch Gill work and listen to the conversation.

He was comfortable in the Dobson's company, and it was quite apparent they felt the same. But Grandpa knew it was time to go home.

He'd been there since early October and now it was going on December. Two months. It had been a month before he could move his leg, let alone get out of bed. He now walked with a limp, but he could move around easily enough and figured he could manage to get on a horse. It would soon be time to try.

A light snow fell on the first night of December, covering the ground with a thin blanket of white. Charlie had surrendered to the fact that he was alone now. Grandpa was gone. He felt the despair of loneliness creep into his life.

He stood on the front stoop and found the Christmas star beaming like a beacon in the northern sky.

"I give up, Jess."

When he spoke, his breath formed a frosty fog, reminding him of the time Big T Cassidy had blown cigarette smoke in his face, but without the putrid smell. That seemed like a hundred years ago.

He wasn't yet eighteen, but he felt old and tired. Over the past several months he'd grown up, but he felt defeated. The cold stung his eyes as tears welled up in the corners. He wiped them away with the back of his coat sleeve.

"Are you ready to surrender, Charlie?" The voice came low and struck to the core.

Charlie blinked against the cold. "Surrender what?"

"Your god."

"My god?" he whispered. "You're the only God I know."

"Not really. There is one other."

Charlie threw his arms up in frustration. "Where? Who?"

"Grandpa," came the reply.

"Grandpa? You want me to give you Grandpa? How can

I give you Grandpa when I don't even know where he is?"

"No, son," answered the calm, peaceful voice. "I don't want you to physically give me Grandpa; I want you to give me the place that he holds in your heart. I want you to make me your hero, your Lord, your God. I want to be the one you hold dear and trust the most. The one you run to for refuge and strength. All the love, respect, and trust that you give your grandpa, I want you to give to me a hundredfold. I don't want anyone to take my place in your life, Charlie."

Charlie lowered his head. "No one can take his place."

"That depends. I did once, a long time ago. Now I'm asking to take his place again, but this time in your life. Give him to me, Charlie. I promise, you won't be sorry."

Charlie's eyes filled with hot tears. He tried to blink them away. "What does that mean?" he moaned.

"I'm not asking you to stop loving him," came the soft reply. "It's not like the old ax in the barn. I'm not asking you to discard him as something old and useless. But in order for me to be Lord of your life, you must learn to put those things or people that are closest to you in second place, and make me first in your thoughts, your words, your actions, everything."

"What you're sayin' is, I can still love Grandpa, only you want me to love you more?"

"That's right, son. I want you to love people, and to trust them, just not more than you love and trust me. And when things of this world crowd your heart, edge their way into first place, surrender them to me again, and *again* if need be."

"There's no one I've loved more than Grandpa," whispered Charlie. "But he's gone, so there's only me left. There's no one else. So it'll have to be me that surrenders. I'll do whatever it is you want me to do, but I need to know what that might be, 'cause right now I don't know what to do."

"Charlie, 'Be still and know that I am God.' You're not alone; you never will be. I am here. I am always here. Learn and understand that those you love will eventually leave you, but I will never leave you. I am your guide, your direction. I am your comfort and your friend. I have even given angels charge over you for the rest of your life; heaven's angels, to minister to your heart when it is tired, to your soul when it is hungry, and to your spirit when it is weak. Just be still and listen."

Charlie closed his eyes and strained to hear something, anything, but there was nothing, not even the wind.

"The answer will come when you're ready to learn, Charlie. Just don't stop listening."

Charlie went back into the cabin and closed the door. He looked around the room, remembering how just a short time ago it felt like he was being smothered in it, like the walls were closing in on him. Now he felt the largeness of the room. He'd give anything for Grandpa to be there sporting his mischievous grin and rambling on about nothing.

He grabbed his Bible off the mantle and pulled the rocking chair closer to the fire. Closing his eyes, he let the Bible fall open on his lap. "Talk to me, Lord," he whispered. "I want to learn." He opened his eyes and read these words:

As you come to him, the living Stone—rejected by men but chosen by God and precious to him—you also, like living stones, are being built into a spiritual house to be a holy priesthood, offering spiritual sacrifices acceptable to God through Jesus Christ. For in Scripture it says: 'See, I lay a stone in Zion, a chosen and precious cornerstone, and the one who trusts in him will never be put to shame.' (1 Peter 2:4-6)

He closed his eyes and rested his head on the back of the rocker. "I surrender, Lord. I give you both of us."

He pushed the rocker back with his feet and started the gentle swaying motion. The fire crackled. Peace filled his heart and he felt its warmth engulf his chilled bones. A small smile curled the corners of his mouth. He didn't know how or why, but he knew everything would be all right.

Earlier in the day he had placed a candle in the front window. With Grandpa gone, it was the only Christmas decoration he could bring himself to use. He pushed himself out of the rocker and struck a match to the hearth. As he held the flame to the wick, a tender voice sounded in his ears. "God has seen and accepted your sacrifices, Charlie."

35

GRANDPA DOZED IN THE ROCKER, LISTENING to the Dobsons' soft whispers that seemed to flutter through the cabin. Then sleep nestled closer and he drifted with the rocking motion.

A voice wafted through the crevices of consciousness.

"Hello, Stuart."

Grandpa knew the voice and didn't stir, but said, "Howdy there, Jess."

"I see you're ready to go home."

"I am if you say so," answered the old man. "I been lookin' forward to this for a long time."

Jess chuckled. "I know you have, old friend. But I don't mean *that* home just yet. I mean back to the cabin."

Grandpa stopped rocking. "Well, I'm ready to go back to that home too, if that's what you want. I'll just gather up Bessie and Charlie, then we'll be off."

"Not so fast, Stuart. I need to ask something of you first."

Grandpa settled back in the chair and looked into the soft brown eyes of his friend. "Anything, Jess. You know that."

"Anything, my friend?"

Grandpa nodded. "Anything."

Jess stood tall and looked down at the old man. "The boy," he said. "I want you to leave the boy with me."

The smile slowly waned from the wrinkled, boney cheeks. "Leave him? What do you mean; leave him?"

"I want the boy to stay with me. He can't go home with you."

Grandpa's gaze drifted across the dirt floor as Jess's words sank deep into his heart. "Can't go home with me . . ." he whispered. The old eyes looked up and searched those of the mountain man. "But Jess, I can't live without my boy."

Jess laid a hand on the bent shoulder. "Look at me, Stuart," he said with stern restraint.

Again, the old clouded eyes searched their way into the soft brown lights of Jess's eyes. "You can, my old friend. I know that boy is your life and has given you much joy. But it's time to truly trust me—with everything."

Grandpa lowered his head and let the tears drip from his chin onto the Indian blanket over his legs. "Will I see him this side of Heaven again?"

"That will be up to you, my friend," whispered Jess.

Grandpa cracked one eye open and looked around the room. Slowly things came into view and he was surprised at what he saw. The room had changed. It didn't look like the room he had been recuperating in since October. It looked more like his own room. But how could that be?

Just then, Charlie walked in and sat down on the bed beside him. He leaned over and kissed his grandfather on the forehead. "Grandpa, you're awake."

"I am?"

Charlie laughed. "Yes, you are."

"But, Micah, how did I get here? We were just at the Dobsons'."

Charlie tried to conceal his confusion. "Calm down, Grandpa. I don't know where the Dobsons live, so I don't know how long it took you, but it's okay now."

"But I was just gettin' ready to come home. You were gonna see to Bessie; and Gill and Orpha were suppose to—"

"Whoa there," said Charlie. "I don't know those people, and I'm not Micah. I'm Charlie. Don't you remember me, Grandpa?"

Grandpa propped himself up against his pillows. When he saw tears streaming down Charlie's face, fear gripped the old man's heart. He reached out and yelled, "Micah, boy, what is it?"

"Grandpa!" Charlie said as he grabbed the old man and held him tight in his arms.

Finally Charlie sat back and wiped his face with his sleeve. "Grandpa, it's been so long. Where were you?"

Puzzled, the old man looked at his grandson, "What do you mean?"

"Don't play with me, Grandpa. I expected you home months ago."

Grandpa looked at his grandson with grave concern, convinced that the boy had been kicked in the head by his horse when he was packing.

"Charlie," Grandpa said slowly, "what are you talkin' about, son? You know where me and Bessie were. We were in an accident, but you were with us the whole time. You found us and nursed us back to health. You and the Dobsons."

Charlie felt agitated but he tried to remain calm. "I knew there was an accident, Grandpa. I saw the tracks in the riverbed, but that was the only place we found them."

Before Grandpa could question that, Charlie continued, "Miller was with me, and neither one of us could figure out what happened after you and Bessie fell. There weren't any tracks leading out of the ravine. Just in and then down. So, I don't know where you've been all this time." Charlie shook his head and searched his grandfather's eyes. "And who are the Dobsons?" The confusion in Charlie's voice clearly reflected in his face.

Grandpa glanced out the window and mumbled to himself. He cocked his head at the boy. "Charlie, if you were here, then who . . . ?"

Grandpa took Charlie by the arm and started to get out of bed. "Help me to my rocker, son."

Charlie helped Grandpa get comfortable in the chair with a warm blanket over his knees.

Bewildered, Grandpa looked around the room. "I am home," he mumbled. Brightening, he said, "Now son, tell me how I got here."

Carefully, Charlie told all he knew.

"Last night I had a nice talk with the Lord, got some things settled, and for the first time in months, was feeling a sense of peace. After reading some Scripture and praying, I got up from the rocker and lit the small candle over there in the window. That's when I saw you."

"You saw me?"

"Yes, sir; comin' down the hill with Bessie."

Grandpa looked at the window and mumbled, "I don't remember none of it. The last thing I remember is talkin' to Jess at the Dobsons' cabin. He was tellin' me that Micah had to stay with him. Couldn't come home with me." Slowly Grandpa turned to Charlie. "I thought he was talkin' about you."

"Nope." Charlie smiled. "I'm right here, but there isn't a Micah to be found."

Grandpa shook his head. "So, you looked out the window and there we were, comin' down the hill."

Charlie nodded. "Yep. At first I just saw movement in the snow. I wasn't sure who it was. I actually recognized Bessie before you, 'cause you were limpin' pretty bad. First time I ever saw you use a cane. But once I knew it was you, I was out there in a flash. Got you and Bessie bedded down and I haven't slept a wink since."

"A cane? What's it made out of?"

"Wood, of course. Why?"

Grandpa threw the blankets off his legs. "Whew," he whispered. "Thank goodness he was just joshin'."

"Who?"

Grandpa chuckled. "Gill. He said he was gonna make a cane out of . . . Ah, never mind."

Grandpa looked back at the window. He shook his head. "No, that can't be," he whispered. "But if you weren't Micah, then who was *he*?" Grandpa looked Charlie square in the eye. "But the boy looked like you, talked like you. He asked me to call him Micah, for my own sake, so I did; but I didn't doubt for a second that he was you."

Charlie stared blankly. "What are you talkin' about?"

Then Grandpa explained the accident and the events that followed as best he could. When he reached the part of how he struggled to sit up before passing out, he explained how Charlie was suddenly at his side, telling him to be still and helping him lie back down on the ground.

In the middle of the explanation, Charlie's words the morning he and Grandpa parted in Denver struck them both at the same time: *I'll be with you every step of the way, Grandpa,* Charlie had said. *Just think of me and I'll be right there.*

"Grandpa," said Charlie, "do you believe in angels?"

Grandpa paused a second before answering. "Charlie, do you mean to tell me that you've been here all this time, just takin' care of the place and prayin' for me?"

"Well, you know I went on the cattle drive 'cause you were with me part of the way. Then when I got back here, I went to Pueblo once, to old man Jacobs' place a couple of times, and then to Mary Lou's funeral out at the graveyard, but that's about it. I promise you, Grandpa. Star and I have spent most of our time right here, hopin' that you would come home."

Turning toward the window, Grandpa's eyes grew wide. "Star," he whispered. "Star wasn't there. Well, I'll be."

Charlie followed his grandpa's glassy stare. "Star's been with me since the day you gave 'im to me."

Grandpa sat back in the rocker and closed his eyes. "Charlie, I believe I met several angels on this journey, but the boy who saved me and Bessie, he was a special gift from

God. He knew if I had you, or thought I had you with me, I'd fight to stay alive and mend properly. Thinking you were safe with me, I'd have no reason to worry; so God brought you to me, in a sense. You were here at the farm, but I thought you were with me, to help me pull through. So, to answer your question, son: Yes, I believe in angels."

The two sat in silence for a long time.

Grandpa finally spoke first. "God certainly does work in mysterious ways, doesn't He, son?"

Charlie nodded, as he thought of God's goodness and how sometimes when things make no sense at all, if you just sit quiet, He'll make sense of it all.

Charlie picked up a match to light the candle. At the window he again caught a glimpse of something out on the prairie, on the crest of the hill. He smiled as he recognized the familiar silhouette of a big mountain man sitting on a big horse. The tail of his coonskin cap fluttered in the wind. The second rider looked vaguely familiar, but he wasn't sure until the stranger lifted his hat and waved it in a wide sweeping arch.

"Miller!" he whispered. "I knew it."

36

CHRISTMAS MORNING DIDN'T BRING CAROLS or bells or angelic choirs, just serene snowfall. Charlie rolled out of bed shivering. A couple of jabs with the poker, and the fire danced merrily on the grate as it did every morning. He struck a match and lit the candle in the window.

Grandpa came out of his room and shuffled to the coffee pot, not saying a word until the smell of hot coffee was mixing with the robust essence of simmering black beans.

Charlie sat on the hearth and rubbed the sleep from his eyes. Grandpa pulled the rocker close to the fire and eased himself onto the padded seat. "Which would you prefer, Charlie? A merry Christmas or a happy birthday?"

Charlie chuckled at the old joke. "I can have both, Grandpa," he said happily. "And I always do." He motioned to the fireplace. "Are you ready for a cup of coffee?"

"Yeah, and while you're up, why not grab that envelope on the mantle."

Charlie fixed Grandpa's coffee then looked on the mantle. Leaning against the clock was a white envelope with Charlie's name printed in bold letters. He picked it up and gave Grandpa a questioning look.

The old man blew on his coffee. "It's a present."

"Then hold on a second. I have one for you, too."

Laying the envelope on the table, he went to his bed-roll, grabbed the pillow, and dumped a small box out of the case.

"I got it on the cattle drive. Traded my belt buckle for it."

Grandpa sputtered his coffee. "You did *what?*"

"I traded my belt buckle for it, with LeFaye." He handed the small box to his grandfather. "I hope you like it. I think it's kinda funny now, after all we've been through."

Grandpa leaned forward to place his cup on the hearth. Sitting back, he took the package from Charlie and held it to his ear, giving it a gentle shake.

Charlie laughed. "Just open it."

The gnarled fingers slowly tore away the brown wrapping. *U.S. Army* was stamped on the box lid in bright blue letters.

"Hmm, wonder what it could be?" he mumbled. Then, with effort he pulled the lid off and slid the gift into his palm. A brass compass glittered in the soft glow of the firelight.

The top of the compass bore the image of an eagle, with its wings unfurled. In its talons it held the words, *United States Army*. Grandpa popped the top up and marveled at the intricate work inside.

"It's beautiful, Charlie," he said softly. "With this, I'll never lose my way home again."

Charlie bent down and hugged the old man. "And I'll never let you."

"Where's your envelope?"

Charlie slid it off of the table. "Right here."

"Okay," said Grandpa. "Your turn."

Charlie ripped the envelope open and peeked inside. "These papers look mighty official," he said.

Grandpa sipped his coffee. "They are. You'll never lose your way home, either."

Charlie unfolded the documents and scanned the pages. "This is the deed to the farm, Grandpa."

Grandpa sat his cup back down and leaned forward. "Yes, son, it is."

"But why?"

"Because I want you to always have a place to come back to, if you want it."

"But, you've already given me so much, Grandpa, I—"

"Well, this place is as much yours as mine. You've worked it just as hard, and you deserve it. That paper just makes it legal. The only thing I ask is that when the time comes, you bury me up there on the hill beside your grandma."

Charlie got up and went to the water basin. Grabbing the counter, he bowed his head.

"Home," he whispered.

The boy's memory raced back a few months to when he stood in this very spot, tormented by the desire to find his own way. He'd seen plenty on the cattle drive, but he'd learned that there was nowhere else he'd rather be than here.

"I'll take care of it till the day I die, Grandpa."

Grandpa pulled himself out of the rocker and limped to the boy. "I know you will, son." He put an arm around Charlie's wide shoulders. "I don't want you to feel obligated to live here. I'm sure life will lead you in another direction; but it's a place that you can call your own for as long as you want. It's your roots, son. It's where you come from."

Charlie hugged his grandfather. "No, sir. This ain't nothin' but a parcel of land and some old buildings that will crumble with time. Don't get me wrong; I love this place and I'll care for it always. But *you're* my roots, Grandpa. You're where I come from and what I'll cherish to my dying day."

Grandpa gently pushed Charlie away and motioned toward the hearth. "I think you better sit back down, son. I need to tell you about a meetin' I had with Mr. Atkins while I was in Denver. You see, he's an attorney. . . .

Acknowledgments

Above all, I thank my Lord and Savior for His strength and guidance as I answered His call and was able to complete this book. As I get older, my life's journey becomes more challenging, but with every step, His grace also becomes more sufficient, and it is because of His grace and goodness that the *Mysterious Ways* series continues.

I also thank my husband, Blaine, whose patience and encouragement have been instrumental in the development of this series of books, and whose love and companionship are my richest blessings.

Thanks to our children, and their spouses and one fiancé: Michealle, Reid, Melanie, Scott, Melissa and Ben. They are my pride and joy, and I thank them, too, for their understanding as I struggled to move forward along so many paths, including the writing and publication of this book.

A special thanks to my mother, Roberta Westover, who, despite her own physical trials, has never let the opportunity to encourage me slip by. She has always believed in me and I still strive to make her proud.

To Char Wixson, my best friend and 'guardian angel,' who has always been there for me; and to her husband, Steve, who never seemed to mind the occasional late dinner when she would get home behind schedule.

Thanks to the Cladach Publishing family, specifically Catherine and Christina, who not only worked diligently to edit and see this work come to fruition, but kept me in their prayers as they did so.

About the Author

Donna Westover Gallup is a poet and musician. She currently works at Colorado State University and holds a B.S. degree in business/pre-law from Liberty University and an M.B.A. from University of Phoenix. Donna is the mother of three grown daughters, and the grandmother of two boys. She and her husband, Blaine, live in Fort Collins, Colorado with their two boxers, Harley and Cheyenne.

In her free time Donna enjoys riding horses and writing stories. Her desire is to convey God's love through fiction.

To order additional copies of the *Mysterious Ways* books

White as Snow
Rock of Refuge

ask at your favorite bookstore or visit
www.cladach.com.
Watch for forthcoming titles in the series.